RICH BOYS

Heather L. Benton

Gold Room Press

Cover design by Slobodan Cedic

This is a work of fiction. Names, characters, places, and incidents are either the product of the author's imagination or are used fictitiously, and any resemblance to actual person, living or dead, business establishments, events or locales in entirely coincidental.

Second Edition

ISBN: 978-0692597668

CONTENTS

MANITOBA, CANADA

DECEMBER, 13 YEARS PRIOR

I stood in front of Tempest Lodge and stared at the sinister looking snowman, with its spindly branch arms. It looked like they reached out to grab me. I stood in the exact spot, the very place where the horrible moment would happen thirteen years later. And I sensed it, that violent end. I had a vision. I gazed up at the giant glass window of the lodge mansion—saw something there. Then I looked back at the snowman and envisioned him choking me, trying to kill me with those cold, scratchy fingers. As soon as it came, it vanished. A shiver shook me and I felt my eight-year-old face contort in confusion. I stepped back from the snowman. Then I paused, my brow furrowed, and I punched the head off of Frosty. I cracked his branch arms in two and then ran inside to wash the bad vibes off of my hands.

This mansion, Tempest Lodge, was the remote vacation chalet on the interior plains of Canada. It was owned by the wealthy Van Ettens, who happened to be our neighbors and closest friends. The vacation house sprawled like a giant on the sloped landscape of pines. The lodge enchanted me beyond any theme park. To me, theme parks were a lie. Just smoke and mirrors, structures of wonder that hid staff lounges and maintenance crews as men greased gears behind the scenes. This lodge, however, was a creation of authentic mystery. Constructed ages before my birth, it had a handful of secret passageways and a bookshelf in one room that opened to reveal a claustrophobic space, with one single vent to allow in air and dismal light. As a child, this seemed only right, magical, a place that every house should imitate. Later as an adult, however, I would wonder about the Van Ettens' ancestors who designed an isolated lodge with such trappings... And how far back the spots of darkness trail in a family's gene pool.

On this maiden visit to Tempest Lodge, I'd laughed outside in the snow the day before with Alex Van Etten—blond haired, one year my senior, and my best friend in the world. We'd erected that snowman, shoddy in our work, which resulted in its deranged esthetic quality. Accessories disheveled, a mangled carrot nose, and spiky branches for arms ready to reach out and snatch anyone who stepped too close. Then Alex carved Frosty a set of hollowed out eyes. Eyes that caused me to avert my own when I stared at them.

"He looks like a madman," I said.

Alex chuckled and drew a grimace on the face with a piece of coal he'd snagged from one of the fireplaces in the lodge. "He's perfect. Don't try to tell him otherwise. You might hurt his feelings," Alex said.

We left our icy comrade out front, and I followed Alex up through one of the not-so-secret passages into his bedroom to build a pillow fort until night fell. When we grew bored, we parted ways. Alex went to play video games, and I ventured on my own into the central great room to find the massive fireplace with its inferno warming the dark space. I approached the fire as it burned like a caged beast, licking and snapping as it craved its escape. I assumed I walked through the room by myself, but I was not alone.

Even at this young age, I'd already selected my path in life and declared that the world of professional dance was for me. So I assigned the fire the role of stage lights, and then spun into a string of *fouettés*, whirling around while I remained in the same spot, eyes trained on the fire.

On the fifth or sixth rotation, I noticed him in the darkness, standing just outside the firelight. I faltered and stopped, startled by the sight of another person in the room with me.

"Sam," I said. Dark-haired Sam, the older of the two Van Etten boys, had six years on me. At fourteen, he appeared so confident, tall and grown up—so intimidating. He edged around the leather armchair and moved in my direction. I grew uneasy in the darkness with him, stepped back and tripped on the hearth, scraping my ankle on a metal fire poker. I groaned and looked down to see blood on my ankle. Sam walked over to help me up and tried to examine the gash, but I stepped away. He looked down at me with solemn eyes.

"Gotta be careful around that fire, Autumn," he said, and then glanced at the flames. His eyes moved back to me. "It could burn you alive."

I bit my lip, fiddled with my hands, and returned his somber expression. Behind me, the fire hissed. A lethal snake sending out its warning.

CHAPTER ONE

CHICAGO: DECEMBER, PRESENT DAY

As I reclined on the cheap IKEA futon in my diminutive apartment, I stared at the miniature Christmas tree lit up on a side table. I listened to holiday music through my ear buds, and hung one of my legs over the side. It bounced against the floor as fast as a rabbit's heartbeat. I tried to visualize the choreography to *The Nutcracker* to keep it fresh for future reference while my roommate, Rachel, sat at the table studying.

Focus, I thought when my mind drifted back to earlier in the evening sitting alone in a restaurant. So alone. Two table settings. Being stood up by Jake. Apologizing to the server as I ordered a drink, and then tipping more than the drink itself cost because I felt rude for occupying the table. And because I didn't want to look like a pathetic casualty of date abandonment. I tried not to cry while I rode Chicago's "L" train home to my apartment. I thought about how little money would be in my bank account after that drink and tip transaction cleared.

Focus, Autumn. I turned my head and stared up at the ceiling when a sharp rapping sounded against my apartment door. I jumped, pulled my ear buds out as I glanced at the clock—midnight.

"Who the hell is here at this ungodly hour?" Rachel asked.

Rachel and I had danced on the same competition team throughout high school, where we formed an effortless friendship. She had flawless Asian features, and was a smart-ass to her core, which explained our instant bond. I liked a good smart-ass sense of humor. When we were both accepted into the same dance program for college, less than an hour's drive from home, rooming together seemed a natural choice. We'd thrived as roomies for the three and a half years since.

Someone pounded on the door again. I stood up and walked over to peek through the peephole, my eyes widening. "What the..? Un-fucking-believable."

I opened the door to find Jake. After he stood me up hours before, he'd also failed to return my calls or voicemails for an explanation as to why he never showed. We'd only been dating for two weeks, but I thought a simple reply would have been nice.

Jake, however, now stood in front of me in a macabre state. He shifted his weight from foot to foot. The area around his eye looked such a dark shade of blue that I jerked my head back. A smear of blood painted the space below his nose, and his lip was split open. He looked... scared. Terrified. Jake, a tall, sturdy guy, who worked out *far* more than necessary, seemed ready to crap himself out of fear.

"What the hell? Oh my God, are you okay?" I asked, and my previous frustration melted into concern.

Jake took a shaky breath. "We're done." His voice wavered from the adrenaline of whatever altercation caused the wounds.

I blinked and shook my head. "What happened to you? What's going on? Seriously... Wait, *what* did you say?" I scrutinized the messed dark hair on one side of his head and the dried blood that had dripped onto his white shirt. I felt strange, as if floating. When I reached out my hand to caress his shoulder and touch his hair he stepped back away from me.

Jake took another breath, trembled, closed his eyes, and held his hand out to keep me at bay. "I wasn't even going to come by. I thought about just never speaking to you again," he said, and glanced up and down the hallway, as if on alert for someone. "But I wanted to make sure you got the message loud and clear, okay? We're done. We're over. I never wanna see you again." His voice quivered.

"What the hell are you talking about?"

Jake's expression changed as if he wanted to punch the wall. "I don't know if you set this up because you're too afraid to break this off yourself or what—sure as hell sounded like that's the case—but I'm checking out of this bullshit," he said, and raised his hands up in surrender. "I'm done. I don't need this. Who *does* that anyway, gets someone to kick someone's ass so they don't have to deal with an insignificant breakup? You're hot, but not worth this."

I blinked again. That stung. And then confusion swarmed. *What* set up? I hadn't even thought about breaking off our new fling.

Jake leaned around me to look through the doorway at Rachel. "Or was it you? I could see you sending out some muscle for Autumn. I ought to just rip that hair right out of your head, you skank." Jake spit the words at her.

I felt flustered. "Whoa, whoa. Watch it," I said.

Jake shoved his body weight forward as if ready to attack. I didn't turn to see Rachel's reaction. An instinctive protective mode took over my body. I blocked the doorway with my arm and hiked my knee up to tap Jake in the crotch, not enough to really hurt him, just enough to make him wince. He stepped a foot back.

"I'm not full of that many good ideas," Rachel said in a deadpan voice from where she remained at the table.

Jake gave her the finger.

I shook my head. "Wait... Jake, I don't know what the hell is going on here. I didn't set up *anything*. But I will tell you, if you don't shut your trap, or if you even think of stepping foot in this door..." I said, trailing off.

Jake laughed for a moment, and then his eyes turned wary as he watched the fury in my cold expression. The realization was visible on his own: he would take me down if a battle ensued, no doubt. But I would, without question, do him some damage in the interim.

"Autumn, just stay away from me. Apparently you associate yourself with douche bags, so I want no part of you," he said, and then began to lumber away. He stubbed his toe against someone's dirty hallway doormat on his way.

My mouth dropped open. "Fine then, leave, asshole!" I yelled just before he stepped into the elevator.

I wiped a hand across my forehead as I gazed down the hall. I hesitated for a moment, mystified. I fidgeted with my hands, and then slammed the door with a rage that seized control of my arm. I stared at the door in confusion and then went to wash my hands, filled with anxiety. I washed them until tears welled up in my eyes, and I forced myself to shut off the water. When I returned to the main room, Rachel looked at me.

"Well, if there was a Ms. Worst Judge of Character in the Universe pageant, you'd certainly win for dating pricks like that," she said.

I moved over to our futon, sat down to stare at the wall, and felt like an idiot. Rachel came and sat next to me.

"I'm sorry," she said. "Even though he's an ass, I know it sucks when a low-life says dumb shit like that... Stuff that doesn't even make sense." She shook her head, confused, too. "But he's not worth being upset over. Besides, you have Alex to go home to over break. I swear, I've said it a thousand times before: the two of you need to stop playing coy. He's smitten with you. So just hook up already, get married, and have ten-thousand babies, okay?"

I let out a small laugh as a tear fell to my cheek. "I appreciate the sentiment, but I can't even... I can't think straight."

Jake's peculiar theories that night fell on my ears like a foreign language, words that evaded my comprehension. I tried to call and text him multiple times during the week, if only to get him to explain what happened, but he never replied. The first night I cried a couple of tears in bed. But by the next day I understood it wasn't worth it. There wasn't much spark between us to begin with, and I could focus more on my dancing without a new guy distracting me.

Two weeks after Jake came to my door bloodied and shaken, I had the fall semester recital, known as the December Showcase, to take my mind off the incident. The morning of the recital began like most of my mornings. I grabbed a small breakfast and rode the "L" from my tiny apartment to school with Rachel.

Commuters and tourists filled the train, read books or played on their phones, pointed out windows, and chatted about what sights to see. One thirty or forty-something man caught my eye sitting across and a few seats down from us. He stared at me, and I stared back. He had dark hair, thick dark eyebrows, pale skin, and looked like he hadn't shaved for a few days. He wore a gray beanie and a navy leather jacket. *Navy leather, peculiar choice.*

His casual posture made me think he was a local. He wouldn't stop staring at me. I began to move my head in the other direction, but kept my eyes on him. He continued to stare. *Rude and creepy*, I thought. I glanced away and back again. He still had his eyes on me, and a chill down my spine made me tremble. Finally, he slowly moved his gaze to the other direction. I pursed my lips and shifted closer to Rachel.

I sucked in a breath. "Sorry I can't stay for your performance. My mom's picking me up, and she has to get to a work meeting after we get back to her house." The comfort of my childhood home in Lake Forest, forty-five minutes north of Chicago, sounded like paradise after the last two weeks.

I bounced my leg with mild anxiety. "I feel like crap about missing your dance. At least I'll see the video, though."

Rachel smoothed her hair, already up in a bun. "Yeah, I know. Whatever. You'll just be missing the dance of the century in person. Your loss." She laughed at her own sarcasm. "But who cares? We'll have fun over break."

I caught the guy in the navy leather jacket staring at me again and I thought of Jake. If Jake had spoken the truth in relating his beating back to me somehow, then someone stalked around Chicago and dished out the unrequested, unwanted assault on Jake on my behalf. And I'll be damned if they weren't good at getting the job done. I shook my head to rid it of the recollection of Jake's wounds.

I'd already sifted through past flings, the occasional ex-boyfriend, and even a patron who bordered on stalker behavior at the restaurant where I waited tables—a man who always, always, *always* sat in my section. I consumed lots of antacids over the previous weeks. The mystery haunted my thoughts every day since Jake staggered away from my apartment and out of my life.

Erase it, I thought. I couldn't dwell on it before my performance today. I had to concentrate, and feeling shaky and disturbed wouldn't help my muscles relax for my routine. That dinging pebble of bewilderment and fear bounced around my head. I made a point to lock it away in a murky box in the corner of my mind. I told myself to think ahead to the stage, think ahead to vacation. My leg bounced faster.

"Yeah, we'll have fun," I whispered in response to Rachel, and I watched passengers board and depart the train one stop before ours. A gust of cold air rushed into the train like a ghost catching a free ride.

Once we arrived at school, Rachel and I headed our separate ways for morning classes. I had a technique course in the morning, but the rest of my day was devoted to the Showcase and then heading home for break.

When I arrived at the performance hall, I hurried to get myself ready backstage. I sat in front of a mirror to apply makeup and false lashes, then blotted my lipstick on a paper napkin. Before long, the moment I'd thought about with anticipation all week was upon me. I heard my name over the speakers and I sidestepped onstage in the darkness.

The lights came up, the music began, and my body moved in memorized motions. The glare of lights obscured most of the audience from my view. All I could make out were the dark silhouettes of the crowd and the occasional shadowed eyes of the people who sat in the front rows. In my lower peripheral vision, I saw the orange fringe that grazed the very tops of my thighs. Sequins from my costume sparkled.

I moved across the black stage, leaped, spun, and slid to the ground in a finely choreographed routine. *Chassé*—step together step—and into a pencil turn, then a fan kick so perfect that my knee came within a centimeter of brushing my face as it swung across the front of my body.

I sailed across the stage in a switch leap, landed as silent as the grave, and then whirled into *fouettés* like a graceful cyclone. The lights felt hot as they warmed my skin like artificial sunlight. The music faded as I moved into my final pose. I smiled as I held it for a moment. The lights dimmed, an auditorium full of hands clapped, and I exited the stage. I panted, felt like I was on high, and hesitated for a moment in the stage wing. I wished so much that it could have lasted longer.

After I packed up my things backstage, I headed out to the performance hall lobby, where the bluish-white winter light filtered through the windows. Most people were still inside the auditorium to watch the showcase, so it took only a moment to spot my mother.

Mom, who aged well despite her years of stress and a bout with cancer, had her purse on her shoulder and a bouquet of flowers in one hand. She smiled as I approached and she held her arms open for a hug. I entered them and hugged her back. She felt warm and comfortable, her floral perfume familiar. It transported me to a younger age, and I felt home already in the embrace.

"You did fantastic, honey," she said, and handed me the flowers. She never failed to present me with flowers after I danced on stage, even when money was at its tightest.

"Thanks. I'm so hungry I could eat someone's face off. Did you eat yet?" I asked.

"No, I figured we could have a late lunch on the way home. I have to get to my meeting by three, so we can't fart around too long, but I need to eat something, too."

We headed out to her car and I tossed my bag onto the back seat. A quick stop by my tiny flat to pick up my bags for vacation, and then we cruised north, parallel to Lake Michigan and out of downtown Chicago.

Lake Forest was one of the affluent neighborhoods on the north side of Chicago. Mom inherited the large house there when I was four years old, left to her by a well-to-do aunt who had no children of her own, and no other nieces or nephews.

My father had left and forever disappeared from our lives before I could even remember him. So Mom struggled in the early years to pay the bills and taxes on the place, even without a mortgage payment to agonize over. She had to make it on her own with two children, a mediocre job managing a store at the mall, and waiting tables on the weekends. But she put herself through school despite the burdens, and now worked as a sales director at a payroll company. My brother Tim, nine years my senior, moved out over a decade ago, so that helped ease the financial load on her, as well.

All was good in the Land of Oz, and then her diagnosis came. A year and a half of battling breast cancer hit the restart button on her life and finances. I watched as my mom lost her hair and I helped shave her head when she said it had gotten too splotchy. I tried to make it seem fun for her. I hooted like we were taking part in an act of rebellion that a young woman might go through with after a breakup.

"Just think of how freeing it's gonna be, not having to deal with conditioner or hairdryers," I'd said to her.

But I had watched her eyes in the moments she thought I wasn't looking—it was evident she only went along with my dumb game to make me feel less frightened. And that made my gut ache. She had the cancer, and there she was, trying to make *me* feel better.

I didn't make a sound when I cried in my room that night, as I imagined how alone in the world I would feel if I lost her. Tim lived in San Francisco; my dad didn't exist to me. If I lost my mom... I tried not to let the idea take over. I dialed Alex Van Etten that night and he let me cry in a hushed tone over the phone for an hour as he whispered consolations to me.

I also came home from college during the chemo treatments, cleaned up Mom's vomit from the bathroom floor, even though I struggled with germaphobia. I scrubbed my hands afterward until they were raw, which made me cry, too, because it was my own mother. God knows how many times she cleaned up disgustingness in all forms from me as a child, and I couldn't stop myself from washing my hands.

I hated myself for that. I knew after years of dealing with it, anxiety was the root of the issue, not germs. But it didn't help me feel any better about myself.

When she went into remission, we celebrated with a pink cake, but an air of fear lingered. Remission sounded like such a fickle word and lacked the guarantee we wanted. Positivity was important to me, though. So things were on the upswing. She had been healthy for a year now and went back to work full time, and I only had one more semester left. *God, just one more.* And I wanted to help Mom with the medical bills. I tried to slip money in her wallet a few times when she wasn't looking, but I waited tables and paid my own tuition. My contribution was practically meaningless. I was dumb enough to think I could do it all. One could say reading up on how to manage personal finances was on my bucket list. And had yet to be checked off.

After the Showcase, Mom and I grabbed a hurried bite to eat at a burger joint near home and we caught up on small talk. I avoided the topic of Jake and pushed the murky box further into the corner of my mind. I wished I could shove it out of my head entirely, where it would fall to the floor and someone would sweep it up and throw it away forever.

"So how've you been? When's the last time you saw the doctor?" I asked her.

"A couple weeks ago. Things are the same. Nothing to worry about, sweetie."

She tucked her blonde hair behind her ears. Mom and I looked very similar. We both had dark blonde hair and brown eyes. Aside from our age and hair length—mine was longer, falling below my shoulders—the main physical difference between us was the smattering of freckles across my nose and cheeks. A trait she claimed I acquired from my father.

Mom cleared her throat. "I get it, you're in college and want to do your own thing. So go ahead and do what you want this evening but tomorrow night, if you don't mind, Camille and I planned on having the annual dinner. It's hard to find a time where everyone can be there at once, and tomorrow evening Sam is off work, Alex will be home, and your brother will fly in during the afternoon."

"Stellar," I said out of nervous awkwardness. I hadn't seen Alex for a month.

The Van Ettens—Camille and her sons, Sam and Alex— were the closest thing we had to family. Closer than any extended family of our own. Years ago, my mother and Camille formed an unlikely friendship when we moved into the inherited house. Camille, a beautiful widow with auburn hair, lived with her two boys next door. Although *next door* meant the next house down, with the Van Etten's massive yard in between. Their Tudor-style home, a legitimate mansion, was vastly larger than our home.

Financial comfort levels aside, Camille and Mom related on raising children alone, had similar tastes in humor, and even more similar tastes in wine. So their friendship bloomed swiftly. Sam and Alex took me in as a part of the clan without question. Sam, the tall brother with hair like chocolate and blue-green eyes of the sea, seemed so much older to me as a child. And, to be honest, a little unapproachable in both his handsomeness and age at times. But Sam was earth: humble, solid, steady, reliable. The kind of person that sometimes made you feel like you were talking too much about yourself, because he listened with interest, and spoke without bragging.

If Sam was earth, then Alex was fire. The sandy-haired one who looked like he belonged on a beach. Wild, fun, and aggressive in sports. He was the outgoing brother who lit up a room with his presence and warmth. Both boys were skilled in athletics and played all kinds throughout high school. But Alex went after them with an obsession. I could remember watching one of Alex's lacrosse games in high school and being amazed at how he dominated the field.

Alex also attracted friends with ease, me included. From the very first summer I moved next door, we did almost everything together. Played in the opulent treehouse in their backyard. Convinced our moms to take us to the beach so we could swim in Lake Michigan. Rode our bikes up and down our street for hours. In the winter, we built snow forts, and when spring came, the Van Ettens' maid scolded us as we tracked mud in across the kitchen floor. We were like a package deal, Autumn and Alex, everywhere we went. I suppose if Sam was earth and Alex fire, then I was like water—going with the flow when it came to Alex and any of his shenanigans.

In more recent years, the last year in particular, I'd tried to suppress a budding attraction to Alex. At first I thought, *Hey, he's good looking; it's only natural for me to notice that.* But over time, I realized the mixture of his attractiveness *and* our close relationship combined in a dangerous way. The result tended toward the side of falling in love, and that equaled complication. Complication in the form of three possibilities:

A) I could tell him and he could love me in return. Fantastic! Rainbows and unicorns and Cupid sits and smiles from the ledge of a diamond-encrusted gazebo.

B) I could tell him and he could want me only as a friend. Nausea. Our relationship would be forever awkward and tainted.

C) I could say nothing, and forever wonder in terms of those dreaded two words: what if? The horror of life seen in retrospect. What if I never said anything and never knew how he felt? I couldn't say for sure yet, but I already suspected *what if* may be one of the most painful phrases that existed.

Alex had taken me to dinner just for the hell of it last winter while he was in Chicago for a visit. That night he had dropped me off at my apartment with both a walk to my door and a spell on my heart. The enchantment lingered. The budding attraction had blossomed, and since that night, the denial of my feelings was futile.

I reminded myself that, at present, I sat across from my mother and tried not to dwell on the memory of Alex—and the arousal from our evening out to dinner last year.

"Stop fidgeting with your hands, sweetheart," Mom said.

I swallowed and set my hands in my lap.

A light snow had begun to fall as we pulled up to our stone house. Although smaller than some of the other homes in the neighborhood it still housed five large bedrooms. It also had a second-story balcony outside on the back, one of my favorite features. My room looked out onto the balcony, with a window large enough to climb in and out of with ease.

I pulled my bags out of the car as snowflakes collected in my hair, and went inside to settle in. I smiled at the garland that ran up the handrail of the staircase—childhood nostalgia. It smelled of pine and cookies in the house.

After a hot shower, I threw my dirty laundry into the washer and I turned on some music. Mom had already returned to work for her meeting. I wandered into the kitchen, grabbed my phone, and sent Alex a text.

When are you getting in? I'm already bored to death.

Within a few minutes, my phone chimed in reply, and my cheeks lifted into a smile before I even read the message. I already knew the answer to the question I had asked. He was due in town tomorrow, coming home from Champaign, where he attended law school at the University of Illinois, a three-hour drive from home. But I wanted to talk to him anyway.

Hoping to get there around 1:00 tomorrow afternoon. Last final in the morning. Can't wait to see you, Auttie.

My insides heated. Alex was the only person who had a nickname for me. I replied:

Don't be late, punk!

He sent a smile back and told me he wouldn't dare think of making me wait around for him. God, I missed him. I bent over and put my forehead on the cold granite countertop.

"Okay, get your mind off of it," I whispered.

I watered the plants around the house—something I enjoyed for a long time—the simple act of keeping them alive. Then I called Rachel to see if she was home yet. She was still backstage after she finished her Showcase performance, just about to leave the dance hall to head back to Lake Forest. Rachel's childhood home was about twenty minutes away from mine.

"My mom is making me eat dinner with the family when I get home," she said. "But I'll come over right after."

I still had hours to kill, so I grabbed my pointe shoes and went to practice in front of the mirrored wall in the basement until she showed up.

Rachel arrived later and stayed for the entire evening. We talked and laughed up in my bedroom like we did before our college years, quoting movies, doing dumb impressions, and Googling dance companies all over the country with lust in our hearts to be a part of any of them. After she left, I sat with Mom and watched a half hour of TV before I headed off to bed. As I stood up to go to my room, Mom spoke.

"You're going to be free for dinner tomorrow night, right?" she asked again. She looked tired as she turned off the television.

"Yeah, I said I'd be there. So I'll be there."

"Okay, good. I love you, honey," she said. She got up and gave me a firm hug. Twenties or not, man, it felt good to be home.

"Love you, too, Mom."

I went upstairs, got ready for bed, and crawled under my old twin comforter. I tried to sleep, and sleep tried to escape me. I looked at the thin sliver of the moon outside my window and thought of Alex. I pictured him crawling through my window in the darkness, pictured him slipping under the covers with me. It could happen so easily. And then, for a second, just the briefest second, Sam filled that image instead of his brother. It caught me off guard. I squeezed my eyes shut and shook the thought away. *No, don't*, I thought, confused as to why my brain shifted the picture so suddenly.

The blustery weather rattled the window, and I opened my eyes again. The prickly branches of the trees swayed outside, bony fingers that waved to me and made me imagine the trees whispering, *Hello Autumn, we can see you. We're watching you and will watch you as you sleep.* I turned my thoughts to Alex again, instead of those bony fingers. Instead of Sam. If only there were a switch to just shut the mind off at night.

"Stop it," I whispered, and rolled onto my side, putting my pillow over my head. But in the late hours, my mind became that of a young girl again and murmured to me about childish things. Things like how it would feel if I changed my name from Autumn Wright to Autumn Van Etten, and how much more elegant it sounded. Just as I reached the dozing place, the moment where I could no longer open my eyes to see what it was, I heard a light scrape against my window and then another. *Just a dead leaf,* I told myself. *A dead leaf, scraping at the windows, trying to escape the cold.* I forced myself to believe it, and then drifted off to sleep.

CHAPTER TWO

In the morning, I awoke from a nightmare. There was a roller coaster, I was strapped in, but somehow I knew the bolts on the tracks began to break loose. No one else seemed to know this, so they screamed from excitement... Just before the *real* screams began. The roller coaster raced forward as tracks broke apart. But I was strapped in, confined. I couldn't escape as the tracks just ahead fell with monstrous clanks to the pavement far below.

I got out of bed as fast as I could and splashed cold water on my face. I needed to burn off the grisly vibe from the nightmare, so I checked with the gym I frequented back in the days I lived at home to see if they had any drop-in kickboxing classes available. They offered one at 11am, so I ate breakfast and dressed for my workout.

To the dismay of my dance teachers, I took regular kickboxing classes from the time I turned fifteen. I wanted to feel secure without a father around, especially after my brother moved across the country. My dance instructors lectured and frowned. I ignored them.

I drove my old Ford Taurus, which remained parked in Mom's garage while I lived downtown during semesters, to the gym. I finally felt awake and the nightmare evaporated in the daylight. After an hour of kicking, punching, and absorbing jabs, I drove home and showered. Knowing I'd see Alex today, I spent an extra half hour in the upstairs bathroom to be certain I looked my best, but appeared as if I didn't need to put work into it. It took a *lot* of effort to look like one needed no effort.

Then I sprayed a light mist of perfume on my shoulders and hair, slipped into a sweater dress, and I pulled on my boots just as Alex's text came in.

I'm home. Get your ass over here :) Unless you're too busy...

I hurried downstairs, checked myself in the gold-framed foyer mirror once more, grabbed my coat and walked outside. The wind slapped me in the face and made me suck in a breath, but I smiled. I hugged my torso as I traversed our yard and up the lawn to the broad cobbled path to the Van Ettens' front door. Camille kept boxwoods in giant pots all along the path, trimmed into soft cone shapes as if they were small pine trees. I noticed Sam's car in the driveway, too. I didn't expect him to be here already. He lived in the north end of downtown Chicago, closer to the hospital where he worked on his residency.

Hmm, weird, I thought and then smirked, delighted at the thought of seeing Sam, as well.

We had a ring-and-immediately-enter policy with the Van Ettens, so I rang the doorbell, but slipped inside the cavernous foyer before the elegant chime finished. The chandelier in the entryway... Good God, I'm pretty sure it had to be the original inspiration for the Phantom of the Opera.

"Alex?" I called. I shivered from the chill but shrugged off my coat and hung it on the hall tree.

I heard footsteps from the hallway ahead toward the kitchen, so I moved in that direction. Just as I neared its entrance, Sam startled me as he stepped around the corner.

"Oh. Sam. Hi!"

He offered me that attractive Van Etten smile. I felt my cheeks flush.

"Autumn," he said, and pulled me into a hug. His body felt nice, and for an instant he seemed reluctant to let me go.

"How are you?" he asked.

I shrugged. "Just, you know... living it. And you? I didn't realize you'd be home already."

"Yeah, I had a shift that ended this morning at ten and had nothing to do today, so I figured I'd head up here since Alex was coming home. And we're doing the big dinner tonight," he said.

"How are things at the hospital?"

"Crazy. But good." Sam offered me a devilish smile.

"So if you just got off at ten this morning... Overnight shifts. Ugh. Are you exhausted all the time?"

"Somewhat, yeah," he said. "But I've gotten pretty used to it. Probably the same way you are used to being on your toes in pointe shoes all day. Which sounds painful to me."

"True," I said. "Being exhausted all the time can make a person insane, though."

He didn't respond but took a sip of what I presumed was coffee in the mug he held. "Want something to drink?" he asked.

"Sure, thanks."

"Coffee? Oh, wait, you want tea, right?"

I smiled to show my appreciation of his memory. "Yes, please."

"I'm on it," he said, and turned back to get water started in a kettle.

I followed him into the kitchen, grazed my hand along the granite counter of the island, and leaned a bit as I walked around to one side, observing him. Sam looked more built than I remembered, as if he'd spent ample time working out in recent months. He wore a white shirt, but still had on his scrub pants. I tried not to stare. Camille had fantastic genes, and her kids received the best of them. Sam and Alex's good looks could irritate a person. Both had the kind of cheekbones and straight noses one would expect out of generations of privileged breeding.

With his back turned to me, Sam spoke again. "Oh, I was flipping through channels the other day and saw a ballet on TV. I actually found myself watching it for a few minutes because I thought of you—thought you'd enjoy it."

I bit my lip for a second and let out a small chuckle. "Really? You watched it for a bit?"

"Yeah. I mean you don't have to go telling all my friends from high school that I was watching ballet on TV alone in my apartment," he said with a laugh. "But it's impressive, some of those twirly moves dancers do, and make it look easy."

I laughed harder at that. "Yeah, my instructors compliment me on my 'twirly moves' when they're in a good mood."

Sam finished up making the tea, and just as he handed me my cup, Alex came beaming around the corner.

"Auttie!" Alex said

I almost spilled the hot water as he pulled me into a hug.

"What took you so long?" he said with sarcasm.

I probably should have waited a little longer before I jumped to come over the moment his text came through.

"I was bored. Tim still hasn't gotten in, Mom is at work. And I wasn't in the mood to watch Public Television or reruns of True Hollywood Stories."

"Hey, I'm not complaining. I'm happy to see you," Alex said. He gestured for me to sit at the giant island.

I pulled up one of the mahogany high-top chairs and held my tea with both hands, letting it warm my fingers. Alex sat across from me, reached forward to grab an apple out of the fruit bowl in the middle, and Sam leaned against the side counter to our left. I sipped the tea and noticed the duffle bag in the doorway between the kitchen and the foyer. Okay, not exactly a duffle—more like a structured bag that looked like the love child of a rendezvous between a duffle and a suitcase. Camille, Sam, and Alex all had this same elegant matching luggage in navy blue that she had custom embroidered with a gold V on the front pocket for their last name. I assumed this bag was Alex's since he'd just arrived home after the three-hour drive from Champaign.

"Haven't even unpacked yet, huh?" I said to Alex, and nodded toward the luggage. "And you're harassing *me* for being eager to hang out?" Alex turned to see what I referred to, but Sam spoke up before he could respond.

"Oh, that's mine. I put in for vacation time a while back so I'd have a break over the holiday. The hospital hasn't given me more than one day off in a row for months, so I needed a breather. And I decided to spend a couple of days up here to catch up with some old friends while I can."

"Oh," I whispered and felt stupid for making it sound as if Alex was that excited to see me.

Alex must have seen the sentiment in my expression, because he said, "I haven't unpacked yet, either. My bag is just upstairs, where people won't trip over it." He grabbed another apple from the bowl in front of him and threw it at Sam, but Sam deftly snatched it with the hand not occupied by the coffee mug. They both smirked with this interaction, and I marveled at the male brain. If Tim threw an apple at me, it would probably hit me in the face and I would either get pissed off or cry.

Sam set the apple on the counter. "Yes, but when I unpack, it won't be dumping out my suitcase into a pile in the corner, and then sifting out whatever I need for the next week from the floor."

I burst into laughter, because Alex did that very thing once, years ago, when both of our families went away for a long weekend together. I figured he no longer did that, but he couldn't come up with any better response than nodding to Sam's scrubs and retorting, "Well, at least I'm not wearing pajama pants." Sam just chuckled.

"Anyway..." Alex said with a sigh, and turned back to me. "I still haven't done any Christmas shopping."

"Of course." I rolled my eyes. "Why bother getting it done early?"

"Exactly. So you up for braving the mall with me?"

"Ugh, gross. A week before Christmas? What the hell is wrong with you?"

"I waited to do it with you so we could hang out," he said.

"No, you waited to do it with me so I'd think of gift ideas for everyone, saving you from having to do it."

"Sounds about right," Sam agreed and took another sip from his mug.

Alex just waved Sam's comment off without looking at him. "Come on, I'll buy you a nice lunch and maybe even a ring pop from that fancy candy store in the mall."

Play it cool, don't seem too overly eager, I thought.

"I don't think even the Hope Diamond would be worth dealing with those crowds," I said with a laugh.

"Can't do anything on your own," Sam muttered toward Alex and then sighed before looking at me. "Just think of all the people-watching you'll get to do, though." The way Sam said it—it was as if he felt exasperated—and I looked over at him. Our eyes locked for a second longer than normal.

"You know Alex will be clueless if you don't help him pick stuff out," Sam continued. "We'll all end up getting gift cards to the Disney Store, along with a packet of fireworks or something."

At that, Alex began to sing the hook to the Aladdin song "A Whole New World" and I covered my face in mock disgust.

I looked up at Sam again. "You're only trying to get me to do it so you won't get dragged along."

He shrugged as if he had no protest.

"Fine," I said. "Only because I'd be bored out of my mind at home." I tried to sound blasé, so much more casual about spending time with Alex than I felt.

Alex clapped his hands together and rubbed them with eagerness. "Fantastic. And as your consolation prize, I'll sing that song for you all the way to the mall."

"Well, you should have led with that. If I knew you'd sing Disney tunes I would have agreed immediately," I joked.

Alex insisted on driving, and he opened the door for me. We crawled into his black Range Rover, and then buckled in. The back seats of the SUV were folded down and a plethora of sporting goods was stored inside. Golf clubs, a football, and some lacrosse gear.

He turned up the music on the radio, looked at me—a long gaze that heated my insides.

"I'm really happy to be home," he said.

I returned the smile and agreed.

Forty minutes later, we were at the mall, and the crowds were even worse than I predicted. People brushed by us on either side while Christmas music echoed through the giant, sterile-lit walkways.

We picked out Alex's gifts to everyone over the course of two hours. As we walked past the food court, he slung his arm around my shoulder. Brotherly? Sensual? I couldn't tell. I peered over at him and felt weak when I realized how close his face was to mine. He looked at me and his eyes, so blue they looked colored in by hand, stirred my shyness.

"Well, we only have one left to go," Alex said.

"Huh?"

"Yours. We still need to pick out my gift to you."

I waved the comment off. "Nah, don't worry about it. There isn't anything I need. I mean, ring pops are fun, but they really don't go with my everyday attire."

Alex smirked. "Nonsense. Christmas isn't about what you need. I'm not going to give you food, water, or air for Christmas. I want to get you something outrageously unnecessary. Like... How about that?" he said, and pointed to the window of a travel accessory shop. There in the middle of the display sat a bejeweled passport holder, covered with pink crystals.

I laughed. "That is absolutely, completely unnecessary. You'd probably have to take your passport out every time you had to show it to customs, anyway. It's lovely, but pointless."

"Then it's perfect," Alex said, and pulled me toward the display.

I leaned to the side to get a glimpse of the price tag and shook my head no. "Astronomical. And for something probably made by a 10-month-old for three cents wage in a third world country. I'm not going to have you spend an obscene amount of money on something so silly for me."

"Maybe it's silly, but you can still use it. And then every time you see your passport you'll think of me. I'm not taking no for an answer."

I stared at the glittery passport holder for a moment. "I guess if I'm lucky enough to end up traveling with a dance career I'll use my passport a lot."

"Then you're getting it."

I tried to protest further, but he dragged me into the store. The warmth of his hand around mine distracted me from any continued objections, and I felt lightheaded when he didn't let go right away. Alex grabbed one of the passport holders from the shelf and then took it to the cashier to pay.

Alex thanked her, grabbed the small bag, and pulled me out of the store. "Okay, pretend you have no idea what I got you for Christmas." He tucked a stray piece of my blonde hair behind one of my ears.

"Huh? Oh, right," I said. "What are you even talking about? You got me something?"

"That's my girl." He smiled at me with an intense gaze, and that smile, the way he uttered *those words*. I was gone, just obliterated. There was no coming back from this, from Alex slithering his way into my heart like this.

And then once again, out of the ethers, I thought of Sam. He loved to travel, and the passport holder made me think of him. Sam and his watchful eyes—intensely watchful blue-green eyes. I needed to think of something other than Sam's eyes. Something other than Alex's *brother's* eyes.

And contemplating those attentive eyes then reminded me of Jake. I quickly suppressed the thought of Jake's black eye, of blood smeared beneath his nose, of someone out there who inflicted violence because of me. I tried so hard to stifle the eerie sensation in my gut. I only quieted it with a mental pillow, but could not suffocate the feeling completely.

CHAPTER THREE

That evening Mom, Tim—who had just arrived home from the airport two hours prior—and I sat down for dinner at the Van Ettens' dining room table. Tim looked like he'd packed on a couple of pounds since I saw him last, and he had given me a tight hug when he walked in the door a few hours earlier. He kept a beard of scruff and his pale brown hair stayed tucked under a baseball cap. Mom still had to remind him to remove it while at the table, even though he was thirty years old.

Just before sitting down to eat, I stared at Camille's Christmas tree, which was a sight to behold: towering high enough that it required a ladder to place the topper at its peak. Every bough dripped with glossy ornaments in shades of pale cream, deep ivory, and gold. Feather plumes reached out like soft limbs, hoping to delight the skin of anyone who stepped too close. And the presents, all wrapped in expensive matching paper, spilled out around the bottom.

We partook of this dinner with the Van Ettens every single year, and the contrast between the elegant setting and the casual, joking, sometimes-obscene conversations never failed to amuse me. Camille sat down at the head of the table, put her cloth napkin on her lap and told us to dig in. Mom sat next to her and they harassed Tim about the swarms of ladies he must be romancing out in California. Alex sat across from me and forked a small roast potato off of my plate as soon as everyone dished up and began eating. I gave him a light kick under the table, having to stretch a little to reach my leg across the distance.

"Alex," Camille said, and gave him a scolding look. Then she rolled her eyes at us for acting like children, and sipped her wine.

Alex remained civilized for a few minutes before discreetly flinging a pea onto my plate.

I sighed and stared at him. "So how about you?" I asked Alex. "You having numerous wild affairs down there at school?"

He shrugged as he stabbed a piece of roast with his fork. "Only with the ladies who don't charge too much per hour," he said, straight-faced, loud enough for everyone at the table to hear.

Sam chuckled under his breath.

"Alex." Camille sounded appalled. "I told you. You get what you pay for. Go for quality," she continued, and then a crooked smirk crept onto her face.

"Sorry, Mom. I'll keep that in mind next time I peruse the street corners."

"Good boy. Keep it classy." She took another long sip of her wine.

Alex huffed out a laugh as he looked at her, and then returned his gaze to me. "Nah, I'm too busy with school. Besides, no one special down there has caught my eye."

"So how is law school?" Tim asked Alex.

"Fine. It's school. How excited about it can I be?"

There lingered a beat of silence. Everyone knew Alex didn't like school, *never* liked it, and that he felt less than thrilled about the profession he had decided to pursue. I asked him once why he didn't do something else, but Alex couldn't think of anything he really wanted to do. And the social pressure among the wealthy... I supposed I lived among them but didn't feel a part of their world when it came to matters of finances. And the high expectations that came with such an upbringing.

Camille transitioned the mood by asking about me. "So what about you, sweetie? How are things with dance?"

"Good," I said. "I'm done after this coming semester. I'm excited to start auditioning for professional dance companies."

My mom cleared her throat and added, "She's going to fly out to New York to see if any of them out there will offer her a spot."

Alex and Sam both looked up at me. My plan for some time was to audition in New York near the end of next semester, and of course I'd audition around Chicago, as well. But Mom knew my dream was to go to New York. I never wanted to do anything but be a professional stage dancer, and everyone knew the place to do it was New York—if you could make it.

"New York?" Sam asked and I turned my attention to him.

"Yeah, but I'll audition around Chicago, too. New York is a long shot, anyway."

I looked back at Alex, but I could feel Sam's continued stare in my peripheral vision, and it pulled my eyes back in his direction. Sam gazed at me for a moment and then lowered his eyes. He poked around at the food on his plate, and I felt my ears go hot.

"Why not San Fran?" Tim asked.

"I'm not opposed to it. I can look into companies out there, too. But New York is kind of the dream, you know?"

"I'm sure they'd love you. My dream, however, is to eat more of that stuffing right now," Alex said, and nodded to the dish in the center.

After dinner, we moved into the living room and sat on the sofas next to the tree. A fire crackled in the corner, Mom and Camille went to the kitchen to get more wine, and Tim excused himself for a few minutes.

"Look at that," Alex said. "It's snowing again."

I squinted to see the snow in the darkness outside, and Alex got up to peer out the window as fat flakes drifted to the ground.

"Has anyone seen the forecast for the next few days?" he asked.

Sam and I both said, "No" at the same time and glanced at each other.

"Jinx," we again muttered in unison, but quietly, as if we both felt silly for saying it.

Alex furrowed his brow. "Hmm. It better be a white Christmas or I'll be effing pissed. Be right back. I'm going to check it real quick." I watched him saunter off into another room and then Sam and I were left alone together.

Sam cleared his throat. "He's probably hoping it will snow enough to build a snow fort."

I laughed. "Yeah, probably." Then silence fell between us.

"So New York, huh?" he asked.

"Yeah, we'll give it a shot. Doesn't hurt to at least try."

"That's true. Too bad you couldn't find something you'd be happy with around Chicago. But I get it. New York would be pretty cool. We'd all be very proud of you."

"I didn't say that I wouldn't be happy around here. I'd be thrilled if one of the top dance companies in Chicago offered me a place. In a way, it would be nice because then I wouldn't have to leave everyone. But New York would be a bigger mountain to climb, I think it would feel more rewarding if I succeeded."

Sam nodded. "I get that. Seems like everyone ends up scattering these days, anyway."

I looked at the glass of wine I held. "Yeah, I guess that's kind of the way our generation does things." All at once, I felt dejected about it. As much as I wanted to chase my dreams, I hated the idea of us all being in different places. Would this thing we always had, the close bond between our families, evaporate over time?

As if reading my thoughts, Sam spoke again. "Well, even if that happens, we won't lose touch. None of us would let that happen. We'll have to make a point to have occasional get-togethers, even if it kills us."

I chuckled, but it felt heavy with melancholy. "Yeah, we'll have to do that," I agreed. "So how long do you have left in your residency?"

"A little over a year."

"And then you will try to get a full-time position with that hospital? Or just look out of state right away?"

Sam shrugged as if to say *maybe*. "Possibly see if I can get a job with them. I'd prefer to work with a private practice, though. I'd love to find a place that sort of gets the link between modern medicine and more natural approaches. You know, treating the whole person, not just throwing a drug at symptoms. But mostly, it'd be nice to develop more ongoing relationships with regular patients, rather than the transient flow of people in a hospital."

That made sense with Sam and his more subdued but loyal personality. The hush fell between us again and I looked at my wine. Camille had instrumental piano holiday songs playing, twinkling notes to fill the silence. The mothers returned with another bottle of wine while laughing about something, and Alex and Tim made their way back into the room a few minutes later. Conversation resumed, but I looked up to see Sam watching me again. The wine broke down any guard I had against blushing.

The following day, as light flurries continued to fall and angry winds beat against the house, I sat on the carpeted floor of my bedroom and wrapped presents. Unlike Alex, I tried to avoid last minute shopping and picked out gifts for everyone a month earlier. I stuffed them in an extra duffle bag, and they made the trek home from school with me.

Thanks to the combination of music in dance classes and the noise of the city, I didn't often experience quiet time to myself. So I savored the peace, hearing nothing but the wind, along with the sound of scissors slicing through paper, tape being torn, and my own inner thoughts. Cut, fold, tape. Cut, fold, tape. I became so engrossed in the monotonous task that it startled me when Alex knocked on my bedroom window.

Alex stood on the second-floor outdoor balcony, an old tradition of his he refused to give up. I rose to open the window and braced myself for the cold. There was only one door to the balcony, located in a tiny vestibule off of the hallway. My room had a large window overlooking the terrace. Ever since we were kids, Alex opted to climb the stairs to the balcony and crawl through my bedroom window, rather than coming through the hallway door.

"God, it's freezing out there," I said. "Can't you let the cold air in downstairs on days like this?" I tried to battle a smile and lost. Despite my shivers, I took pleasure in the sight of Alex crawling into my bedroom.

"The cold is good for you," Alex said.

He ruffled a hand through his hair to remove the snowflakes, and I shut the window. He slipped off his shoes and set them on a mat I left below the window for that very purpose from the time I was young. Mom knew of his habit and insisted that he not track dirt on the carpet if he kept entering the house this way.

"Busy?" he asked.

"So very," I said, and returned to the presents, relieved his gift was already wrapped.

Alex sat on the floor across from me and leaned against my bed to watch as I scrolled an elegant design in gold marker on one of the wrapped presents. "Maybe you should give up dance and become a professional gift wrapper," he said as he touched a handmade decorative bow, adorned with a tiny snowflake I cut from thick glitter paper.

He examined the perfect folds of paper on the box. "It's weird that you're so tidy and disciplined while still being creative. I thought creative people were supposed to be kind of sloppy and free-flowing."

"I don't think Martha Stewart is sloppy. And anyway, being disciplined and creative is a combination that works well for dance. So I think I'll stick with that, but thanks."

Alex shrugged. "Suit yourself. All I'm saying is that you could wow the world with your skills if you opened a Hallmark store." I rolled my eyes but laughed.

A minute later he stroked the tulle that still encircled my nightstand, like a long tutu skirt. My bedroom had changed very little from the time I was twelve.

"So what are you doing this evening? Strutting the catwalk for some high-end designer, then going out with some celebrity who is in town? Or just staying in, watching TV in footie pajamas?" he asked.

"Very funny."

"I know it's last minute, but Sam and I are trying to pull together a party tonight. The Sergeant gave us the go ahead as long as we keep it quarantined to the rec wing," he said, referring to Camille.

The rec wing was an overindulgence of ridiculous proportions. Rather than an actual wing, it encompassed the entire walk out basement of their house, which was, naturally, mammoth. When the boys were younger, Camille outfitted it with an indoor basketball court on one end, a partial wall down the middle, along with sofas and an enormous television on the other side. Later came the pool table, a full-sized refrigerator, and the dark wooden bar.

It was Camille's effort to get the boys to spend most of their time with friends at the house, rather than roaming the streets, all while keeping the destruction sectioned off to a dedicated area. She instated the rule that once she furnished it, Sam and Alex had to replace anything with their own money that was ever damaged from irresponsible behavior—as well as reimburse her for what she initially spent on the item in question. As a result, the rec wing remained in impeccable condition.

"How do you guys expect to wrangle together enough people for a party in one day?" I asked.

Alex looked at me like I should know better, and I did. With his extensive list of acquaintances he kept in touch with, he could get two dozen people to come by with minimal effort. The rec wing's ambiance didn't hurt in luring people, either.

"So you aren't busy, are you? You think you can pencil it into your gift wrapping schedule?" he asked as he moved up to sit on my bed, and gave me a teasing smile.

"Well, I *suppose* I could manage to make it, between that, staring in my mom's kitchen pantry out of boredom, and practicing routines in my basement."

"Good. Please convince any of your friends you can that they should come by, too. We've got a handful of girls coming, but not enough to keep it from being a sausage fest."

"I'll do what I can."

"So, you want to wrap my gifts for me?" he asked.

"No."

Alex leaned back on his hands. The wind rattled my window and I shivered; a peculiar chill raised goose bumps on my arms.

"Eh, I think plastic garbage bags will be just as easy," he said. "That's pretty much what Bed Bath & Beyond does, but with their logo printed on it, right? Besides, I don't want people to think I have so much time on my hands that I have to fill it by spending hours wrapping gifts." He smiled, trying to get a rise out of me.

I gave him a half-hearted glare. "Like your mom would allow anything so vulgar under her Christmas tree."

"She'd probably have me strung up for that, wouldn't she?"

I chuckled and then sighed. Alcohol, loud music, Alex and myself all mixed into one evening at this party in question. The result might hurt, bad. But if I wasn't delusional about the sexual tension between us yesterday, it might also be the perfect opportunity for us to let down our guards.

All at once, I looked forward to the evening more than I ought to. And yet, there was something in my gut, some deep instinct—a premonition. The party. It was as if I could hear the distant echoes of those screams, of the bolts rumbling loose on that roller coaster. The sound of them, like clairaudience, that resonated before something dreadful occurred. Before the tracks ahead led to something ghastly.

CHAPTER FOUR

I agreed to head over early to help Sam and Alex get things ready for the party. So after I spent a full hour primping myself, I walked to the back of their house wearing a tight red sweater and even tighter jeans under my long jacket. Letting myself in through the basement doors, I realized there was nothing to do. They would order pizzas once enough people showed up, and the fridge was stocked with booze. The only contribution I made was in finding bowls to pour some chips into, instead of forcing people to grab handfuls out of the bags like the guys would have done. Sam fiddled with the music in the corner. Alex started to hand me a beer and then pulled it back.

"Will the beer do for now, my lady?" he asked in a less-than-stellar British accent.

"Indeed, fine sir," I said. I would have preferred a shot of something hard to get my inhibitions running away faster, but the beer was physically closer.

He opened it for me and I took long gulps when he turned away. Tim came over about a half hour after I did, and he and Sam played billiards as they fell into their own conversation. The crack of pool balls hitting each other snapped through the air. Rachel came by soon after.

Rachel started on a drink herself and stared at the guys.

I turned away from them and looked at Rachel. "Tell me the best book you've read lately. Or a movie you've seen. I need to get my mind off of being stupid and obsessing over—"

"God, is it me or did Sam and Alex get hotter since I last saw them?" she interrupted.

"You tell me. And you're no help at all right now."

"Oh please, like you don't notice these things," she said.

It embarrassed me to admit something like that when Alex was actually in my presence, so I shrugged it off even though Rachel would see right through it.

"They're like brothers to me. It's too weird."

Rachel's laugh was so loud that all three of the guys looked over at us. I mentally thanked her for making me appear funny.

"Psh, 'like brothers... Too weird'. My ass," she mumbled before sipping her drink again. "Your actual brother is getting a little fat. But he's still cute, too. I'd make out with him."

"Gross," I said.

She nodded and grinned. "Yep. See? When it's *really* like a brother, you find that appalling. But I don't think you'd find it appalling in the same way if I wanted to make out with those Van Etten boys. I think you'd want to scratch my eyes out, in that case, rather than vomiting in your mouth a little."

"You assume a lot here. You seem to think I feel such ownership over them. And *both* of them at that."

"Oh, you do. Trust me. You do. With both of them... Yep."

Rachel continued gazing at the guys. For a moment it was just me looking at her, her looking at them, and me realizing that Rachel had a sort of clarity in the way she saw the world that others lacked. I took a lengthy gulp of my beer, finishing the bottle.

Before long, people came in hordes through the basement doors. Pizzas arrived, Sam mixed drinks for a handful of people, and the music was turned up to be heard over the buzz of conversations. A group of guys shot basketballs on the court side of the wing, and from the sound of it, the alcohol did nothing for their aim. A few more of my friends from high school arrived, and we sat on one of the couches as we caught up on life.

After a half hour, I got up and crossed the room to get another drink. My eyes darted around as I searched for Alex. I didn't see him until his arm was around my shoulders and his face was right next to mine.

"Need a refill, lovely lady?" he asked. His eyes and lips were so close.

"You're correct, handsome," I said, and felt a little embarrassed saying that to him.

Sam stood near the bar and watched us approach. He smiled from the conversation he engaged in with someone I didn't bother to notice, but his eyes turned slightly serious as he observed us.

"The lady would like a drink," Alex said to him.

"What'll it be?" Sam asked me.

"I don't know. Something simple. Rum and diet, I guess."

Sam gave me one nod and slipped behind the counter to pour me the beverage, then turned back around and slid it to me. I sipped the drink. Then Sam resumed his conversation with some friend again. Alex leaned back against the bar.

"So how's life, Auttie? Really, no-holds-barred honesty. Naked truth. How is it?" He offered me a devious smile.

"Good. Exceptional at this exact moment."

Alex lifted an eyebrow. "True?"

"True story. And you?"

"Fantastic. Want to go on a crime spree with me?"

I threw my head back in a laugh. "A crime spree?"

"Yeah, hell yeah. We could rob banks, pillage petty cash from local businesses, and hell... Even the snack drawers from the cubicles of those businesses while we're at it. Just run off with a dump truck full of money and snacks. Then you could woo every man you see with your beauty and your scandalous, criminal money."

"And fun sized candy bars," I added, my voice dropping. I felt the frown on my face, the wilt in my emotions. If he wanted me, he wouldn't want me to woo other men.

"You don't need the money," I said.

"It sounds fun, though. We could be the new Bonnie and Clyde."

I gave him an expression as if considering the idea. "You could charm any woman with your money and snacks, too," I said, trying to sound lighthearted... and failing.

Alex leaned in toward me. "I'm just joking with you." He brushed a hand through my hair, tucking it behind my ear. "Okay? You know I'm just kidding."

He moved close to me, and I felt hot all over.

"Okay, yeah... I know. So are you glad to be home for the break?" I asked and took a breath to release the momentary gloom, to slow my quickening pulse.

"Quite." He righted himself and indicated with a quick tilt of his head that I should walk with him.

And so I did, strolling around the groups of people until we found a deserted corner to occupy. We both leaned against adjoining walls. He held a beer with one hand and put his other hand in the pocket of his jeans. I could see the definition of his arms through his long-sleeved shirt.

"Yeah, I'm very glad to be home," he said.

"What, law school isn't all it's cracked up to be?"

Alex didn't answer but gave me a look as if to say, *please, you know I hate it.*

"You'll be good at it, though," I said. "You have a way with people."

"There are a million jobs that I could do with that. I could sell vacuum cleaners door-to-door. It doesn't make me care about it."

"Well, maybe you can do it for ten years until you figure out what you want to do—the thing you'll end up being passionate about. By that time, I'll probably have to transition into something different, too. Dance related, but a stage career won't last forever. Maybe teaching or working as a choreographer."

"Oh, I'm sure you'll be able to dance for a very long time," he said, but he seemed depressed.

So I tried to ease back into the inklings of flirtation we had going a moment earlier.

"Sorry that I couldn't get more girls to come, but you didn't give me much notice. It does appear they're occupying some of the guys, though," I said, and nodded to my friends, now playing pool with the males that were their eye candy earlier.

The hint of a smile returned to his face. "You did fine. You're here, too, and that helps."

"I'm not sure it does. Not getting much in the way of being hit on." Oh yes... yes, I was playing the game.

"No?" he asked and gave me a long, meaningful stare. "You sure about that?"

My insides softened. I wanted to skip all of this and just make out with him. If it were any other guy, maybe I would. But my wits were still with me enough to know that it would make tomorrow very uncomfortable. Something had to be said.

We had to say *something* to the effect of this being a thing we both wanted and thought about beyond just this evening.

"I think I'm pretty sure. Yeah, not getting hit on at all," I said, the smile cracking through my façade.

I waited for him to say something else to further the banter, to bring us closer. But all he muttered was, "Hmm."

I looked around, trying to think of something else to say. I saw Sam on the other side of the room, and he glanced my way again. It conjured a memory for some reason, Sam over there, seeing us. If I kissed Alex right now it wouldn't be the first time, technically, that we kissed. And it wouldn't be the first time that Sam had witnessed something like that.

~~~

A couple of years after our first visit to Tempest Lodge, Camille invited us again. It was the second and last time I ever visited the lodge, because we usually went to places with beaches when we vacationed with the Van Ettens. On this second trip, we went for a week in the summer. Everyone lingered outside, enjoying the hot summer breeze as we hiked around the large pond and towering pines off in the distance behind the house. The grass was tall, reaching my ten-year-old shins. It undulated in the wind like waves. Our moms walked somewhere up ahead, beyond the trees. So did Sam and Tim, at least so I thought. I trailed behind and looked at flowers as I strolled. Occasionally I glanced at Alex, his sandy hair gold in the sunlight, as he found rocks and chucked them at nothing in particular. And then, when we were in the middle of talking about something I couldn't remember, Alex suddenly turned, walked over to me, and kissed me. It was a quick, juvenile kiss. We were still kids. Shock was my dominant feeling. Sure, I felt a little lightheaded, a little weak. But surprised more than anything.

When I looked around after he resumed walking again, I saw Sam off to the side. I hadn't realized he had walked parallel to us, about twenty yards away. His expression revealed nothing. I assumed he thought it was stupid—him being a teenager, older than us. He looked ahead then and kept moving as if nothing had happened. But I flushed and felt more alarmed, more flustered that Sam had witnessed the kiss Alex gave me than from the actual kiss itself.

~~~

I blinked away the memory and sipped my drink. Someone changed the tunes to dance music, and the liquor made my body want to move. It also loosened my grip on self-control. I thought getting away from Alex might be a good idea until I sobered up a little, or until he drank more to keep up with me. I didn't want to—God I didn't want to—but I made myself pull away.

I threw him a coquettish smile. "I think I should spend a little more time with the girls. It's been a while since we've seen each other."

"And just when I got you alone."

"What? Oh, you didn't want to see us girls get in a pillow fight?" I said, jerking a thumb over my shoulder at them. "Because that's what we do when we catch up. We strip down to our underwear and have pillow fights. Just an all-out giggle fest while we discuss final exams and our opinion on politics. I was about to grab some of the cushions off the sofa and pass them around."

Alex laughed and gently pushed me as we walked back to the crowd of people. "Now that... I would be willing to watch."

"I bet you would. Some of them are probably wearing hot matching bra and panty sets, too."

Alex moved behind me, leaned in, and whispered in my ear. "I'd only be looking at yours."

I glanced back at him, my heart pounding. He smiled and then wandered off, leaving me to my friends. I watched the lines of his muscles on his back as he walked away. I downed the rest of my drink in a few rapid gulps.

Someone cranked the music up even more, and before long almost all of the girls danced in the ample space between the bar and couches. Then a handful of guys were there, too, dancing with the girls. I was drunk. Really drunk. Too drunk. I danced by myself among my friends and still held my emptied glass in my hand. Alex reappeared and maneuvered his way in through the crowd. He gave me another drink, taking my empty glass. Then he started to dance with me, putting one arm around my waist. I allowed myself to touch his arm, but my new drink was full and I needed to focus to keep from spilling it. I drank at least a quarter of it right away, just to reduce the amount of liquid that tried to abandon the glass onto the floor. I had to lean in and talk loud for him to hear me.

"This is too much," I said, referring to the alcohol.

"Do you want me to take it?" He kept smiling as if the sexual tension between us kept him from being able to put on a straight face.

"Mmm, no. It's good." I took another taste.

"I'm glad you like it," Alex said with more innuendo than necessary when referring to any beverage. He moved in closer. I let him. My skin felt hot and dewy, so aware of how close his body was to mine. I felt his hand on my hip, and there was nothing platonic about the sensation. A few songs breezed by, and we continued to dance. I danced with him as long as I could, but after a bit, I thought I might burst. Too much liquid. I had to use the restroom.

"I need to do the, you know, proverbial powdering my nose kind of thing," I said. My intoxication leaked into my communication skills, my words lacking proper enunciation.

"Alright. Hurry back," Alex said, and let me go with heavy reluctance.

I walked over to the rec wing's bathroom and had to wait a minute for someone to finish and leave. I went in, used the toilet as the room wobbled, and then looked in the mirror as I washed my hands.

"Shit, I'm so drunk," I whispered. What was it about bathrooms that made drunkenness so much more obvious than a dance floor?

"Too drunk. Too drunk," I mumbled as I dried my hands on a plush hand towel and checked the mirror to smooth my hair.

When I reemerged, I couldn't find Alex anywhere. I searched through the dancing crowd but did not see him. I leaned around the corner to the basketball court, but he wasn't there, either. I walked back over to the bar and set my drink down. Sam stood at the edge of the bar, halfway behind it.

"Sam, please. Take this from me. Now. Before I finish it."

"That bad?" he asked.

"Are you referring to my opinion of the drink or my condition?" I asked.

Sam laughed and looked like he'd had a little too much of the hard stuff, as well. "Your condition."

"Ah. Yes. That bad. The drink was good. But too much. Too much."

"Good, I made that drink myself. You almost hurt my feelings," Sam joked. He took the drink and dumped it down the drain of the tiny sink behind the bar. Then he came around and leaned against the bar next to me. We watched the party as it moved and gyrated in front of us.

"What am I gonna do with myself?" I said.

"I'm sure you'll be fine. Are you having fun?"

"Very much."

"Good. Then don't worry about it." Sam had a gentle smile on his face as he watched everyone. I couldn't help but smile as I looked at him.

"So what's new, Sam? Want me to hook you up with one of my friends?"

He laughed and swigged his beer. "Ha, no. But thanks."

"Ooooh, why's that? Have a girl downtown already?"

"No. I don't have a ton of extra time on my hands right now to date."

I felt a peculiar relief in hearing him say that. "I guess not. When's the last time you had a girlfriend? Like two years ago or something?"

"Three," he admitted, looking pained.

"God. You must need to get laid." In the abyss of my thoughts, I shouted at myself to sober up.

Sam was mid-sip and choked a little on his drink, and then laughed. "Well, I didn't say it has been three years for *that*."

"Oooooh," I said again, teasing.

Sam wore a crooked smile and looked a little embarrassed.

"That doesn't surprise me," I said. "Probably doesn't take much effort for you, does it? With all that." I gestured up and down the length of him. "And being a doctor, too."

"I wouldn't say it's all that easy. Maybe if I were as forward as Alex it would be. But I'm not."

"Hmm, I don't know," I said. I felt unsure about how else to respond, so I changed the subject.

"So if you look for jobs all over the country when you're done with your residence," I said, aware I screwed up the word and pretended I didn't. "I think I just decided I'd be bummed if you moved away."

"Is that so?" he asked and gave me a coy look. "Why would you be bummed if you're off in New York anyway?"

"Hey. No guarantee of that. And I don't know why, I just would be."

"Well, what if by coincidence I found a job in New York, and you happened to get a place with a dance company there, too? Would you still be bummed then?"

I pursed my lips. "No. I would *not* be. I'd love that."

Sam shrugged and took another drink. "Well, there you have it. Until life happens, you can't be prematurely disappointed about it. You never know where the road might lead."

"Are you planning on looking for jobs in New York?" I asked.

"I'll look everywhere and anywhere decent. I love Chicago. But I'd also love the adventure of moving somewhere else. New York would be cool. I'm sure I'll at least check for positions out there. Hell, especially if you're out there already."

I blushed, felt my heart race again. "Yeah, true. I forgot for a second that was your thing—travel."

Sam went on more exotic trips than anyone I knew. Not that he had five million stamps in his passport or anything, but Sam did the cliché backpacking through Europe thing the summer he graduated high school. He also spent a semester in Australia when he was an undergrad, and took a trip to Thailand a few years ago, in addition to numerous road trips around the U.S. He had pictures with friends in front of places like the Washington Monument, next to the Grand Canyon, with a fishing boat captain on some charter trip in New

England, and in front of a place called SurfFace Surf Shop where he'd taken lessons in California.

"I enjoy seeing new places, new cultures, yeah," he said.

"I look forward to doing more of it myself."

Sam sipped his drink. "I think it's a good way to expand your world. And sometimes, you know, you just need to see some new scenery."

"Yeah. I get that. The whole change-of-pace thing. There are some beautiful places out there, I'm sure... The scenery is nice around here, though," I said, staring at him.

Wait, what the hell? Was I flirting with Sam? I took note of my posture and assessed how I gazed at his deep-set eyes and strong jaw. Yes. Yes, I was. He looked back at me and I saw the surprise on his face. He appeared pleased by the interaction. I thought I sensed him move closer to me.

"You don't mind it, huh?"

"Nope. Don't mind it at all." *Oh my God, stop it!* I thought.

"Well, if it's any consolation, I don't mind the scenery, either," Sam said.

Oh, shit. I nodded. Surprise bloomed in me like a poisonous flower—both pleasant and alarming. Did Sam, *Sam*, just admit he found me attractive? This felt exquisite. Disastrous. The word *tease* floated through my thoughts as I reminded myself of my increasing devotion to Alex.

"That's good. Yeah, good consolation," I said. I blinked and it seemed like it took longer to close and reopen my eyes than it should.

Sam's crooked grin was back, and he gazed at me with tenderness. The surprise lingered there again, but he appeared elated.

"So... travel," I said, trying to steer away from my transgression.

"Yes. Travel," Sam said, and set down his drink, still leaning on the bar. He moved his hands back to rest on them against the ledge.

"Do you have any trips planned right now?" I asked as I turned my body toward him.

"Not at the moment. Do you?"

"Just New York in the spring."

"Oh, right. Yeah."

"Do you know where to go next? Next time you trip, take one, I meant?" I asked fumbling over the words.

He looked thoughtful for a moment. "Hmm. Maybe South America? Or maybe Japan? I don't know."

"South America seems sexy," I said. "I mean, parts. Brazil, you know?" I felt like I became less coherent as the minutes passed. I scooted an inch in his direction, in part because he smelled good, and in part because my concern about fainting grew larger with each passing moment.

"Yeah, I guess you could say that. Brazil would be awesome. I'd love to see it. You could, you know... You could go with me someday. If you wanted," he said. This was unlike Sam, to be so bold. He definitely had an ample amount of alcohol in him.

My cheeks, already flushed from the liquor, heated even more. I swallowed. "Ha... Yeah, sure. Uh, that'd be awesome."

We had traveled together as families countless times. The prospect of going to Brazil with Sam shouldn't, in theory, have shaken me the way it did. But alone with Sam, it sounded like an entirely different sort of vacation. It scared me. It excited me.

Sam moved closer to my ear and whispered, "I think it would be awesome, too." As soon as he said it, he seemed embarrassed, as if he knew he had crossed some invisible boundary, so he steered the conversation into another direction.

We continued to talk, but I lost track of parts of the conversation. I only knew that we continued to flirt. Sam rested his hand on the small of my back—another un-Sam-like move—and I gazed up at him to evaluate if he was really as drunk as I figured he must be. I couldn't tell, but I felt woozy, so I leaned into him. His face turned toward mine and he looked down at me with warmth.

I reached the point of drunkenness where I became wrong, so very, very wrong. The kind of drunk where the filaments of thought that typically lay dormant in the darkest recesses of my mind crept out into the light, and nothing kept them restrained. Thoughts such as, not only how attractive Sam was in an objective sense, but how much I thought of him as *hot*. How good he smelled. How desirable I found him at the moment without my guard up. And then, how horrible a person I was for thinking those things.

I saw Alex again across the room then, and I was too drunk to understand what he was up to. I looked back and forth at them, from brother to brother, and marveled at how appealing they both were.

"You two," I said to Sam, gesturing at Alex and back to him. "How do I *live* next to you two?"

"What do you mean?" he asked with a small grin on his face, amused.

"You're both just so... Both of you. You're both so attractive... And fun, and rich. And funny. I don't belong here."

Sam laughed. "There is nowhere you belong more, Autumn. Besides, our mom is rich, not us."

"*Psh*, please."

"I'm serious. Money is sort of nonsense. It's just a superficial thing. It's a nice, helpful superficial thing. But that's it. And come on, you're like family. How could you say you don't belong here?"

"Well, you know what I mean," I said.

"Not really. You live right next door, are about to be a glamorous dancer, and you're beautiful. If anything..." He didn't finish his sentence, and I was about to ask him to continue when Alex approached.

"Don't be such a creeper," Alex said, throwing a faux punch at Sam's shoulder. The gesture came off as carefree, but I detected the trace of truth in it. Sam retracted his hand from my lower back.

Alex shifted his gaze to me. "What are you drinking?"

"Nothing. I had to put my drink down earlier."

"Want another?" Alex asked.

My intellect said no, but I shrugged and agreed to one anyway. Alex fetched me another drink, and even while I waited for it I realized I was farther gone than I should have been at this point. Most of the time, I could hold it together better than this—had a higher tolerance than this.

"You sure you want another?" Sam leaned in toward my ear to ask.

"I'm just barely going to drink any of it. He already started making it. But I won't drink it all."

"You don't have to drink any if you don't want to. It's not a big deal if one little drink goes to waste."

"It's okay. I'll just have two sips. That's all."

After I sipped from the next glass a few times, it was virtual amnesia, with fragments of coherence burning hazy imprints into my memory. There was Rachel hugging me and telling me she'd get a ride home with our friend Bethany. And then I had a deep conversation with my brother and Sam about the merits of sushi. And then Sam, Tim, Alex and I all discussed a trip we should take together. And then it was just Sam and me talking about travel yet again. Then Alex and I flirting, and back to Sam again. Alex, Sam, and me horsing around outside for a few minutes in the freezing night air. Me laughing with some of my girlfriends. Sam and I alone in the corner. Sam. Alex. Sam. Alex. Tim. Some guy I didn't know. Alex. Sam... Sam whispering so close to my ear that I could almost feel his lips on me. A swirl of wooziness and heavy eyelids.

And then, at some God-forsaken hour, one of the strangest conversations I've ever had took place. His face was close to mine, his eyes intense. We talked about taking a little trip, a little getaway. Something out of the ordinary, something both of us would only come up with this drunk. Even as we discussed it, I kept thinking *this might be the weirdest idea on Earth*. So unexpected. So irresponsible. And then we were off, and the party was behind us. The party—the freefall on the roller coaster—was such a blissful drop. Pure, uninhibited joy that left my stomach with a weightless sensation.

But then, *clink*, the first bolt on the tracks came loose. The pressure of the coaster shook the others out of place, readying them for liberation. The beautiful thing about tracks: they keep one sailing forth in a fixed direction, on course. The dreadful thing about tracks: they keep one sailing forth in a fixed direction, with no escape. The party was behind us, and then... Blackness.

~~~

When I awoke, I emerged from a deep blackout. I felt complete disorientation. My stomach rolled. I rocked back and forth. At first, I thought it was all dizziness from the hangover. After a bewildered moment, I realized the surface I was sprawled on moved to and fro, making my stomach lurch in protest. I blinked a few times, trying to decipher where I was, and my brain locked in confusion.

I registered my surroundings. I was lying on a minuscule bed of some kind. To my right was a small window, close enough to touch, with bright sunshine peeking around thick, beige curtains made for blocking out light. I lifted the curtain back with a finger, and the sunlight looked like... What? Late afternoon? Some kind of low surface hovered a couple of feet above my head, and to my left was an open space—a room, if it was even large enough to be called a room.

Over and over, I both heard and felt a sort of clunk-*clank*, clunk-*clank*, clunk-*clank*. It timed itself with the rocking. I realized it wasn't just the bed I was on; the entire room rocked in a subtle motion. I sat up as slowly as I could, unsure whether I'd be able to keep the contents of my stomach down. I burped and my head throbbed. The same clothes I wore to the party were still on my body. I eased my feet onto the floor, sitting on the bed while I hunched forward because of the surface above me. A moment later, I realized it was another bed, a bunk bed.

The party. Where was the block of time between the party and where I was now? I took slow, deep breaths, thinking. It felt like pulling memories out of tar—I had to struggle to bring them to the daylight, and even then they were murky, coated in residue. I remembered leaving the party with him, some kind of impulsive idea, one faint flash of walking down an elegant hallway with red carpet as I stumbled, and his warm hands caught my arm to steady me. That was it.

Covering my mouth with my hands, I processed the shock of where I thought I might be. I hung onto the corner post of the bed as I stood up, struggled to balance with my spinning head and the rocking, and turned to see if he was in the upper bunk. He was not. I turned back around to face the door, and stared at his bag, with the signature gold V embroidered on the front pocket.

A train. We boarded a train. *I must be in some kind of sleeper car or something*, I thought. The train rocked—clunk-*clank*, clunk-*clank*, clunk-*clank*. I had to remind myself to breathe.

"Why... The fuck... Did I get on a train?" I whispered. And then the doorknob rattled, and he came back into the sleeper room. I looked up, alarmed.

He smiled. "Ah, you're up," Alex said.

CHAPTER FIVE

It took me a moment to respond to Alex. At first, all I could do was stare at him, wide-eyed. He'd changed his clothes since the party. I felt both comforted and nervous at the sight of him, which confused me even more. *Why nervous?*

"When did you wake up?" he asked.

"Uh, just now. What happened? What are we doing?"

"You don't remember?" he asked, turning his face to the side.

"Only parts of it. Not much."

I surveyed the tiny room for a moment and saw a small chair and low-pile carpet, as well as two doors—one straight ahead, and one on an angled wall that jutted out to my right. I looked at the floor and took a deep breath as a wave of nausea hit me again. Alex watched me for a moment.

"Is that a bathroom?" I asked, nodding to the door on the angled wall.

"Yeah," he said.

"I have to puke." I hurried into the tiny bathroom and threw up. Somewhere in there I asked what the hell was going on, why we were on a train, but I couldn't discern if Alex answered me because my attention was on being sick.

Alex waited outside the door, then helped me stand up when I flushed the toilet. He assisted me as I moved over to the sink to scrub my hands, which shook to an upsetting degree. Then I rinsed my mouth out.

Alex cleared his throat. "Come on. We'll get you something to help the hangover in the dining car and you'll feel better. We can talk there."

Food sounded both helpful and simultaneously repulsive, but I wanted to get out of the claustrophobic room, so I didn't protest when he put an arm around me and led the way.

Alex ushered me out of the room and into the hallway, where I felt like I could breathe a little easier. Crimson carpet with a pattern of small golden medallions covered the floor. I felt the ripples of movement beneath my feet and kept a hand on the wall to steady myself. Small windows lined the wall opposite the sleeper rooms. Outside, the landscape gave nothing away but winter. I looked at the flat countryside with barren trees and felt like I was in a dream from which I couldn't wake up.

"This way," Alex said, placing his hand on my lower back to lead me to the right—toward what was the back of the train, judging by the direction the outside view blew past. It felt good to have Alex's hand on me when I felt so unsettled.

We walked to the end of our car. Alex opened a small metal door to a connecting platform that felt unsteady beneath my feet. Then through another small metal door, one more sleeper car, and then into the dining car. When we entered the dining car, the sight of a few other passengers and the gentle clank of dishes relaxed me a little. I brushed a hand over my hair.

White linen clothed tables and booth seats lined each side of the dining car. We found an empty table and Alex nodded for me to sit, then he took the seat across from me. I sat with my hands on the ledge of the table, stunned into silence. I observed my surroundings—the china place settings, the small lamp sconce bolted to the wall just beneath our window. When I glanced up, I realized gold painted tin tiles covered the ceiling, and three small chandeliers hung along the length of the dining car, their crystals swaying with the movement. Old music, standards from the likes of Frank Sinatra and Ella Fitzgerald, played in the background. I noticed the exit signs were in two languages, English and what looked like French. I don't think I'd ever felt this confused in my life.

"This isn't Amtrak, is it?" I asked.

Alex snorted out a laugh. "No."

"What... Where are we?"

"It's a private rail, we're traveling in style." His eyebrow lifted as if to impress me.

"I see that. But where are we? I mean, what the hell are we doing?"

"You really don't remember deciding to do this last night?"

I squeezed my eyes shut and propping one elbow on the table, I leaned my forehead on my hand. "Vaguely. No. Not really. I remember leaving the party, and sort of remember discussing trains a little when we were still at your house."

A waitress approached, set a basket of bread in front of us, and then handed us each a short menu labeled *Dinner / Dîner* with four items to select from. The entire menu was also in both English and evidently French.

I tapped my thumb against the menu. "Dinner. I slept away most of the day. So gross and wasteful."

Alex opened the cloth napkin in the basket to reveal all of the steaming bread rolls. "You should eat one. Get yourself leveled out a little."

I swallowed hard, grabbed a roll, ripped off a small piece and ate it. At first I thought I might be sick again right there, but after it sat for a moment in my stomach it helped ease the nausea.

"I think you mentioned the idea of sleeper trains," I said. "Or maybe someone else did, and I remember saying how cool it sounded to take a trip on one. Did I say that?"

Alex bit his lip and then answered. "Yeah. We had a long conversation about it. And don't you remember us deciding we should go on a trip for the hell of it, because it's your last semester before you finish school and head off to New York?"

"No." Bits and pieces of conversations were there, but portions of the night still were gone for good. I was pretty sure I'd never get them back, no matter how long I tried to pull the memories up.

"You seemed pretty excited about the idea," he said.

"That might be. But Alex, I was so drunk. *So* drunk. That might have been fun to talk about then, but we're sober now. What the hell are we doing? Answer me. Where are we going?"

He leaned back and rested one of his arms along the back of the cloth booth. "A small town to turn around, okay? Yeah, we're sober now. But we're already here. Look at it this way. We have a few days to kill before there are any real plans at home for the holidays, so why not enjoy ourselves? Like I said, we're just going to stop at a small tourist town where our tickets are set to turn around on another train. This line has two actual trains, I think. We're boarding the other one to head back home in one day. A couple of days, total. It's not that big of a deal. So why not just relax?"

I squeezed my eyes shut and then looked at him again. "Because, this is effing crazy, that's why. Our moms are going to be pissed and in a complete panic."

Alex shook his head. "I already called my mom and had her tell your mom, too. Yeah, they thought it was irresponsible, but

I told them we'd be back in a couple days. They'll get over it." He offered me the most sincere, puppy-eyed expression.

I believed him.

My shoulders dropped an inch in relief. "Oh. Okay... Oh. I guess that's good."

I swallowed another bite of bread. The waitress returned and asked what we'd like for dinner. Alex looked at me to let me order first. I didn't even bother to register the choices on the menu. I glanced over them quickly and picked something settling for my stomach, some kind of pasta. I waited for a moment after the waitress left with the menus before I spoke again.

"So there's no way to depart earlier? This is the dumbest thing I've ever done. I can't believe I got that drunk. I'm sorry. I just don't know..."

Alex looked a little hurt, which made me feel guilty. We partook in a million crazy things over the years—granted, nothing even close to this level. But I was sort of his partner in crime, and it was as if I rejected him by saying this.

"Well, we can get off at the next stop and try and find a way home, if that's what you want." Alex appeared despondent. He sat for a moment looking at the tablecloth, and it made my insides ache. Was I being ungrateful and rude for however much money he'd spent on the tickets? And it was only one day. I was probably being ridiculous.

"The other option is that we just finish out the ride," he said, his eyes were sweet, genuine, and pleading. "It's only a couple of days, total. It'd be easier than figuring out another way to get home and—if you let yourself—you could have a good time. The ride will be over with days to spare before Christmas, if that's what you're worried about."

I sat in silence for a few minutes. Alex stared out the window as he allowed me to consider the prospect. I pondered for a moment the idea that I was confined to this train with him, with Alex all to myself, and with no distractions around from home. And the sleeper car... Sharing a room with Alex. Even if there were two beds, the thought of him being that close at night twisted my insides in pleasant anticipation. He looked so delicious, so appealing. This was stupid and I felt panicky. But I also felt so lucky to be the one sitting here with him.

I kicked him under the table to get his attention. "Okay, look. I'd like to call my mom and talk to her myself. I know that means I'll have to deal with her anger now, but at least then I'll know she won't be in a freak-out the whole time. Just a couple days, right?"

His eyes lit up. "Yeah, two more days in all. That's it. We'll be home in the evening the day after tomorrow."

Giving into the idea—for a second it thrilled me. Two days didn't sound all that bad. We didn't have any plans at home. Mom would be at work most of the time, and I'd just be hanging out with Alex anyway. *Just enjoy the moment.*

"Okay. I really don't like stressing her like this. But I guess there isn't much I can do about that now."

"I was drinking last night, too, otherwise I would have thought about that," he said.

"But obviously not as much as me. You were coherent enough to get us on this train."

"That's true. I'm sorry." Alex leaned forward onto his forearms, looked down at the table and then back up at me. "You can call her as soon as we get back to the room," he said, and regarded me from under his brows. Something in his expression told me I wasn't the only one here hyper aware that we shared such a small room. And I wasn't the only one thinking about the possibilities that offered.

The waitress returned with our food a few minutes later. The portions were small but elegant. I ate my pasta at a cautious pace, and with each bite my stomach normalized.

Alex glanced out the window as he severed the rare filet in front of him. "You have to admit, for a drunken idea, it was kind of an awesome one."

I watched the snowy scenery pass by. "Yeah, I suppose. It's kind of ridiculous in the worst-best way. How did you even know about this train? I didn't realize there was a private line nearby."

"My mom. She took us on this train when we were small, and some of her friends vacationed on it once."

"Hmm," I muttered. "The things money can get you."

"Yeah, whatever," he said, acting self-conscious. "But yeah. I guess you're right. It's not too shabby, huh?"

I glanced around. "Not at all. I feel like I'm sort of out of place, though." This wasn't the typical college student type of vacation. I also felt grubby, like I needed to wash off the party from last night.

"You're fine. Your sweater even matches the carpet," he said.

I smirked. "Ugh. I can't wait to change my clothes. Do I have spare clothes?"

"Yes, you do." Alex nodded and I saw, clear as a blue sky, the male gears turning behind his blue eyes: me, changing my clothes, stripping down to put new ones on. We both stared at our dishes with half-grins as we continued dinner. After we finished eating, I played with my napkin for a moment.

"Okay, so I need to call my mom, and I need a shower. Are there showers in the bathrooms? I didn't really look at it when I was in there."

"Yeah, there's a shower in there."

I stared at him, amazed that the diminutive bathroom could actually house a shower stall. "For real?"

"It's true. Our own little fully-equipped private bathroom." Again, the flicker of sexual tension passed between us. Such a small room. Just the two of us.

"Where are my clothes?"

"You have some in your bag. We packed a little last night. Don't remember that, either?"

"No," I said. That memory was obliterated. Not even a fragment of it remained.

"Well, you have clean clothes, so don't worry about that," he said. "Ready to go?"

"Don't we have to pay?"

"It's all part of the fare. It's covered."

"Like a cruise," I said.

"I guess. But not so... working class."

I looked down, unsure how to stomach the haughtiness of the comment.

We walked back through the halls, flying forward in the direction of the train's destination with effortless momentum. It felt like striding on a moving walkway at an airport. When we returned to the room, Alex unlocked the door with a key card and gestured for me to go ahead.

"Your bag is in the corner," he said, nodding to it.

There, at the base of the bed, shoved against the edge of the bed frame and the wall, was my duffle bag. My purse leaned against it. I moved over and squatted next to them, then began to sort through my purse for my phone. It wasn't in the pocket

I normally kept it in, so I shuffled through the contents in the main part of the bag. I still couldn't find my cell. Impatience gnashed inside my gut, and I emptied my handbag onto the floor, scattering everything around. The phone was nowhere to be found. I threw everything back into my purse and searched through my duffle bag. I looked under every item of clothing, in every pocket. Nothing.

"I can't find my phone. Have you seen it? Do you remember me bringing it with us last night?" I asked.

Alex was reclined on the lower bunk, leaning back on his elbows and holding one of the curtains out with the fingers of one hand, watching the landscape outside. "No. Haven't seen it. It's possible you left it at home or at the party."

I took a deep breath, ran my hands through my hair and then stood up. "What am I gonna do? I need my phone. Alex, I need to call my mom." I couldn't locate the exact root cause of my anxiety. I hated to lose things, and sure, I'd become dependent on having my cell on me all of the time. It gave me anxiety if I accidentally went to the store without it. *That must be it*, I thought. *I'm an idiot for freaking out this much to be without my phone for only two days.*

"Okay, relax. You can use my phone," Alex said, then got up and pulled his phone out of the back pocket of his pants.

I wanted to kiss him. But I couldn't concentrate on that until I talked to Mom and got the hard part out of the way.

He handed me his phone and I clicked the button to illuminate the screen. Nothing happened. I clicked it again, and still, nothing happened.

"Alex..." There was a growing alarm in my voice.

"Let me see it," he said, so I handed it to him. He pressed the button, and nothing happened. He held down the power—

maybe it was turned off. Still nothing. We both looked up and our eyes met.

"It must be dead," he said, and walked over to his bag. "I don't remember if I brought my charger."

I watched as he unzipped a side pocket and shuffled his hand through it. I glanced over his shoulder. Inside the pocket was an electric shaver in a small case, and an mp3 player. It looked like the only electronics he packed aside from his phone.

He turned and looked at me. "I must have forgotten to pack it." We both stared at each other with unease, but then his expression smoothed. "Don't worry, okay? As I mentioned, I already called my mom before my phone died, and she told your mom the situation. I know you want to talk to her yourself. I know, I know. I get it. But she's already aware of the situation, and she's probably already on her way to cooling down and not being so angry, okay? It'll be fine."

I cracked my knuckles with anxiety. "Are you sure?"

Alex walked over to me and put his hands on my upper arms. I felt warm at his touch. "Yes. And I understand," he said. "But what can we do about it right now? Just take a deep breath, and try and see this in the big picture. A year from now, this will just be something your mom rolls her eyes at when she remembers it. It'll just be a story we laugh at. Can you try and relax—just try and enjoy it, since we're already here?"

I looked at the floor and sighed. "I guess."

"It's going to be okay, alright? Like I said, it's not like your mom doesn't even know where you are or anything. You just want to talk to her yourself, but she knows what's going on. It'll be okay."

I nodded.

"Maybe you'll feel better after a shower," he suggested.

"Okay. Yeah. Probably."

I grabbed my bag and opened the small door to the bathroom. I switched on the light and assessed the situation now that I wasn't rushing to the toilet. It was practically a doll-sized bathroom, but it would do.

The shower stall might have been miniscule, but the water was hot, and it did soothe my nerves. Afterward I dressed, brushed my teeth, and dried my hair with the hairdryer built into the wall. Then I exited the bathroom feeling a little more prepared to enjoy my time on this ludicrous, lunatic trip. God, we were fools. So stupid of us to come up with an idea like this as drunken idiots, bother to pack, but fail to bring my phone and his charger.

"You look a little less rolled in terror," Alex said.

"I feel a little less. Turns out terror washes off with hot water and fancy train soap."

"Good. Want to check out the game car?" he asked.

"The game car?"

"Yeah. I haven't seen it yet, I'm curious. Grab your ID," he said.

Alex rose from the bed and took hold of my hand. The nerves in my fingers tingled. He led me out the door and down to the left this time. The sun had dropped below the horizon while I showered. We passed through two sleeper cars, no one else in sight. I kept waiting—dreading—the moment Alex released my hand. But he didn't. I made sure to hold his tight, letting him know I didn't want the connection to end.

When we crossed the third threshold into another car, a new array of lights and sounds met our senses. There were three card tables, the kind used for poker in casinos, each with a group of people at them and a dealer. On the far end sat a small bar with a brass countertop, and along one wall there were five slot machines. A few armchairs and sofas were placed around the room, and a television, too.

"It's like mini Vegas on a train," I whispered.

Alex laughed at the glory of a space dedicated to such entertainment.

"Alex, they have to have a phone in here somewhere. I need to at least try and check with one of the staff to call my mom."

He sighed and then shrugged. "Okay, go ahead. Maybe they have one for emergencies they'll let you use."

I walked over to the bartender and explained I had to contact my mother but my phone was dead. He was kind enough to offer his own phone for me to use. But as I went to dial, I stopped seven digits in. *Shit.* My stomach sank. Mom had gone so frugal during the worst of her financial issues and piles of medical bills that she temporarily used a prepaid cell. Then she had gotten a new number this past year when she bought a phone plan again. I stood there staring at the buttons, and could not for the life of me recall the entire number. I thought I'd memorized it, but my brain refused to retrieve anything beyond the first seven digits.

"I can't... I can't remember," I whispered.

"What's that?" Alex asked.

"I can't remember her whole number. The new one. I have to have my phone to get the contact."

"It's okay, it's all right," Alex said, and rubbed my shoulder. "She already knows anyway, like I said. It's going to be fine."

I handed the phone back to the bartender feeling stunned. "I'm sorry. I mean thank you, but I..."

"No worries," the bartender said, trying to make me feel better. "I don't know anyone's number anymore, just what their name is in my contact list."

"Thanks anyway, man," Alex said to him.

Then he turned to me. "Let's have a seat and get a drink, okay? It'll calm you down, and you have nothing to worry about anyway. Sound good?"

I nodded, took a long, deep breath, and followed him to an open sofa bench. A couple of waitresses wearing white buttoned shirts with bowties, black shorts, and black nylons walked around with drinks. We took in the surroundings for a couple of minutes. A waitress approached and asked if we wanted anything to drink. She spoke with some kind of beautiful accent; it sounded French.

Alex looked at me. "A little hair of the dog that bit you?"

I sighed. "Sure, just one," I said, and then turned to the waitress. "I'll have a vodka and ginger ale, I guess."

"A Johnnie Black for me, please," Alex added.

"May I see your identification?" she asked. *Definitely a French accent.*

We had to let go of each other's hands to pull them out, but he took my hand again once we put our IDs away. We sat there, watching a few people at the tables, and glanced at the television now and then. It was hard to pay attention to much other than the warmth of Alex's hand around mine, but news of a potential winter storm flashed across the television screen. A couple of people laughed at one of the card tables.

The waitress returned with our drinks. I sipped mine and within a few minutes, the booze relaxed my shoulders, and I told myself to let the whole thing go. Forget about it for the moment. Slowly, I felt a budding anxious excitement about the rest of the evening. Two people got up from one of the card tables to leave, and Alex turned to look at me.

"Mind if I play a few hands?"

"Not at all," I said.

Alex grabbed my hand again. We walked over to the table and took a seat. Alex gave the dealer our room card to purchase chips, and he played a few hands—losing on two of them, winning on the last. As I finished my drink, my inhibitions retreated. I smiled, loving the atmosphere. Alex put a hand on my thigh. Apparently his inhibitions retreated, as well. We looked at each other, and I felt the buzz between us. His hand moved against my leg and I went soft.

"Shall I quit while I'm ahead?" he asked. I sensed another question beneath his words.

"Yes. To the game, I mean," I answered.

His eyes met mine with a devious expression. Then Alex stunned me by gently grabbing the back of my head and pulling me in for a kiss. I felt shy about the public display of affection, but it was as if Alex wanted everyone in the game car to see it. When our lips parted, I saw a few people turn their heads, trying to hide the fact that they had watched us kiss. My face felt hot.

We got up and held hands all the way back to our room, only letting go when he got out the card key to open the door. I walked into the room, feeling the hangover subside. Feeling relaxed from the vodka and ginger. Feeling every nerve in my body standing on edge in anticipation of what was to come next.

Alex shut the door behind us. I turned to look at him. A dim night light kept the room from total darkness. He stood there staring back at me—unabashed, bold. I felt an enchanting fear about the moment, but I stood my ground and stared back. With each passing second my knees felt weaker, my insides turned softer.

Alex walked over to kiss me again. This was going to happen; this was actually going to happen. He reached around my waist with one hand and brushed his other hand around my face, pulling me to him. And then his lips were on mine— the feel of his soft mouth pressing against my own, with his warm breath on my upper lip. I felt his whole body against me, and I reached my arms around his shoulders.

The kiss turned heated and passionate within seconds when his tongue found mine. And then he was kissing my neck, and then my mouth again, and his body pushed against mine to lead us toward the bunks. I put one hand behind my head, grasping the ledge of the upper bunk. He grabbed it, too, holding me around the waist with one arm and steadying us against the bunk with the other. Then both of his arms wrapped around my hips again, he lifted me up, moving me onto the lower bed. Then eased himself on top of me, just rough enough that I enjoyed it. The faint scent of his cologne and the warmth of his hands on my body excited me.

I didn't care what it would be like tomorrow, how it might feel like a glaring silence in the sober light of morning. I believed I could make that kiss, that embrace, that connection, last forever.

And I didn't feel any holding back from him. I knew by the way he touched my hair and kissed me that this was not just a whim for him. He'd thought of this on previous occasions, and wanted it, too. After all the years upon years, it felt natural to kiss him. When his shirt came off and I felt his skin against mine, it felt as if it were something that should have happened a long time ago. He tugged lightly on my hair, and kissed me harder. I wondered how we managed to keep from doing this for so long.

But who cared? We had the rest of our lives to make up for lost time, and I envisioned that with such optimism—as a long string of years that stretched out before us. Into the night, I lost myself in him.

CHAPTER SIX

In the morning, I felt the rocking of the train before I opened my eyes. I remained still for a moment, both hearing and feeling the clunk-*clank*, clunk-*clank*, clunk-*clank*. Alex's arm was under my head, leaving my neck with a small kink, and one of my hands rested on his bare chest. He felt warm, and by the rhythm of his breathing, I knew he was still asleep. A slow smile spread across my face, and I tugged the blanket up over myself, nuzzling into his shoulder, taking in his scent. He let out a soft, pleasured sound and rolled toward me. It was a moment in life where desire meets reality, and reality felt unreal as a result.

I opened my eyes, and in the dimness of the room—lit only by pale morning light peeking around the curtains—I saw that his sandy hair was ruffled. The line of his nose and lips and jaw looked so perfect that my chest ached. I didn't want to leave that bed, ever. I wrapped my arm around him tighter, and he moaned again. I could see the shadow of a smile twitch on his mouth, and without opening his eyes, his face nestled toward mine.

I drew closer still, and it was enough to ease him into consciousness. He didn't say a word before he began kissing my neck again, and then moved on top of me. In the silence, we started a repeat of the previous night. The bit of concern I felt about it being something Alex would regret in the morning vanished as he moved into me once more. With the morning light, he still wanted me.

When we finished, I felt weak with hunger and my arms trembled. I pulled the blanket up over my chest and sighed, feeling uneasiness in my torso. I rationalized that it was too much rocking of the train, too little sleep, too little food, and too many hormones running through my veins. I could feel the chemicals infiltrating my limbs—microscopic snakes of emotion slithering through every vessel, turning me into a lovesick weakling.

I also felt cramped next to the wall with the window. Alex turned onto his back, putting his hands behind his head as a pillow. He stared at the bunk above us, and it felt like he slipped away from me a little. What it was... I don't know. A look in his eyes, his posture, or just a vibration in the air.

"I think I need to eat," I whispered.

"Yeah, we both need to recharge the tanks, I'm sure," he said, and remained still, looking at the bunk for a moment.

"Okay, food then," he said, whipping the blanket off of himself and standing up to stretch. He pulled on his boxer shorts as he spoke. "Do you want to eat in the dining car, or order something to have brought to the room?" Alex sat down on the edge of the bed and I lifted myself onto my elbows.

"We can stay in the room all day if you like," he said.

"I didn't even know that was an option—room service."

Alex swept a piece of my hair back behind my ear. "Of course it is. I think even Amtrak has that service, but I can't say for sure. This line does, though." His tone sounded a little sweeter, but he still had that testosterone marinade working in his system, making me feel just a little... as if he thought he'd conquered me. That was the feeling. I couldn't say I'd never experienced that kind of post-sex vibe from any of the few men I had been with. But it bothered me coming from Alex. I thought the years of friendship leading up to this event would turn this experience into one of a little more softness. Love, if I were going to be mushy and honest about it. It troubled me, and when I felt uneasy, I needed air.

"Nah, let's go to the dining car," I said and sat up all the way, letting my head settle into the movement of the train before I rose completely.

Alex slipped into the bathroom, and I dressed. Then I threw on some socks and my boots and waited for Alex to finish in the restroom.

My stomach was a mess of knots, mixed up between continued dread of what waited for me when I returned home, and feeling a sort of shocked exhilaration about Alex. I wasn't the type to immediately wonder where a relationship headed. I didn't mind dating someone for a while and just seeing where it led. But something about the weight of knowing Alex the way I did gave me a disquiet about sitting there in that kind of limbo. I wanted to know the direction with him—whether it be into a relationship or the acknowledgment that it was just a night of fun. I swallowed hard at the thought of the latter.

I distracted myself by searching for my phone again. I hated not being able to just hear my mom's voice lash out at me and get it over with. The anticipation, I believed, had to be worse than whatever punishment I would receive at this point.

Alex emerged from the bathroom and saw me sifting through the contents of my bag, looking frustrated.

He stood there for a moment, just watching. "I'm pretty sure you left it at home. Just give it a rest."

"You're certain you didn't see it? You don't remember me packing it or anything? You're absolutely sure?"

"Yes. *Calmer.*" he said, using French, and caressed my shoulder.

I gave him a look of irritated confusion.

"Seriously, Autumn, listen—*your mom already knows,* alright? Just relax."

I sighed and nodded, then bent down to get my toiletries satchel out of my bag. "Just give me a second."

"Sure thing. I've got all day," he said, and lay on the bed with his hands behind his head.

I brushed my teeth, combed my hair, and applied minimal makeup. I reemerged through the tiny door and looked at him. He was still on the bed, staring up at the bunk over his head. His blue eyes eased over to me, and there was something I didn't recognize in them. Something... sinister? *Couldn't be. Why on Earth would he look at me like that?*

"Ready?" he asked. I nodded.

We walked to the dining car and found an open booth. I felt ravenous as soon as I smelled the aroma of warm breakfast dishes being served to the sparse group of fellow passengers. The scenery outside was breathtaking. We passed a landscape blotched with areas of barren winter trees surrounding small frozen lakes. Then the land would open up into a snowy easy roll of ground, and then another frozen lake would pass by. The trees' delicate, twiggy branches were frosted with snow on their tops, like layers of icing. Fog crept over the countryside in a soft mist, and the sky was overcast. I didn't think there was an ounce of yellow in the lighting out there—just endless muted tones of blues and grays. The contrast of the warm red interior of the train seemed haunting to me. Like blood on ice.

A waiter approached and I looked up at him.

"Good morning. Can I bring you two anything besides water?" he asked.

"I'll have a coffee," Alex said.

"Hot tea," I said.

"Very good," he replied and handed us each a menu. When the server left, Alex looked at me.

"So…" he said, and the hint of a smile lifted the corner of his mouth.

"So," I said.

We both regarded each other in silence for a moment. I fiddled with the edge of the thick, one-page menu, and then Alex's hands rushed forward and took hold of mine—so fast it took me a second to realize what happened. The heat of his hands around mine made me tremble.

"So," he repeated.

I laughed. He glanced down for a second, sighed, and then looked back at me. His eyes were so bright, as if all of the cool illumination outside the window condensed into pools of light to shine through them.

He cleared his throat. "I'd be full of shit if I said I hadn't dreamed of that happening many, many, many times."

I let out another small laugh, feeling my tension depart—surprised and delighted. "I would be, too," I admitted.

He grinned. "That makes me… *very* happy to hear." Another beat of silence passed, filled with the hum of conversations around us, dishes being stacked, and the clanking of the train. I could hear that old music again as if the dining car were a time capsule from the 1940s. I recognized Dean Martin's song from a dance performance I did years before, "You Belong To Me".

I blushed and ran a hand through my hair. "So what now?"

"Breakfast," he said, and his eyebrows lifted as he looked up to see our waiter return from behind me.

"Your tea, miss. And your coffee, sir," he said, setting the drinks in front of us. "May I take your order?"

We ordered and then Alex handed the server the menus. Alex grabbed my hand again across the table when the waiter left.

"Just so you know. With us... I'm in it. Like, all the way in. If you were wondering," he said.

I bit my lower lip and nodded my head a bit, reassured, but surprised by such a sudden declaration. "I guess that's kind of a relief to hear. I mean, if this were just going to be a friends-with-benefits type of thing, that'd be okay, I suppose. It just seems like, with us though, we know each other so well that—"

"It would be weird," he interrupted.

"Exactly."

"Yeah, I've thought about this a lot," he said. "I don't think I would've gone there if I weren't certain about it. Don't worry. I'm not going anywhere."

I nodded again, and Alex looked out the window, gazing at the landscape. I smiled for a moment. But then my brow creased just a bit as I continued to stare at him and it occurred to me that, all at once, I was in a relationship. Without giving more than an ounce of an opinion on the matter. Yet, this was what I wanted, for a long time. This was what I wanted. And less than an hour ago. So elation settled on top of the disquiet like oil on water. I took a deep breath. I probably just needed time to process it. That had to be it. I should have no other reason to feel strange about getting what I wanted. At least that's what I told myself.

"I'm going to sound like such a chick, God, I shouldn't even say it," he said.

I raised one eyebrow. "Say what?"

"Kids. You know, I mean we've been friends for so damn long, and I've wanted this for so damn long. I even heard a name once that I really liked and thought to myself, *that would be a good name for a kid*, you know. If you and I ever had one."

I froze in place. I couldn't think of a response.

"Finnegan, if you're wondering," he said. "That was the name. It could be used for a girl or a boy, I think."

I swallowed. Don't panic. It's not that weird. Girls do that kind of stuff in their heads all the time, I reminded myself.

Jesus, though, I could see now why it freaked men out so much when women did stuff like this. I wanted this man, wanted him for ages, loved him to death—but Alex having a name picked out for our future child? *Slow your roll*, I thought. I wanted a dance career. I didn't even know if I wanted to have kids.

"Hmm. Yeah. It's a nice name," I said. I didn't know what I really thought of the name. I couldn't think about it objectively as I tried to talk myself down from the alarm. *Alex is just impulsive*, I repeated mentally.

My foot began tapping, bouncing my knee. "Is there anywhere I can stretch out on this train? I'm starting to feel bound up. It's making me anxious that I haven't practiced. I need to stretch out at the very least."

Alex shrugged. "I don't think there's a whole lot of extra room anywhere. There might be a sitting car with a little space, but we'll be making our stop today, so you could stretch a little when we get outside."

"Oh. Good. I guess that makes sense if we have to turn around to get back by tomorrow." Alex looked out the window again and said nothing.

"Where are we, anyway?" I asked.

"Minnesota."

"It's pretty."

"It is," he agreed, continuing to view the world outside the window. "I love winter. It's so quiet." I squinted my eyes a little, and supposed I knew what he meant. It lacked the outdoor noise of summertime. Snow had to be the most silent thing in nature, drifting to the ground, muffling the world with softened acoustics.

I didn't hate winter the way some people did, but it wasn't my favorite season. I lied and told people I liked springtime best. I did enjoy the temperate weather and the blooming flowers, but autumn was my absolute favorite.

I felt like an idiot admitting it, however, because I never held any faith that people would think I liked it for any reason other than my name. That kind of self-obsessed vanity was not an impression I wanted to give off. So spring it was—to most of the world, at least. Mom knew my true favoritism because I didn't worry that she would get the wrong impression. I probably told Alex the truth at some point, too. And Sam... Sam knew. Out of the recesses of my mind, a memory revealed itself, the way they sometimes did with an insignificant provocation.

~~~

It had been Halloween, a few weeks after my eighteenth birthday. Alex returned home for a weekend in his first year of college, and Sam decided to come back to visit, too. I'd headed over to their house to hang out with Alex in the afternoon, and Camille decided to invite my mom over to have some cider— doubtless a spiked version. Their backyard looked like a fall wonderland, with birch trees showering yellow leaves onto both the ground and the boughs of neighboring spruce trees. Farther back, in the thin strip of forest at the end of their property, an array of deciduous trees stood in a flamboyant chorus of color. I'd sat on the edge of the Van Etten's back patio—a stonework masterpiece that was raised up a couple of feet so it was level with the doors of the rec wing. Watching the leaves dropping like confetti, I wrapped my arms around myself to pull my jacket tighter. Alex kicked the leaves as he told me about school and such.

Alex hopped off onto the grass. "I don't know. How the hell do they expect you to decide what you want to do for the rest of your life before you're even twenty years old?"

I understood his aggravation, even though I didn't relate to it. I already had dance, and I'd always known I wanted to be involved in it somehow, some way, no matter what happened. But if I didn't have that? Perhaps I would be as lost as he was.

"What about something art-related? You're so good at drawing. *So* good at it," I said.

Alex scoffed. "Right. Be serious, Autumn. They don't call it 'starving artist' just to make creative people sound thin and attractive." He kicked another leaf.

"There are some jobs out there, graphic design, whatever."

Alex stared up at his family home for a moment. "I don't think you understand the pressure that comes with being brought up in a family like mine. The history, the expectations. Especially being a male. Not that women don't have that pressure now, too. But you know what I'm saying?" His eyes had looked sad and sincere.

I nodded. I understood the best I could.

Sam had come out to join us for a bit and to listen to Alex ramble on as he continued his rant against societal conventions. Alex could get anyone fired up about them, myself included, even when I felt like I had very little to complain about. Sam sat down next to me on the edge of the patio and looked at me at one point with a smile, as if to say, *yeah this is Alex.* We sat there, occasionally adding to his tirade with a statement of agreement or understanding, but it was *The Alex Show.*

After about fifteen minutes, Alex ran out of frustrations to vent and stood looking at nothing in particular with his hands on his hips. His shoulders looked strong in the old rugby shirt he'd put on that day.

"I need to take a piss," Alex said, and Sam and I sat there unresponsive.

Then Sam nodded and said, "Alright."

Alex went inside, and there Sam and I were, sitting on the patio watching the leaves. I could smell a hint of cologne or aftershave on Sam, and it mingled with the nostalgic bouquet of rotting foliage. A gust of wind blew through the trees with a loud whooshing sound, and a thick litter of leaves had come down with it. It felt like we were in the middle of a New Year's ball drop for a moment, all natural confetti. I felt comfortable in the silence with Sam there, but also aware of his presence in excess. He let out a soft laugh, and I looked at him.

Sam smiled at me. "Autumn in autumn," he said as he pulled a leaf from my hair.

My cheeks had felt hot at the gesture. "It's your favorite, isn't it? The season, I mean," he said.

I looked down and smirked. "Yeah. But don't tell anyone."

He twirled the leaf between his index finger and thumb, watching it spin. I watched it, too, entranced by the rotating whirl of crimson-tipped gold. Entranced by his observation of me.

Then Sam's eyes met mine again, and I had to force myself not to shy away from his gaze.

"Your secret's safe with me," Sam said, and smiled.

~~~

I shifted in my seat in the train's dining car, remembering the way Sam had looked as he whispered those words to me. After breakfast, Alex and I strolled back to our room. Although I felt a bit caged in by the conversation in the dining car concerning a relationship, I couldn't help it; being in that small room with him aroused my instincts again. We sat on the bed, and before I knew it we were kissing, touching, and kissing more. It seemed like an hour or two passed, just making out with him—going no further—but enjoying the delicious feeling of my lips on his. I was so caught up in the moment that I jumped when a voice came over a PA system throughout the train. We stopped, and Alex lifted his head away from mine as we listened.

"Ladies and gentlemen, your attention, please. We will be crossing the border into Canada shortly and will be stopping to check passports. Please return to your rooms so our attendants can efficiently check each passenger's passport and collect customs slips. Again, please return to your rooms, and our check will be through shortly. Thank you, and enjoy your day." The entire message was then repeated in French.

My stomach felt queasy. I looked at Alex, but he didn't look me in the eye. He stared at the door instead.

I jolted upright in alarm, pushing him off of me. "Canada? Wait, what? Passports? Alex, what the hell is going on? I thought we were getting off and boarding another train today."

"I told you the train was stopping today," he said, and scratched his head. "But I might have been mistaken on whether it was today or tomorrow that we turn around. Let me check."

"Yeah, but... Wait, what? Shit. *Canada?* Alex, hold on. You might have been mistaken about which *day* we depart? What the hell?" I stood up in the middle of the room, and Alex rose, too. "What the hell is going on? You told me we were going to be home tomorrow. How can we get home tomorrow if we are headed into Canada? Passports? We don't have our passports."

"Yes, we do," he said.

"What?"

"We got them when we packed. But you don't remember packing, so of course you don't remember grabbing them."

"No. Wait. How the hell would we think to bring our passports but forget my phone?"

"You were... A little drunk. I don't know what to tell you."

"Okay, well that doesn't answer my question about going into Canada."

"Our stop to turn around is a bit after we cross the border. Let me check if I was right about it being today."

"I thought you said..." And then I recalled that he'd only specified it was a tourist town we were stopping in, not exactly *where* the tourist town was.

Alex opened his bag, searched for a moment, and pulled out both of our passports, along with boarding passes. He evaluated the tickets for a moment and ran a hand over his mouth.

"Ah, shit," he said. "Don't be mad, Auttie. Remember, I was drunk, too. It's tomorrow. We depart tomorrow, not today."

"*What?*" A slow, seething anger rose inside me.

"I made a mistake, okay? I'm sorry. We'll still have days to spare at home, so it's really not a big deal. You've got to remember we were both drunk. I'm really, really sorry. I mean it."

Alex held the ticket up to show me the date—the following day—as our scheduled departure. Although he retracted the ticket and put it back in his bag, and I felt livid as hell, but it soothed me a bit to see it printed on the boarding pass, that we were indeed scheduled to get off of this train tomorrow, for sure.

Alex then handed me my passport, and I looked down with my mouth hanging open as I held it, encased in glittery pink crystals. I could feel the train lurching to a slow, jerky stop, and the whistle blew a few times.

"You'll have to remove it from that case when they check it, I'm sure," he said.

It took me a minute to find words. "Why did you have my passport in your bag?"

"Because I figured you might as well get some use out of your Christmas present. We got our passports, and I said I would keep them safe. I wanted to put yours in the gift I got for you. Why do you seem so worried?"

"I'm angry," I corrected him. But I did feel worried. I couldn't explain to myself, let alone to Alex, why a wisp of fear went through me.

"I'm sorry, okay? I really am," he said.

I brushed my fingertips over the bumpy crystals and took a breath. Maybe I just needed fresh air. Being cooped up on the train made me jumpy.

I tried to calm myself and removed my passport from the silly, beautiful case. I sat down on the edge of the bed again, looking at it as we waited for the train attendant to come by. After about five minutes, there was a knock on our door. Alex got up to open it, and I rose and walked to the door, too. A middle-aged woman in the train attendant uniform stood there. She chewed gum, but I could tell she tried to be discrete about it. She had a list on a clipboard.

"Hello, *Bonjour*. Passports and customs slips," she said. We both handed her the passports, and Alex gave her custom slips, already filled out. I shot a confused glance at him. She examined each one, looking up at us to confirm that we were the rightful owners. She handed them back and checked something off on her list.

"Anything to declare?" she asked.

We both said no.

"Any weapons, fruit, or drugs with you?"

We both replied no.

"What is your reason for traveling to Canada?"

"Vacation," Alex answered without hesitation.

"How long do you plan to stay?" she asked.

"Just a day," he said.

She looked up at him from under her brow as if she thought that was a strange answer, but said nothing about it. "Okay, thank you. Have a nice trip," she said.

Alex thanked her and shut the door. I walked into the middle of the room, pacing as I ran my hands through my hair and twisted it over my shoulder.

"Autumn, why are you so tense? We've done riff-raff shit before. This isn't the first stupid thing we've done together. And you've never freaked out on me like this. You usually go along with the program, hooting and hollering the whole way."

"Because we've never done anything *this* crazy before. And I thought it was just two days total. So now it's what? Four?"

He gave me an intense look. "Yeah, I guess it's four. Still not the end of the world when you look at the big picture. And are you sure that's why, because we've never done anything this crazy? It's nothing else? It's not what's going on between us that's freaking you out?"

I swallowed and stood there for a moment in silence. There was something; I couldn't put my finger on it. Again, I needed to process how fast we moved from old friends into a relationship. And naming our future children already...

"It's not that. It's just that I keep worrying about my mom," I said, telling the half-truth.

"Chill out," he said, but rather than his typical calm tone it sounded like a command.

I glared at him. "Don't tell me what to do. I'll freak out if I want."

"Okay, does it feel good? Are you enjoying your freak out?"

I looked at the wall to avoid his glare. "Yeah, maybe. Fuck off. I need a drink," I said.

"Geez. Yes, you do."

We left the room in silence, went to the game car, and walked straight up to the bartender. I didn't care to have an enchanted handholding moment—I just barreled forward with a mission to obtain alcohol. Anything to get rid of the anxiety that continued to build without any real explanation.

"Is it too early to order a drink?" I asked the bartender.

"No, miss. What can I get for you?" It still seemed early in the day, maybe just past noon. I rummaged through a list of brunch type drinks in my head since I hadn't eaten lunch yet. It seemed appropriate.

"Can you do a Bloody Mary?"

"Sure. Anything for you, sir?" he asked Alex.

"I guess I'll have the same."

He made our beverages, handed them to us, and we went to sit on a sofa to drink them. I decided I didn't like Bloody Marys. The name sounded bad enough, but it felt like I had to choke down the thick tomato juice. We watched the television a little, and I gave Alex the silent treatment until I returned to a level-headed state. More news of the approaching blizzard filled the screen. I turned my gaze toward the landscape outside the window. At first it remained still, and then gradually began moving past as the train started up again and chugged forward.

The whistle blew, and the speed increased until it reached its normal cruising pace, dragging us across international lines.

"Canada," I said.

"Yeah... Canada," Alex repeated.

"Okay, good. It'll be fine." I exhaled, trying to feel relief.

Alex put his hand on mine, and I stared at him.

"I sincerely hope you enjoy this time, Auttie. I really do," he said—genuine, serious, and a little strange.

I nodded. "Me, too," I agreed. "I do, too."

CHAPTER SEVEN

"I need to shower," Alex said, when he finished his Bloody Mary.

I'd abandoned mine about halfway through, deciding I couldn't stomach it.

"I need a nap," I added as my budding headache worsened by the minute.

"Likewise," he said, quite serious, but then he glanced at me and a flicker crossed his expression.

I knew that look: us, in bed again. I was still furious about the schedule mix-up, but with that look in his eyes, it was difficult to remain angry with Alex. We walked over to the bartender and handed him our glasses, and he nodded in thanks. Alex left him a tip and then held my hand as we walked back to our room—through clanking connecting platforms, and down elegant halls.

Alex unlocked the door to our room and held it open for me. I slid through the doorway and surveyed the bed. The tangle of sheets we'd left behind had turned into a tidy, tucked bed of fresh linen with a small wrapped chocolate on the pillow.

"Room keeping was fast," Alex said as he shut the door behind us.

"Guess so."

"I'm going to hop in the shower and then I'll join you for that nap," he said.

"Okay." I smiled. He wrapped his arms around me and gave me a long, slow kiss that tasted of Bloody Mary. Then he took off his shirt and stepped into the tiny bathroom. I watched his bare back and thought that it didn't matter how tired I felt, there was no way I could sleep with his body next to mine, regardless of my apprehension about getting home.

I heard the shower turn on and I sat on the small chair in the corner to remove my boots. As I wiggled my socked feet to stretch them out, I thought stretching my whole body for a minute might be a good idea. So I stood up and bent over, pressing my forehead to my knees as I grasped the back of my calves. The train rocked on uneven terrain, and I wobbled. I stood upright and my head pounded.

I stood there for a minute and decided to check for painkillers in my purse. Squatting down to sort through my things, I found my pill case, but all I had in it was a couple of antacids, no Advil or Tylenol. I also noticed my other pill container and realized that I'd missed a day of my birth control, so I took out two and swallowed them down without water.

I checked my duffle bag for painkillers but found none in there, either. I crouched on the floor and eyed Alex's bag for a moment. Doubtful, but it seemed worth checking at this point. I unzipped the front pocket with the embroidered V on it and found a few toiletries, but no pills. I glanced in the main portion of the bag, but it just looked like clothes in there, so I didn't bother looking under anything much. Then I opened the side pocket where I had seen his electric shaver.

I froze as soon as I rummaged around and peeked inside. There was his electric shaver along with his mp3 player, and below them a dark sock covered most of a device, but not all of it. I moved the sock out of the way, reached in. I stared. I gaped.

My mouth opened as I pulled out my phone.

My phone. He had it in his bag this entire time. Hidden. My face went stoic, but I swallowed hard. I held it in my hand as if it were the Holy Grail itself. Then my eyes eased down into the pocket again, and next to where my phone had been I saw a phone battery. I illuminated my phone and it worked, so I guessed Alex must have taken the battery out of his own phone to make it appear dead. I stood up and illuminated my phone once more.

I felt my face go vacant as I stood there, rocking with the train. Clunk-*clank*, clunk-*clank*, clunk-*clank*. I had seventeen missed calls. Most were from Mom, along with a couple from Sam and Tim. I also had numerous text messages. At first, I felt utter confusion when I saw that I had apparently responded to my mother. Today. This morning. I read the message sent from my phone.

Hey Mom, I'm super sorry if I worried you! Alex and I are fine, and we'll be back soon. Please don't worry, K? Love you.

That didn't even sound like me—the way I texted. I swallowed back a sick feeling as I scrolled through her nine or ten angry, troubled replies. Alex had sent a text from my phone posing as me? This couldn't be right. I felt lightheaded. Most of the other texts were from Sam with a few from Tim. Tim's were calm but annoyed, telling me that he was off to see a couple of friends downtown for a few days, but that I needed to stop being selfish and give Mom a call. Sam's messages worried me. I read the newest one first. They were more concerned than the ones sent earlier. I read through them, starting at the oldest.

Are you okay? I'm concerned. What the hell is going on?

I read another.

Autumn, what's happening? This doesn't seem like you. Alex, maybe, but not you. Can you please call or text back?

And an older one.

Hey, what are you guys doing? Alex left me a voicemail saying you guys were doing some spontaneous getaway, but your mom is freaked out. You need to call her.

I typed out a text as fast as I could, panicked by all of the missed correspondence. I figured I could call Mom right away, too, but I wanted to shoot Sam a text first to get word there right away in case my mom didn't pick up the phone. My fingers stumbled over the letters.

Sam, just got your texts. We're on a train, not sure exactly what is going on now. Thought it was fun, now I'm a little worried. If you talk to my mom before I do, please don't let her stress too much.

I was about to type more, but the shower shut off. I hit send as fast as I could, and watched as the status was sending.

"Come on, come on," I whispered. Shit, I had almost no bars in whatever wasteland of civilization we were in. "Come on!"

I thought I had another minute or so before Alex would emerge from the bathroom, but the door opened then, startling me. Alex had on pants, but no shirt. I looked up at him. His eyes met mine, and then they lowered to the phone in my hand. For a second we were both frozen still as ice. I glanced at the message again and it showed that it had delivered. *Thank God*, I thought. Then Alex moved toward me so fast I didn't have time to react. He ripped the phone out of my hand, shoved it back into the pocket of his bag, stood up, and put a firm hand on my shoulder. He pressed on me, not quite pushing me, but forcing me to sit on the bed.

"Let it go, Autumn." He was livid.

"What the hell?" I said, pissed, and pushed his hand off of my shoulder.

"I just put it away so you wouldn't be distracted the whole time we were here," he said, crouching in front of me.

I shook my head, and I felt my body tremble with anger. "No. No. No, you don't get to do that."

"Don't take it so personally."

"Take it *personally*? Oh, it's beyond taking it personally at this point."

"Don't be angry."

"Alex..." I said, and took a shaky breath.

Odd gears clanked into place, as peculiar realizations crept into my head. I took another breath, and my body felt off as it submitted to a sudden release of chemicals. Oddities that seemed not quite right before. My complete lack of memory getting on the train, and inability to remember my mom's phone number the next day. *Clank*. Comprehension falling into place, the feeling of being caged, of things moving too fast. *Clank*. My gut instinct of anxiety, and a whispered memory from many years ago. A premonition. Winter. Canada. Danger. *Clank.*

I closed my eyes slowly, and then opened them again. It became clear to me in a matter of seconds.

I cleared my throat. "I'm not... I'm not here by choice, am I?" It was more a statement than a question.

He looked at the phone in his hand for a long moment, and then back up at me. "I'd like you to be."

It felt like the longest moment of silence in my entire life, as I comprehended those words.

I swallowed hard. "Alex..."

"You seemed happy enough to be here last night."

"You know what I mean," I said.

He was silent.

"Alex. Say something."

"What do you want me to say?" He glared at me. His tone matched his expression.

"Answer me. Am I here by choice?"

"You agreed to get on the train, didn't you?"

"I don't even know for sure! And if I wanted to leave right now... If I *insisted* on getting off this train and going home, right now?"

"You can't make them stop the train."

"But if I *could*. If the train was stopped and I wanted to leave and go home right now?"

The shake of his head was miniscule, but it was enough to answer me.

"You won't *let* me?" I said. The defiance in my core rose up to spit itself out with my words.

"Autumn, just enjoy yourself, will you?"

"Alex."

"Stop. Just stop," he said. His face filled with resentment.

What the hell? I was being held captive? By Alex? I slapped him across the face as hard as I could, so hard that my palm stung. The expression he returned was so dark it scared me. I'd never seen that look on him before. I'd never seen that look on any other person in my life.

When he spoke his tone was even, but stern. "I will let that one go. That *one*. Don't... do it again."

I watched as his cheek reddened from the smack. I couldn't find any words to say. I sat on the bed, the awareness that this train was a prison revealing itself as if a giant stage curtain dropped away.

Alex stood up and pulled out a fresh shirt to put on. He turned away from me to hide the phone in a different spot in his bag, but his body blocked my view, so I didn't see where he hid it.

Then he turned back around to face me. "Now. We're going to take a nap. We didn't get a lot of sleep last night, and we need sleep."

I didn't know where the Alex I knew was, but he wasn't here. This voice coming from him now, it sounded like another person. I still couldn't make myself move. My thoughts used all of my energy trying to find a way out of my situation. I couldn't come up with any tangible solutions this fast. So when he moved over to the bed, threw the small, wrapped chocolate onto the floor, and pulled back the sheets, I hesitated but slid next to the window and lay down facing away from him.

I let him get in next to me and hold me with one arm because I wanted to think this through, to be rational about what was happening. I glared at the wall, just inches from my face, and then eased my eyes up to the sky outside the window. The train rocked, and clanked, and took me farther into the reaches of the north. I didn't know for sure where we were headed, but I had a pretty damn good idea. And so my mind went to work trying to find a way out.

CHAPTER EIGHT

I didn't sleep at all during our nap, but Alex did. I felt his breathing go rhythmic and heavy. He slept for so long that I thought I'd lose my mental stability tucked into the cramped corner. Alex could be a light sleeper, though, so I didn't want to risk waking him by jumping out of bed once he fell asleep—fearing the backlash.

Advantage: Alex. He could sleep through this new, sick opposition between us. Finally, he awoke and stretched. Then he caressed my side. I stared at the sky out the window again without him seeing my expression, resentment creasing the shadows and angles of my face. A pleasured sound came from his throat.

"How'd you sleep?" he asked as if nothing had happened.

I remained silent for a moment. "Good," I lied.

"Mmm. Me too."

I felt his nose in my hair as he nuzzled closer. My body went into a living version of rigor mortis, resisting his approach. In my head, I danced in a surreal world in that confined corner on the bed, trapped by him—facing the outside world but so far from it. When we got off of the train, there had to be a way to flee. If we were boarding another train, it was probably taking us farther north. But there had to be another one headed in the other direction, headed back home. I could run fast. I could run when we got off the train.

I also told myself Alex couldn't be all that serious about this. This was Alex, "My Alex" as my brain just began to think of him as I'd always known him. I'd known him forever. I'd known him from the time he was in kindergarten! Part of me refused to believe the darkness of the situation to be true.

And, just in case, there was Sam. He must have seen my text by now. Maybe I didn't have the chance to communicate the full situation, but at least I conveyed that I was worried. I had to get that damn phone out of Alex's bag again, but the room was so diminutive. I knew there was no chance he'd let me sleep on the outside of the bed, especially now that I knew I was a prisoner. But I would find a way to get into that bag.

"Want to go play cards or something?" he asked.

How could he think about doing something so lighthearted? It was as if he wanted to bring things back to normal, like nothing happened.

"No," I said, and then regretted it. We needed to get out of this room, out where I could see other people. "Maybe I could play a slot machine or something instead?"

He remained silent for a long moment as he stared up at the bunk over our heads. "Maybe." The weight of that word felt heavy in the air. "I need another drink," he continued.

"Okay."

"Come on, let's play poker. You don't have to play if you don't want to, but sit next to me and you'll be my good luck charm." He stood up and held out a hand to help me out of the tight space. I sighed and took it. When I stood up he kissed me, and I backed away.

He looked at me, disappointed. "Please. Live a little, will you?"

"Are you kidding me?"

He clenched his jaw, and then his normal expression returned as if it never left. There he was, My Alex. Sincere, loving eyes.

"It doesn't have to be so bad," he said.

I looked down at the floor. I was so sick of the motion of the train I thought I might scream. Would I ever feel like I wasn't rocking back and forth again?

"Can I brush my teeth first?" I asked.

"Sure." He watched my every move as I brushed my teeth. Then he held out his hand as I slipped out of the bathroom, and I grabbed it, now disgusted by the feel of his skin on mine.

"To the game room," he said.

Who was this man who held my hand and led me down the narrow train corridor? Never in my life did I ever think Alex would hurt me on purpose, in any way. But now? I thought back to some of his more wild moments—convincing me to graffiti the side of a building, shoplifting a pair of earrings for me when we were in our early teens, getting in a small scuffle with another kid when he was in the ninth grade, ranting in anger about sundry topics from time to time. Small but consistent rebellions and bursts of anger.

They still seemed relatively harmless. But combined with the icy glares he gave me a few times today, they painted a new picture of Alex for me. One that was there all along, but which I had turned a blind eye to all my life. The Mona Lisa did not wear a contented smile; all at once, she looked passively pissed off. Once I saw it, I couldn't un-see it.

But part of my mind would not relent on arguing on behalf of My Alex. It couldn't be. This couldn't be happening. What if I was confused? What if this was a big joke? I wanted to come up with an excuse to keep this from being real. And if I screamed for help, would I possibly screw up the rest of Alex's life, if by chance this was all some misunderstanding or prank? My instincts wanted to kick my logic's ass for trying to excuse any of it. But my logic kept whispering, *It's Alex, for crying out loud. It's Alex. You know him better than anyone.* What if I got help on this train, and the whole thing was just an elaborate practical joke, but Alex ended up with a police record that would potentially ruin his career?

I sighed as we stepped through the connecting threshold into the game car. It was busier than the last time. The sight of fellow passengers was a comfort, yet also frustrating. I wanted to muster that scream, and I began to gather the energy to do it when Alex gripped my hand so tight his fingers started to claw into my flesh. He looked at me with such warning I decided to wait. Tears petitioned to cover my eyes, but I declined them.

He was gone from me. He was right there next to me but gone. At any other time, he'd have been one of the first I would tell about this kind of traumatic event, and now he was the cause of it. The void of that friend in my life sucked in my gut like a black hole. I felt the breath go out of me.

"Here we go, an open spot," he said, pulling me toward a card table.

We sat down at two open seats and in the next hand Alex was in the game. I couldn't focus. My ears felt so pricked to attention that they rang a little.

"Quelque chose à boire, mademoiselle?" a cocktail waitress asked me.

I jumped, startled to find her right next to me. I spoke almost no French, only had one year of it from high school under my belt, and remembered nothing except what I used for dance. Why was this woman speaking French? I stared at her with confusion, but then turned it into such an intense gaze—

trying to communicate my need for help—that she looked at me, confused herself, and backed up a step. I tried to locate the French word for *help* in my head, but could not find it. Then I felt Alex's hand on my shoulder, and he caressed the back of my neck under my hair.

"Nous aurons tous les deux un Jack et Coke," Alex said.

I knew he spoke French. Camille enlisted both Sam and Alex in private classes from the time they were small. But I almost never heard him use it. It made him sound richer. More mysterious. The woman nodded and walked away.

"I just ordered us Jack and Cokes. Hope that's okay," he said.

I bit my lip in anger and lowered my gaze, staring at nothing in particular. "Fine. That's fine. Whatever." I wrung my hands. "Why is she speaking French?"

"It's a Canadian line. It travels to Québec. A lot of the staff speaks French."

I sat there and kept my mouth pursed, running my tongue over my teeth as I felt the walls close in.

A minute later, she returned with the drinks, approaching on Alex's side. He took both drinks, shuffled them on the table for a second as he signed them to the room charge, and handed one to me. I let it sit on the table for a couple of minutes, watching the condensation drip down the side of the glass, forming a ring on the cardboard coaster below it.

"A drink might not hurt," Alex whispered. "Unwind."

I turned my head and gave him an atrocious glare. I let the drink sit there for another ten minutes or so as he continued to play a couple of hands. My obstinacy faded as he ignored my show of defiance toward the drink. I grew so bored that I grabbed it and took a sip, and then another. Within minutes most of the drink was inside me. My head started to swim. The rocking of the train seemed to increase, or maybe I just noticed it more. I furrowed my brow, trying to figure out why the alcohol hit me so hard.

"Did you order us doubles?" I asked.

"No. But you need to eat," Alex said, noticing my state.

"Yeah. Yeah, I probably do." The alcohol lessened my fear and fury toward him, which I didn't like.

He bowed out of the game he was in and helped me out of my seat, then led me to the dining car. We sat down at a booth and I let out a quiet hiccup. A server handed us a menu, and I ordered the first thing I saw. Just when the server began to walk away I said, "Wait…" but he didn't hear me.

I sat with my hands in my lap, staring out the window, and wanted to cry. Everything felt slow, my reactions, my motions—they all felt too involuntarily slow. No more alcohol. Alex would have to shove it down my throat if he wanted me to drink any more. Holding onto anger seemed important in keeping me from becoming some kind of victim in this situation.

"The gears are turning in there, even if they're a little slower at the moment. I can see it," Alex said.

"How could they not be?"

"I'll take you home again, okay? What do you think we're going to do, stay on this train forever?"

"You tell me."

"It has to end somewhere, don't you think?" he said.

"Oh, I know it does." I meant something more with that comment but didn't expand.

Alex sighed. "I'll take you home. Just try and have a good time while we're here."

I didn't believe him. "Swear it. Swear it on your life. Swear on your *life* that you'll take me home."

"I swear it on my life, okay?"

My eyes trailed back to the window and I said nothing. And in my tipsy state I thought maybe I was being held captive for this few day getaway, but that was it. That *had* to be it. Nothing else made sense. Alex was being stupid, but he couldn't possibly have anything further planned than this train trip. I'd go with him anywhere, willingly. So what reason would he have to do anything further? I knew there were gaps in my logic, but the alcohol made them fuzzy.

We ate in a tense silence, but the food didn't seem to help my wooziness. Too late, the alcohol already permeated my bloodstream. I was also running on too little sleep at this point. If I was going to get out of this, I had to get some rest. God, I felt so irate I wanted to pull my hair out.

"How's your food?" Alex asked.

"Fucking delicious. How is yours?"

He tilted his head at my tone with the air of a father looking at an annoying teenage daughter. "Also fucking delicious."

"I bet it is." I didn't even know what I tried to say with my sarcasm and attitude, but my intoxication smashed down the gate holding in the bucking antagonism.

"You're having fun. You just need to stop fighting it and realize that."

"Keep telling yourself that. Maybe you'll keep one of us convinced of the idea."

His eyes looked so dark for being so bright. He said nothing else to me while we finished our food. We headed back to the room and I sat down to remove my shoes. Alex stood with his hands on his hips for a minute and the quiet between us persisted. The little room felt more like a prison with every passing second. I began to think I would never be anywhere but on this train.

"I need a shower," I said.

"It's all yours." His tenor sounded sullen.

I stood up, being careful not to fall over, and got a few things together to clean up. In the shower, I tried to clear my thoughts and sort them into tidy rows.

I was on the train.

We were to depart tomorrow.

Alex had no weapons, to my knowledge, so I could just bolt when we got off of the train.

He said he'd take me home, and he seemed back to his old self by the time we returned to the room, so maybe this was all a big, appalling joke.

If it was a joke, it wasn't funny; it was demented. Which made it not a joke at all, but frightening.

I tried to stay in the shower forever, but the water went cold and I shut it off. I stood there in the stall, rocking with the clunk-*clank* below my feet. *Don't cry, you cream puff,* I told myself. *Don't you dare cry. Suck it up. You're getting out of this.* I opened the stall and grabbed a fresh towel. I dried my hair, brushed my teeth, and slipped into the lounge clothes I grabbed from my bag before the shower. Then I leaned forward on the sink, resting on my hands and trying to muster up whatever kind of life force I needed to get out of the bathroom and get into that bed.

I had to get that phone again. It was absolutely imperative. The new Alex would not give me the phone even if I demanded it, though—I knew that. So it was on me. Get that phone, however I could. He needed to go to sleep, and I needed to stay awake. This was a small problem, since he slept most of the afternoon, and I felt exhausted. If I could get him to fall asleep before me, I could get that phone and get the hell out of this room. I swallowed back the lump in my throat and opened the door. Alex sat on the chair with his legs crossed, one ankle resting on his opposite thigh, and looked deep in thought. He raised his eyes to assess me.

"Hey," he said.

"Hey."

"Feeling new and improved?"

"A bit." I moved toward my bag to put my toiletries back, and he jumped to his feet and grabbed my arm.

I whipped my head around to look at him. "I'm just putting my stuff back."

He lessened his grip and nodded, but didn't let go completely. I tried to shake him off and dropped my small satchel. He resisted my attempt to make him let go, taking hold of me around the waist with his other arm. He pulled me around to him and then eased in to kiss me. I tried to shove him off and he clenched his jaw, pulling me to him again.

"Stop," I said and yanked away.

"What happened? You wanted this last night. And this morning," he said angry.

"You can't be serious. What *happened*? No, you did *not* just ask me that."

He yanked me to him once more and kissed me. I tried to smack him across the face again, but he grabbed my wrist, forced me onto the bed, and moved on top of me. He felt so heavy on me, and one of his hands grabbed the back of my thigh to wrench my leg around him.

"No, stop," I said, but it was muffled against his mouth on mine. "Alex, stop!"

I hefted the knee of my opposite leg up to try and catch him in the crotch, but it missed and jammed him in the top of his inner thigh instead. One of his hands held me down by my shoulder. I knew I should have more fight in me than this, but the alcohol weakened my physical state so much it seemed like

I was echoing the movements I should have tried—a diluted form of self-defense. That alcohol seemed too strong for just one drink.

He let go of my shoulder just long enough to move my other leg up and around him, too.

"Stop, damn it, Alex, stop," I continued, but it was hard to get enough breath with him on me and his mouth against mine. I began to panic, a kind of panic I'd never felt before. This was not happening, this was not happening, this was not happening. It couldn't, it absolutely could not. I felt like I would do anything, *anything*, to keep it from occurring.

So my mind went quiet for a moment, and I evaluated the situation as best as I could in the chaos. How could I keep myself from suffering this? I was too weak to fight him right now. I was already in a defeated position, my body felt drained despite the adrenaline now coursing through it, and he was a strong male to begin with. I was not going to be able to fight him off. I considered biting him as hard as I could for a second but knew that would cause an even bigger backlash for me.

I saw just one other option in the midst of him pressing against me: slow him down. Just slow him down, and gain control in whatever way I could. He left my clothes on aside from yanking my pants down a little and my heart pounded with fear. I didn't have time to consider it at any length, so I reacted by instinct and decided on that course of action. In an instant, I went from fighting him to kissing him in return. He pulled back, surprised by it. I reached up in the moment he afforded me and wrapped my hand around his shoulders, and though it made me want to puke, I moved in to kiss him again as he tried to figure out what was happening.

For a minute, he reacted with anger, frustrated by his loss of control in the situation, and became more aggressive with me. But I kept up the charade and continued to kiss him and go along with it. He let go of the hostility, and the ocean calmed from a thrashing sea into more manageable waves. And then, at least from a voyeur's perspective, it looked as though we were merely repeating the events from the night before.

It was only my mind that screamed in protest. Tears welled in my eyes, and I blinked them away. One rogue tear ran down my cheekbone and into my hair. But I figured it was better to go willingly into this with extreme aversion than to forever carry the deeper emotional scar of him painfully forcing himself on me. At least that was my scrambled, intoxicated thought process in those moments.

Afterward, it seemed like it took him forever to fall asleep. The nap of the afternoon left him with energy to spare. After he had finished with me, I pulled my clothes back in order while he continued to kiss my neck and cheeks. Finally, *finally*, he grew tired and just curled up next to me, holding me down with the weight of his arm. I was cramped in the corner of the bunk again, and waited for his breathing to go into a sleep cadence for a while before I got up the nerve to try and escape this spot.

When I believed him to be in a deep enough sleep, I must have spent five full minutes easing myself out from under his arm and over the top of him without touching his body—slowly, so slowly. I slipped onto the floor as quietly as I could, moving with such gradual progress so that the bed would not squeak. I crouched down just to breathe for a moment when I made it to the floor, and then eased myself over to his bag. I unzipped his bag with another round of silence so unhurried it felt agonizing, making sure the zipper never sounded louder than the clanking of the train. I stooped in near complete darkness, the nightlight too dim to reveal anything in his bag, so I had to fish around with my hand to find the phone.

I grabbed an object that I thought was my phone at first. But after handling it for a moment I realized the shape was longer and a little thicker, and then I felt a handle at the end. I froze for a second, and my sense of touch computed what I had in my hand. It felt like a knife in a sheath—maybe a four or five inch blade, I estimated.

My pulse raced again and I tried not to hyperventilate. I set the knife on top of the bag so I could hide it somewhere beyond Alex's knowledge. All at once, the need to find my phone became more urgent, and I clutched around in the bag with more speed. I found it in the very bottom corner and pulled it out. Before I illuminated it, I contemplated whether I should try to send a message for help out first or just grab it and run out the door. *I'm so tired I can barely think straight.* I knew if I opened that door Alex would be up in a flash, so I opted to get a message out first, and then flee.

I illuminated the phone and hunkered down over it to hide the light. I felt overwhelmed by the number of missed calls and texts I received. All evening it was tucked away in here on silent, buzzing with activity. I clicked the first text in my inbox, from Sam, and began typing a message. I planned to tell him to help me, that we were on a train now in Canada, and that I suspected Alex might be taking me to their vacation home, to Tempest Lodge. But all I had time to type was:

Sam help m

Alex pushed me aside, out of bed before I even realized he was awake. The phone fell from my hand, and I scrambled to grab it, hitting send before he could rip it from my fingers. I didn't see the message go through. I could only pray that it did while he clutched the device in rage.

"You trying to play me?" he said, spitting the words at me.

I stared at the phone in his hand and didn't answer. *Please go through, please go through*, I thought at the message. It would have to be enough. If that message got to Sam, he would have to know the situation was desperate.

"You think this is a game, kitten?" he said. He approached with a measured step, and then another.

I stared at the phone.

"Don't act like a fool. You know better. Don't fuck this up for yourself. Because..." Alex huffed out a humorless laugh. "Man, Auttie. You could really fuck this up for yourself if you try. Who were you trying to contact, anyway? Your mom? Or maybe... Sam? You want him to come save you from his own *brother*?"

A chill tightened the skin on the back of my neck until it hurt. I took deliberate breaths.

"This shit?" he said, holding up the phone. "We're done with this shit."

I watched him open the bathroom door and flick on the light. I had to squint against the blinding glare as it assaulted the darkness. He turned on the faucet of the sink, popped the back of the phone off, took out the battery, and then threw the phone and the battery into the sink under the running water.

I bit my lip for one second, and then bolted for the door. It flung open and smacked against the wall of the bathroom, and I ran to the right, toward the dining car. There had to be someone in the hallway that could help me. I tried to yell out, "Help!" but I felt so breathless and weak that it came out almost as a whisper. I made it to the threshold without seeing another person, and panicked. In through the connecting platform, which wobbled beneath my feet, and then I passed through the next door.

The hallway of the next sleeper car was empty, too, and my stomach sank. It was late. Most people were probably in the game car or in bed. I glanced back and saw through the windows of the doors that Alex was just now leaving our room and beginning to chase me. Why did he hesitate so long? Then I remembered the knife, cursing myself for forgetting to pick it up and take it with me. My feet pounded against the thin carpet of the hallway, and I had to brush my hand against the wall at one point as the train rocked against an uneven portion of the tracks.

I arrived at the connecting platform to the dining car and my heart sank. The lights were out and there was no one to be found. All of the china was cleared from the tables. I kept running, keeping my eye on the door to the next car, but I had no idea what laid beyond the dining car. I held onto the hope that maybe it was the staff quarters, and that some of them were still up even though night had fallen a while ago. I heard Alex make it through the connecting doors and his feet pounding up behind me. I slammed into the door to the next connecting threshold and screamed, "Help!" But there was no one to hear me. Through the window of the doors, I could see that it was the kitchen, and it was dark, as well. The door to that car was locked, and I realized I was cornered and alone.

My shoulders tensed and I squeezed my eyes shut as I continued to yank on the door. I heard his steps come up on me. Then a violent yank of my hair whipped my head back and I was on the floor, slammed onto my back. Alex squatted down next to me, still holding my hair. I tried to catch my breath from the pain in my scalp and neck, as well as having the wind knocked out of me. He watched me for a second, his face absent of expression.

When I felt like I could breathe again, he lifted an object in his other hand for me to see. I lay there on the floor, with him crouched beside me, and watched as he released my hair so he could remove the knife from the sheath. He surveyed the blade of the knife as he spoke.

"Let's play nice, okay Auttie?" The contrast between his violence, the threat of the object in his hand, and the complete normalcy of his tone seemed wicked. "Let's just... play nice."

I swallowed hard, and watched the dim hall lights from the previous sleeper car dance against the blade. "Okay," I whispered.

He sighed and hefted me to my feet. My entire body trembled as he pocketed his knife and led me back to our room with a firm grip on my shoulder. When we got to our room, he shut the door behind us, moved the chair in front of it, and looked at me.

"Lie down on the bed," he said.

He couldn't have it in him to attack me in that way again so soon, could he? I complied, fearing a stab wound, and he kept a steady eye on me as he sifted through his bag and pulled out a scarf and two long socks. I tried to keep steady as he approached. He grabbed my hands first, binding them together with the scarf, rolling me on my side toward the window, and then tied the end of the scarf to a post against the wall leading to the bunk above. Then he tied my feet together with the long socks and secured them to the post at the bottom of the bed.

He got in next to me, covered us with the blanket, and within a half hour or so, he fell asleep. Silent tears rolled down my face. It was a battle, but I forced myself to stop crying after a while because I couldn't wipe the tears away. They tickled and itched my face, and I had to try and smear my cheek against the upper sleeve of my shirt.

Any part of me that hoped this was some kind of sick practical joke was abandoned far behind us on the tracks. This morning I loved him. Tonight he'd raped me and then threatened me with a knife. The world I thought I always knew with Alex disappeared, vanished like a child pictured in a "Missing" alert. My own face would probably appear soon in one, as well. Finally, after hours and hours, when I could see the faint slivers of gray morning light peeking around the curtains of the window, my body gave up. I fell into a deep depression and gave into sleep.

CHAPTER NINE

When I awoke, I felt stiff all over and not even close to being rested. My back was cold, and I realized Alex no longer lay next to me. I lifted my head a little, turned it as far to the side as I could, and saw that he was in the bathroom brushing his teeth, leaving the door open to keep a lookout in case I figured out how to untie myself. I dropped my head down to the bed again and stared at the wall. What now? What the hell now? When he finished in the bathroom, I heard him come out and felt his eyes on my back. I lifted my head again to look at him.

"Alex," I pleaded.

He paused a beat. "You must be hungry," he said.

I rested my head again. "I am," I muttered.

"I already ordered us some breakfast."

I looked around the room, wondering how he ordered it, searching for a phone or something on the wall; but I saw none. After a moment of evaluating me on the bed, he walked over, untied me, helped me sit up, and then looked me face on.

"Don't say a word to them when they come to the door. Understand? Just, bring out that proper little ballerina side of yourself, okay?"

I thought about the blade of his knife shining in the dim light from the night before. I imagined the way a piercing jab through my flesh might feel. I nodded.

Alex leaned against the door of the room, watching me as we waited for our food to arrive. After a minute, he slid down to sit on the floor, leaning against the door with his arms on his propped knees. We just looked at each other, like a sick version of a staring contest. Blinking did not declare a loser. What would decide the loser was seemed much darker. Who would break first? The train clanked away.

A few minutes passed, and Alex grew tired of the stare-down, so he fiddled with his fingers, but remained against the door. A train attendant came by a short while later with a platter of food. Alex stepped out into the hall to take it from him, so I still didn't see the man, but I stood up and began to muster the nerve to scream. I heard the train attendant speaking French, and Alex replying in kind. Damn the language barrier on this train. Quick internal debates ran through my head, the hesitation ruining my chance. I thought of that knife again. I thought of it being worth the risk. And then the transaction was over too fast. Within a second, Alex came back into the room and I heard the man walk away. I saw the hot coffee on the tray, and sat down when I imagined it being thrown in my face at the first sign of defiance.

Alex set the tray down on the small end table and shuffled things around with his back to me. I tried to lean around to watch what he was doing but couldn't see anything. When he stepped to the side, I saw he had ordered two cups of coffee, and a breakfast sandwich for each of us.

"Here. Eat. I'm sorry, Autumn. I know things have been... Rough. And I... I am sorry." He turned and handed me a small plate with one of the sandwiches on it. I took it, stared at it, and then took a bite. Alex brushed a hand over my hair and I flinched away, but then I glanced at his eyes, and they looked like the eyes of My Alex. I softened, and wanted to weep. He ran his hand over my hair again, tucking it behind my ear. After swallowing my bite of the sandwich, I realized how famished I felt, and ate the rest of it quickly.

"Coffee?" Alex asked.

"No, thanks." As I finished my last couple bites of food, my head experienced a strange bout of swaying, and I felt dizzy. I shook it off, paused for a second, and then swallowed my last bit of sandwich. Again, the woozy feeling infiltrated. I glanced up at Alex and realized he watched me, as if he knew what I felt. All at once, my body felt relaxed and loopy.

"Wait. Wait. What?" I said. I went to set the plate on the carpeted floor but ended up halfway dropping it. "Stop, wait... Wait. What's happening? What did you do?" I asked, my words beginning to slur.

Alex regarded me for a moment before answering. "We get off the train tonight, but you're kind of exhausting me with your antics."

"What? My *antics*?"

"You just won't calm down and enjoy the ride, so I thought I'd help you."

I jerked my head back to look at him in confused disgust, realizing the motion looked like that of a drunk person's. "Help me? What the hell? What did you do?"

"You'll just take a little nap, that's all. It should just be enough to help you sleep for a few hours. You'll probably feel back to normal this evening."

"Wait, wait... You..." My brain decelerated so much that I had to concentrate to finish my sentence. "You put something... in there. You drugged me?"

"I just gave you a little something to relax you. Well, to make you sleep, really. It'll help you sleep."

I leaned forward and put my head in my hands, trying to connect the dots. I wasn't sure where the dots were that needed connecting. "Hold up. This... isn't the first time. Wait. You did this to me before, didn't you? You bastard. You did this before."

"I thought I might need a little help convincing you to get on the train in the first place. Once you let go of your inhibitions, you were pretty easy to convince."

I swayed with the movement of the train, and fuzzy memories of the night we boarded the train came through, made even fuzzier by my current state. Blacked out segments of time, drunkenness that seemed too drunk for the amount of alcohol I'd consumed, the decision to do something as stupid as agreeing to this trip. And then I remembered last night in the game car, feeling too tipsy for only one drink.

"And last night," I slurred.

"Yeah, I hardly put any in there. Just a touch. Just enough to help you be at peace a little bit. Don't tell me it's not more enjoyable when you let go of some of that tension."

I glowered at him and shook my head. I gripped the edge of the bed for a second. "Fiend!" I said, emphasizing the sound of the 'f' as I spit the word at him and leaned forward. I lost my balance and fell to my face on the floor, but it didn't hurt with the sedative in my system. I stared at the corner where the carpet met with the wall, noticing the cheap plastic molding, and a few crumbs on the floor.

Laying there with my cheek against the carpet, I had two thoughts. One, how disgusting it was that my face was on the floor with its plethora of germs. But the drug made me care so little. And two, I thought of Sam. *Please Sam, God.... Please have gotten that message.* I would try to get out on my own; I would do everything I could. But in that moment, overtaken by the tranquilizer, I felt helpless and drained of any fight. All of my hope rested on Sam. I heard Alex shuffle around near my head, and he began to lift me by the shoulders up off the floor, but I blacked out before I even made it to the bed.

When I woke up out of the drugged slumber, I lay on the bed facing the window and felt ill. Staring at the sky outside, a memory surfaced from the deep recesses of my mind, brought to life from the situation in which I found myself.

~~~

Alex and I were children, somewhere around six or seven years old, and a mouse had been wreaking havoc in the bottom cupboards of the Van Ettens' house. Camille had set a mouse trap, and Alex and I were near the entrance of the kitchen when we heard it snap—indicating that something set it off. We ran over to the cupboard and looked inside to find a frightened little mouse, caught by the end of its tail in the trap. It was alive, and it had urinated out of fear on the wooden part of the trap. I told Alex we should take it out to the back of the property, or down to the park to set it free. Instead, Alex grabbed hold of the mouse, lifted the metal part of the trap, and forced it to snap back down again on the mouse's neck, killing it instantly.

~~~

I flinched as I thought of the incident for the first time in at least a decade. An authentic memory, a red flag, whitewashed back then into something like a dingy streamer at a carnival. It seemed like nothing back then. It meant everything now.

As I opened my eyes again, I assessed that my hands and feet were free of restraints, but I could feel Alex's presence in the room. My stomach twisted. I turned my head and saw him sitting in the chair reading a book.

He looked up at me. "Awake?" he asked.

I stared at him for a moment. "That's a dumb question."

He glared back at me with a sardonic expression. "Don't be such a crab-ass." I narrowed my eyes, but then realized how gross my stomach felt and I gave up on the interaction. The movement of the train did not agree with the amount of sedative he gave me. My head spun a little, and I realized I was going to be sick. Again.

"I need to use the bathroom," I said sitting up as fast as I could without making my head swirl even more. I didn't wait for him to answer, I just stood up, stumbled forward, and headed straight for the toilet.

When I was done, Alex came in and put a hand on my back. "You okay?" he asked, as if he were My Alex.

I turned and smacked his hand off me. "Don't touch me." I flushed the toilet, went to the sink to scrub my hands and face with a vengeance, and then brushed my teeth.

He stood in the doorway to the bathroom surveying me. "I didn't mean for you to get sick," he said.

I glared at him. "Oh, is that right? You drugged me, threatened me with a knife, you're holding me captive, but you didn't *mean for me to get sick*?" Sarcasm gnashed through my voice like a feral beast.

"I was just trying to settle you down and let you rest. It's not like I shot you up with heroine out of a dirty street needle, for God's sake."

"Really? *Really?* You're going to justify this to yourself?" I rested on the bathroom counter with one hand, rinsed my mouth and spit again.

"This whole manner doesn't suit you very well," he said gesturing in my general direction and then crossing his arms over his chest.

"Well, then do please beg my pardon, fine sir, while I invite you to go fuck yourself."

"Auttie." His expression was severe.

"And *don't* call me that," I said. "You've lost the right to call me that stupid nickname ever again." I knew showing anger toward him was a poor idea, but I still felt off from the drug. I couldn't control it. Like having too much alcohol, it destroyed my self-restraint and amplified my anger.

He let out an exasperated sigh. "Whatever. It's almost dinnertime. Do you think you'll be able to eat? More importantly, do you think you'll be able to behave yourself? I really, really don't want to do anything unpleasant to you."

I let out a hard, wicked laugh. "*Sure* you don't."

"I see the stuff is still working its way through your system. It can have that affect, so I'll let some of your snippiness slide for now. But I'm asking you. Will you be able to contain yourself if we go to the dining car, or would you rather stay in the room and eat again?"

The thought of staying in the room any longer made me want to scream. "I can contain myself."

"Good. I'm getting bored in here. We have to go soon. The dining car is closing early tonight because we're heading for the next stop. We get off the train tonight."

I couldn't find any words, and I realized I needed to sober up as fast as I could if we were departing this evening. Help had to be there waiting for me. Even if it weren't, once I set foot outside, it would be my chance. Dart off into a crowd in a train station, and grab anyone who could help me.

I changed into jeans and a sweatshirt—something that would keep me warm once we departed the train. The dining car was already almost full, but we found an open table near the back. I tried not to look at the spot where Alex had yanked me to the ground and threatened me with the knife the night before, but we sat right next to it. The music seemed louder than normal. Some old crooner finished a song over the speakers, and Etta James came on with another old standard. I brushed my hand over the smooth fabric of the bench I sat on and looked at the swaying crystals of the small chandeliers. I existed in some kind of demented art deco nightmare.

Outside the window, large pines clustered along the Canadian landscape and flurries fell from the heavens. They sky was thick with overcast, furthering my claustrophobic sensation. A waiter came by and I decided I should push as much water and food into my system as it could handle. I didn't know what to expect after we departed the train. I would probably be at a police station for a long time answering questions. And I needed to get my head back into sorts.

I ordered a sandwich from our server—who had such a thick French lilt I had to repeat my order—and drank my first glass of water as fast as my stomach allowed. Alex said nothing to me throughout the entire meal, and I said nothing to him. He just watched me, keeping his guard up in case I bolted or screamed. I saw him toying with the knife on the table from the silverware setting.

After the food arrived, I ate half of the sandwich, and my stomach felt pretty good. So I downed another glass of water. My head began to clear, and Alex scrutinized me. I finished the sandwich and then started to stand up, but despite my speed, he beat me to it and grabbed my arm across the table, yanking me back down. He picked up his knife again and stabbed at his food.

"I'm fast, Autumn," he whispered. "Think of the damage I could do if you try to run. Even if someone helped you, I could break a bone or two of yours before anyone took me down."

I did not blink for a long time as I stared at him. I waited for our server to return, and when he did, I swallowed hard and looked at him with all the seriousness my face could muster. I thought it worth the risk if a man stood at the end of the table between Alex and myself.

"Please help me! I'm being held here against my will. Please, please help. He kidnapped me," I said indicating to Alex. I started to rise.

A brief flicker of fury crossed Alex's expression, and then he burst out laughing, releasing my hand and the silverware for a moment to clap once. He brushed a hand over mine in a way that appeared to anyone else as a reassurance—a caress of friendly inside jokes—but against my own skin the gesture felt like a the warning.

"Don't mess with people like that," Alex said to me, his performance so fine he almost fooled me. "You're just going to confuse him and make him feel weird and embarrassed. Do you feel awkward now?" Alex asked the waiter, who appeared confused into stillness—a perplexed sculpture of a man.

"Um, *oui*, yes," he said.

"She's just messing with you. I'm sorry. She messes with people a lot. It's a thing we do. One time she dared me to walk by someone, bump into them, and when they told me to watch where I was walking say, 'You can see me? But... I've been dead for fifty years. How can you see me?!' I told her not to screw with you, but she never listens," Alex said and gave me a poignant glare at the end of his statement, timed just right as the waiter looked away from Alex to stare at me.

I was so surprised by his cover, by his lie—so impressed by it—that I just sat there with my mouth gaping. The server took a moment to compute the story, some of which he probably did not understand in a second language, and looked at me to confirm whether or not it was true. But he didn't give me enough time to respond. I just muttered, "Uh..." and he apparently took that to mean that Alex's story was valid. He looked offended, and walked away. Alex glanced down at the table for a second, took in a measured breath, ground his teeth, and then he looked back at me.

"You said you would contain yourself," he whispered, so irate that my hands shook with fear of the consequences for what I just attempted.

"I said I *could* contain myself."

"When we get up, control yourself, or I'll snap your leg so fast you won't have time to even explain a word to anyone in this car, little dancer," he whispered back.

I swallowed. I saw Alex's speed during his sporting events, his strength. I believed him. If he wanted to break my legs, I was sure he could do it before I had a chance to run.

He took one last drink from his glass and then gripped my wrist and led me back to the room. He jerked me in through the doorway of our room and shut the door behind us. He took a breath when we stood there, and it almost sounded like a growl.

"Autumn," he said moving forward and touching my hair. It began as a caress, and then, as he stroked down its length, it morphed into a tug. He slowly pulled my head back by my hair, exposing the front of my neck. His other hand clutched me around my waist, and he surveyed the skin of my neck, moving up to inspect every inch of the side of my face. "How am I going to get you to stop being so damn obstinate? Hmm? What is it that I have to do? How can I convince you that this is what you want?" I didn't answer, I just tried to keep breathing. He moved me over to the bed.

"Lie down," he said.

I complied, shaking as the full extent of terror sank in. I didn't fight as he tied me up again. Then he sat down on the bed facing away from me, hunched forward like he felt burdened by grief. I looked at his back, and felt so much inside: horror, hate, confusion. But worst of all, longing. I missed him so much, and wished I could call out for the old Alex to help me. Where the hell was he?

He sat there for a long time, leaning forward. Finally, he ran a hand through his hair, stood up, and began to pack up our things. There wasn't much to stuff into our bags, but he checked the bathroom to make sure we had everything, and then zipped the bags and set them near the door. He sat down and leaned one elbow on one of the arms of the side chair, putting one hand to his face in thought. He stayed that way, staring at nothing as if devising a plan, until the train began to lurch and slow. The train whistled a few times, and it slowed further. A voice resonated over the PA system.

"Ladies and Gentlemen, we have arrived at stop number six. Please check your tickets to confirm your departure station. If you are departing the train tonight, please ensure that you have all of your belongings and meet with the attendant in the hallway of your car with your tickets out. If you are continuing on with us, please remain in your room and have your tickets available, as attendants will be coming by to check them. Thank you." As before, the message was repeated in French.

Alex stood up and came over to untie me, avoiding eye contact as he did. I rubbed my wrists. He had tied the scarf much tighter this time than last. I scooted to the edge of the bed and watched as he crouched down by his bag and pulled something from it. I didn't need to set eyes on it to know what it was, but he stood up and faced me so I could see it anyway. He drew the knife out and inspected the blade.

"We're not going to have any trouble getting off this train, are we?" he said.

I shook my head. "No," I whispered. Police would be outside. I knew it. They had to be waiting at the stop. Sam must have received my last text message, and they certainly would have tracked down our location by now. No need to fight, I would have help waiting. They had *days* to catch up with us. They would be there.

Alex put the knife in his pocket and pulled his shirt down over it to make sure it was covered. I held back a smile, because that knife on him would be incriminating to the police. He could try and come up with some elaborate story, but my text messages to Sam, and that knife under his shirt would be evidence on my side. He handed me my coat, donned his own, and then he pulled two tickets out of a side pocket in his bag, along with a set of keys.

I furrowed my brow as I looked at the keys. Brief visions of being buried alive or meeting with some other heinous end came out of nowhere, assaulting my thoughts. I shook them out of my head and reminded myself help would be here waiting for me. If not, just run into the crowd. Alex grabbed my hand, handed me my bag, and hefted his bag over his free shoulder. He held the tickets with his unoccupied hand, but kept my hand close to his leg, so that it brushed up against the knife in his pocket now and then as a reminder.

"It would take me two seconds," he whispered into my ear. "Two seconds to pull it out and inflict a wound you wouldn't believe. Two seconds."

I stared forward, saying nothing, trying not to cry.

We left the room, and a few people departed at the far end of our car. I could feel the frigid night air blowing in from the open door to the outdoor platform, and I felt dizzy from terror. *Help will be here.* We approached the attendant, a heavy-set woman, and even though I clutched onto hope, each step felt like one stride closer to the grave. *Sam, help me. Please have people here to help me.* The phones *had* to have tracked our location. Maybe the squad car lights were off to avoid scaring Alex into fleeing. As we neared the attendant, it began to feel as if I didn't have any legs. I just floated along, disconnected from the floor beneath me.

"Did you two have a nice journey with us?" she asked as he handed her our tickets.

I looked out into the dark night through the windows, searching. Maybe police were behind the building that served as the train station, which sat maybe twenty yards from the tracks.

"We had the best time," Alex said.

"Wonderful. We look forward to you traveling with us again. You have a good night now," she said.

"Thanks, you too," Alex said, and she stepped aside to let us off.

I tried to give her a pleading look, just in case, but she turned away to meet with the next people departing behind us. It felt unreal getting off of that train and stepping onto solid ground. The wind felt like ice, pure ice, in breathable form. It stung the skin on my face and hands. I gave one last glance back at the warm light of the train as Alex led me into the dark, arctic night, and I realized no one waited for us. I let out a terrified "Help me!" A feeble yell as it left my mouth, and useless as the words evaporated into the night. My stomach sank and I felt weak. He held on tight and pulled me into oblivion, and no one was there to help.

CHAPTER TEN

I started to hyperventilate and yanked against his grip. The night was black, and only a tiny train station with sickly lighting sat before us, virtually barren of people. We passed through it—glass doors, florescent lighting, pallid green walls, with a couple of vending machines to one side. I'd thought there would be more people. Any people. But the station was empty, and only a few passengers appeared to depart the train minutes behind us. Beyond, there was a parking lot with just three cars in it. Alex pulled me toward a black SUV in a hurry, and I resisted harder, wrenching at his grasp. He tugged harder and growled.

"Help! Help me! Someone, help!" I screamed, and he pulled me into the shadows.

If anyone heard me, they must have thought I joked around or worse, they didn't want to get involved. I screamed again. Alex whipped his free hand across his body and drew the knife from his pocket. He jerked me in front of him, switched his grasp on me to his other hand, and led me to a vehicle with the knife at my back. I could feel the tip of the blade through my jacket, the point pressing against where one of my kidneys resided. We arrived at the trunk of the vehicle. He let go of my arm for a moment but kept the knife pushing against my back, and hit a button on the key fob to unlock the black SUV.

"Oh God, please... Alex, please," I whimpered.

"Put your bag in the trunk," he said.

I opened the trunk and set my bag in there, and then he tossed his in next to mine. He shut the trunk, led me around to the passenger seat, and opened the door. I slid in and the leather seats of the SUV were so cold I shivered on contact. As soon as Alex shut my door, he locked the vehicle. As he walked around the front of it to get in on the driver's side, I pushed the lock up and tried to open the door, yanking on the handle like a wild animal. It wouldn't open. He unlocked his door, slid in next to me, and locked the whole vehicle again when he saw that I had pushed up the lock on my side. Our eyes met in the dark.

"Child locks," I whispered.

"Yeah," he said. Irritation painted his face, and I swallowed back a lump in my throat.

I'd missed my chance. Now I was trapped in this next step of imprisonment, wrapped in the blackness of the night in the middle of God-Knows-Where, Canada. And I'd missed my chance. Now he was pissed.

"Where are we going?" I asked while looking at my hands.

"You don't know yet?"

"I suppose I have a good idea."

The lodge—it was the only place I could imagine him taking me to in this part of the world. Maybe he would torture me for a while there before killing me. If he just wanted to drown me under the ice in some frozen lake or something that simple, he didn't have to bring me this far to do it. It had to be Tempest Lodge we were headed for.

He turned the ignition. It protested at first with the cold weather, but started when he turned it over again. He flipped on the windshield wipers to clear the accumulating snow. I wrapped my arms around myself, unable to control my shaking. I thought Chicago felt frigid in the winter. This was a new level of bitter cold—like the arctic itself swept a giant arm across the land to knock down any life forms foolish enough to attempt survival here. It felt unnatural to be in a place this devoid of warmth—alien even.

Alex backed the vehicle out of the parking space, and then pulled out onto a two-lane road. At first, we passed a few small shops and neighborhoods, but then civilization vanished behind us, shrinking in the rearview mirrors. Just on the outskirts of the small town we went by a quaint airport, and it was like déjà vu—a place, a memory, from another lifetime. I didn't realize how familiar somewhere so far away could be when I had not laid eyes on it, or even thought of it, since I was small. But there the airport sat, to prove that it never left, and it looked like it never even changed at all. We'd flown onto that very landing strip on a small connecting flight both times we came to stay with the Van Ettens in their vacation home up here. The sight of it was also the last confirmation I needed to be sure that we were indeed going to that house. Knowing we were headed somewhere I had visited before, somewhere I had fond memories of, felt disturbing.

The airport drifted behind us, and we cruised into blackness, with snow-frosted pines on either side of the road. The snow fell harder, and the windshield wipers filled the silence with a steady rhythm. We followed the headlights into the night, and I envisioned deer or other creatures bolting onto the slick road, leaving us no time to react. It didn't seem like Alex watched for them. He just stared ahead, his jaw tense.

It felt like we were flying over the pavement. The speed of the car twisted uncomfortable knots in my shoulders. I knew the highway had to be slippery from the snow and ice.

Everything was all black night, headlights against snowfall, windshield wipers cutting the awkward silence, trees in the darkness, and the glossy interior of the SUV. The dash lights illuminated Alex's face in a soft glow. I brushed my hand along the chrome-edged leather interior of my passenger door.

"Where did you get the car?" I asked, finding it difficult to speak at full volume.

"I bought it from someone in the region. Then had it delivered to the parking lot yesterday," he replied.

The things money could buy you, I thought.

"You planned this, far in advance. Oh my God, you *planned* this." Even though I sort of knew it, I hadn't confirmed it out loud, and hadn't even confirmed it for certain even to myself. A diminutive part of me still thought he decided on the whole thing on a whim—took advantage of the situation the night of the party at their house. I realized now that every bit was premeditated. And it made me feel betrayed with such intensity that I had to bend forward to ease the ache in my gut. The Alex I thought I knew slipped even farther out of my grasp, like watching that person drop from my hands and fall into the blackness of a bottomless well. An abyss that consumed him, leaving me to wonder if I'd ever held him in my hands at all.

"Oh my God," I said sitting up again as another realization hit me. "It was you."

"Me?" he asked glancing at me for a second and then back to the road.

"You're the one. You kicked Jake's ass, didn't you? The guy I was dating, you assaulted him." I watched Alex for a reaction.

The muscle of his jaw flexed and he took a moment to respond. "You didn't need him around."

"Yeah. I would have come to that conclusion myself. But you freaking came up to Chicago, didn't even tell me you were in town, apparently stalked me or something, and decided on your own to assault someone just because I was sort of dating him?"

"It didn't sound all that casual from what I heard."

"Oh, so you're going to take second-hand gossip from our mothers to decide on something like that?" My head said I should control my response more, but I couldn't.

"Don't piss me off any further, Autumn."

I relaxed back into my seat a little and tried to keep myself from seething. When I spoke again, I made sure my tone was quieter. "Did you stalk me a lot? I mean, you could have just told me you were in town and I would have wanted to spend time with you."

"No, I didn't stalk you at all. Well, *almost* not at all. I'm aware that wasn't necessary to spend time with you. I was just trying to tie up some loose ends."

"What was the point? If you were going to steal me anyway, why did you bother with him?"

His jaw clenched again. "I just... I didn't like the guy. I wanted him out of the picture."

I turned my head away. The distortion of Alex's mental faculties continued to revealed themselves, but I didn't want to see it. I wanted to run the other way, to close my eyes and cover my ears to block it all out.

We sped along for what felt like a half hour before Alex made a right onto another deserted highway. I had no idea of the lodge's exact location. All I knew was that it was in Manitoba, about an hour or two from Lake Winnipeg—but on which side, in which direction, I had no idea.

The snowfall eased up the farther we drove, but the windshield wipers continued to smear themselves across our vision. We passed a long patch of deciduous trees, naked of their leaves and scratching, clawing, scraping at the sky for warmth. Finding none.

Another twenty to thirty minutes later, Alex made a left onto another two-lane road. I spotted a few houses down side streets, as well—not mansions, but large homes for an area so remote. This locale jogged memories from before, too. We were getting close.

The landscape changed to a pure sea of lofty pines. They towered overhead, their boughs hanging heavy with snow.

Alex made another turn, and we passed the last house before the lodge. I could remember from my childhood visits being able to look out far in the distance and see that house on clear days if I squinted, a large log cabin-style home. The trees became sparse again and we headed down a road that sloped lower, and then pulled back up again as we neared the Van Etten chalet.

And then it appeared: Tempest Lodge. The mansion loomed before us—a giant dwelling—dark against the overcast night of bright winter clouds. My trembling subsided a bit during the drive as the car heat warmed my body, but now I tried not to hyperventilate, and the shaking returned.

Soaring pines surrounded the shadowy castle of a house in patches, with a handful of the trees hugging closer to the house itself. Facing the road stood the giant main gable—the triangular shape of the roof capping off the main window that jutted out from the rest of the home, like a tall bay window. The glass stretched nearly floor to ceiling under the gable. It always seemed as if the house itself was looking out over the horizon, or watching anyone who stood before it.

Alex pulled off the road onto the long dirt driveway, now covered in snow. The driveway itself must have extended at least a quarter of a mile, and it circled around in a cul-de-sac near the entrance. Alex put the car into park, and I gazed up at the lodge. It was constructed of a stone base and stone chimneys, with the remainder made of dark wooden logs. The design was heavy with windows, and the foundation was so thick that the front door was about five feet above the ground with a porch leading up to it.

Because it was a vacation home, and the Van Ettens' trips up here were so infrequent, the landscaping had to be maintenance-free. As a result, the ground right around the house was covered in intermittent slabs of stepping stones surrounded by smaller river rocks.

At the end of the driveway, a cobbled walking path led the way to the front door. And lining the cobbled path were wooden stakes—about three feet tall—with spikes at their tops, softened very little by weather and time. Landscape art that required almost no upkeep. On the narrow poles, designs were carved to portray totems of the native art from this region.

I didn't want to go into that house as I sat in the SUV looking up at it.

"Give me your jacket," Alex said.

"What?"

"I said give me your jacket."

I hesitated, but took off my jacket and handed it to him, and within seconds my body began to quake.

"Now. We're going inside," he said. "You'd prefer to go inside than freeze to death out here in the cold without a jacket, right? You would die before you even made it to the closest house."

I clenched my jaw, wrapping my arms around myself. "Fine, yes. I want to go inside."

Alex got out and came around to my door to let me out. Clutching my arm, he led me to the trunk where we retrieved our bags, and then he locked up the SUV, stowing the keys in his pocket. He pulled out another set of keys and we shuffled through the snow up the cobbled path. I slipped a little on a patch of ice, and Alex balanced me with the firm grip of his hand. A violent shaking had overtaken me as soon as we were outside again, but I couldn't resist reaching out and brushing my hand over the top of one of the snow-capped totem spikes. My hand burned with cold as the snow melted against my skin.

The air here smelled so fresh and unpolluted. Crisp pine blew in with the wind. The sound of the north woods echoed far in the distance, so far that I wasn't sure if it was just my imagination, but I thought I heard the howl of a wolf.

Alex unlocked the large wooden door and gestured for me to enter first. I walked into total darkness, and my trembling bordered on convulsions.

"Can I have my jacket now? It's freezing in here."

Alex shut the door behind us, flipped a couple of locks, and switched on the light. I squinted as the sizeable chandelier—made of heavy wrought iron molded into an array of scrolls and maple leaf motifs—illuminated the great room. It hung in front of the giant main window, and had more than enough candelabra bulbs to light the enormous space.

"Yeah, sure," Alex said, handing me my jacket. "The heat is on to keep the pipes from freezing, but I kept the dial around ten degrees Celsius, fifty degrees Fahrenheit, so it'll take a little while to warm up."

I furrowed my brow as he moved over to the thermostat to turn it up.

"You kept it at fifty degrees? What do you mean you *kept* it at a certain temperature?"

He just threw me a patronizing look in response.

I moved into the room and surveyed the place I hadn't seen since my childhood. A giant room sprawled before me with brown leather sofas featuring nail head trim, pale wooden walls, tasteful tapestries depicting northern scenes, and a few expensive art pieces in that same native style as the totems outside. To the left stood a giant bookshelf with a decorative boat oar above it, and next to the bookshelf was a fancy globe made of polished stones, on a stand that reached the height of my waist.

Toward the back of the room sat an oversized dining table. And of course, there was the fireplace. To our right was the colossal polished stone fireplace, surrounded by a few more leather armchairs. It was free of fire at the moment, but it was cleaned and set with fresh logs in place, ready to be ignited. I stepped toward it and thought I could detect the faintest scent of smoke. I rested a hand on one of the chairs, recoiling at first from the cold leather beneath my skin. I placed my hand there again, and stared at the fireplace, remembering it from what seemed like so long ago.

Every night that we had stayed here, eating dinner at the table in this same room, that fireplace had burned. One evening we'd played charades around the fire, and on another Alex, Sam, and I had stood by the giant windows, watching for shooting stars while the reflection of the fire off to the side flickered in the glass. And then, of course, there was the night Sam had caught me dancing.

I smiled a little, even now, at the memory of twirling around by the firelight, imagining it was a set of stage lights on me. Sam, standing there, seeming so unapproachable and handsome and grown up, just watching me.

My smile melted, dropping into a bleak expression, and my stomach sank. *Where are you Sam? Where the hell are you?* I thought. Even if that final text did not go through, there couldn't be any doubt back home that I was in trouble now. I would never decide to be away from home this long, this close to the holidays, giving zero notice.

With that reflection, my pleasant memories evaporated. Alex stood behind me, and I was not in this house to have fun this time. I was here to fight or be held in an imprisonment that would certainly include things I didn't want to think about. I turned to look at him, and he stared back. It seemed like he might be relaxing, letting go of some of the stress that transporting me off the train and to this place gave him.

He could choke down all of the poisonous stress in the world for all I cared, but it did benefit me if he was in a more pleasant mood. So I relaxed one tiny notch, as well. Just one. The heat kicked on and I could smell dust burning on the tops of radiators too infrequently used.

"What now?" I asked, fearing the answer.

"Now we unpack and get comfortable. I'm sure we could both use a little cleaning up after the long train ride. And I don't know about you, but I'm getting hungry again."

I wrinkled my brow again. "Where are we going to get food?" But I had a feeling I knew the answer before I finished the question.

"I brought some up last time I was here. We have plenty," he said.

I tilted my head as I watched him. I looked around the room, confused, and that was when I fully took notice of the artificial Christmas tree in front of the giant front window. It was not lit up, but ornaments dripped from its branches and a star perched on top. Not done the way Camille or my mother would decorate a tree, but enough to give a rudimentary air of holiday cheer. I stepped toward it, and the sick feeling of deception and betrayal writhed in my gut again.

"You did this?" I asked, indicating to the tree.

Alex walked over and plugged it into the outlet just beneath the huge window. "Yeah. I wanted it to feel homey for Christmas."

I swallowed, thinking of Christmas. Thinking of him planning on us being here for Christmas.

"You... were here recently," I said.

"Yes."

"When?"

"About a month ago, I guess it was. I flew up here on a weekend."

I paused, trying to breathe, and nodded my head. "To prepare," I said.

"Yes."

"So why didn't we just fly up here this time? Why the train?"

"It's easier to get onto a train, not so much inspection and all that. I didn't think the TSA would take too kindly to your condition that night. Trains are... well, you know, you just walk right on. Buy a ticket and there you are. But that wasn't all. I really thought it would be a nice trip. It was an exceptional train, you have to admit. I thought it'd be a great time for us. It ended up a lot more stressful than I would have liked. But it could have been a pleasant experience if you would have let it be. I mean, it *was* for one night there, at least."

Almost gagging at the thought of having sex with him, I scrunched up my face for a second. I remembered his knife and thought about that at any airport security, too. I stared at the tree, depression weighing down my shoulders. He brought a knife with a four-inch blade, and thought I would enjoy myself. I had to admit my hopes had soared when I first settled onto the train. It made me feel nauseated to think of it now.

"You thought I wouldn't figure this all out until farther along?" I asked.

He shrugged in response. "I'm not sure. I guess. I thought I could be more convincing, I suppose. I thought a part of you would really want to be here with me, to run away with me. I still think a part of you does. But you got all pigheaded, and the second that drop of plague entered your mind, it grew and spread so fast you wouldn't even stop for a second to control it. And now you're fighting me, and so here we are."

"I'm not stupid enough to allow you to blame even a hair of this on me. You brought a knife with you, for God's sake. If you were reasonable, you would have let me go when I said I didn't want to do this."

He put his hands in the pockets of his pants and looked at the floor for a moment. "Nah. You were going to run off at some point. To New York or wherever. And it's not what should happen."

I scoffed. "Since when are you against me going to New York? You always acted like you supported my dreams."

"Well, early on I didn't believe you would actually do it. In the last couple years, though, you got pretty serious about it. And come on, Autumn, like that would be okay. You'd what? Go out there and start screwing guys out in New York?" His tone turned to ice. "No. No. Not happening. It's so obvious that we're supposed to be together, it's ridiculous. But then you started planning things like you could care less about us happening, and fuck that. No. You're not going to New York."

"So, what's your plan? Just keep me a slave here?" I asked, my voice trailing off into a whisper. If he hadn't thought of options worse than that, I didn't want him to think of them now.

He shrugged again. "My hope is that you'll just calm yourself the fuck down and realize that it's still me. I'm still Alex, still your friend. And maybe then you will think about how great this could be. I mean, look at this place! We could stay here together, and stop pretending that we're just friends and nothing more."

"Why didn't you just tell me how you felt? Alex, come on. Why go to these great lengths without at least *talking* to me?"

In response, Alex simply shook his head, cleared his throat, and shook his head again. "Look at this place. You could love it."

I knew he'd gone off the deep end already, but nothing confirmed it to me like that statement. He had no sense of consequences or of the future if he thought like that. How would we get money and food, even if his wildest fantasies played out? How did he think no one would come looking for us? And how on Earth did he think I could ever feel love toward him after he held me captive, raped me, tied me up, and threatened me with a knife?

Unable to find words, and feeling my gut sucked inward, I stood there and observed the lights on the Christmas tree. The ornaments glistened in all shades of scarlet—crimson bulbs and scrolling ornaments that shimmered like ruby slippers. The night looked so dark through the window behind it, making the tree seem small and lonesome there by itself. Heat emanated from the radiators as they knocked to life, but the house still felt frigid. Nothing about it seemed inviting or cozy now, just cavernous and oppressive.

"Anyway," Alex continued. "Like I said, I'm hungry. I'm going to heat up some chili or something."

"Fine," I whispered. I felt like my insides were dying.

He looked at me standing there, unmoving. "Well, would you like to join me?" he asked.

I sighed, and followed. The kitchen was to the back of the great room and to the left, down a wood-walled hallway. It opened up into a large room with an island in the center. The countertops were granite in an almost identical shade to the pale wood floor and beams overhead. The cabinets were a dusty, elegant pale green. Alex flipped on the light and went to a cabinet, pulling out a can of chili and a box of crackers. He opened up the crackers and set them on the island counter, then went to the stove to make the chili.

I felt like I couldn't move. My thoughts clogged themselves with possibilities—ideas of how to escape, and immediate consequences to each idea. I could try to knock him out with a frying pan, steal the keys to the SUV, and take off. But I held little confidence in my ability to knock someone out cold like that. Sure, I saw it a few times in movies, but how realistic was that? It would probably just hurt Alex and piss him off, and I'd pay a steep price as a result. He must still have some of the drug he slipped me in his bag, so I could try to find that once he was asleep. But I had no idea if Alex planned to tie me up at night, and I felt certain he'd at least keep me very close. So if it were stashed somewhere difficult to find, he would probably wake up before I could get to it.

I moved closer and sat at one of the high top chairs at the island. He stirred the chili and kept me in his peripheral vision. Once the chili was heated, he pulled out two bowls and spoons, then divvied up the food. He gave me a bowl and I took a hesitant slurp, and noticed it was room temperature. I looked up at him from under my lashes. Maybe Alex wanted to keep it cool enough that it wouldn't burn him if I threw the bowl at him. I hadn't thought of the idea until then, but now it was locked in as a possibility for the future.

We ate in silence, the heat continued to run, and the lodge eased to a temperature that felt somewhat bearable. I could smell the faint aroma of the log walls, a fragrance that again made me feel nostalgic about the trips here as a kid, now tainted. Alex finished his food within minutes, and went to rinse his bowl in the sink. He sniffed and then let the water run. I could smell the sulfur of the well water from where I sat, but it began to clear after a couple of minutes as Alex left the faucet on full blast.

"We'll have to clear the pipes in the bathrooms, too," he said.

"Sure." I sat there for a moment, and couldn't eat anymore, feeling ill with anxiety. I couldn't take it anymore, I had to try and clear the air, knowing it was in vain, like trying to clear smoke from a house fire as it continued to burn.

"Are you going to kill me?" I asked.

Alex stood still, resting his hands on the sink. "*Kill* you? Why would you ask me that?"

"You're holding me prisoner. It's not crazy for me to wonder."

"Prisoner is an extreme term."

"It's not. Answer the question."

"I love you, Autumn," he said, turning to me. "Why would I kill you?"

My gut fluttered and then went queasy at his declaration. "Because I don't want to stay here with you." I realized I shouldn't provoke the idea a moment too late.

He stood quiet for a second. "But you will."

"What if I don't?"

"You will." His face hardened into that frosty glare.

"And if I don't?" I persisted. I knew I should shut up, but I couldn't stop myself as a panic attack rose inside.

He turned and looked out the window over the sink, staring off into the blackness of the night. "We'll cross that bridge when we come to it, kitten." His voice sounded like another person's, and that seemed all the answer I needed to hear.

I tried not to vomit.

Alex took my bowl from me, and then made me follow him around the house, unpacking some of his bag, running the faucets in the bathrooms, and getting a fire started in the huge fireplace.

I stood behind him, and as he coaxed the embers to life, I eased my eyes toward the front door, trying to estimate if I could run to it before he would catch me. But then I noticed something I'd missed when we first entered the house. There was a combination deadbolt lock installed in reverse on the door. The Van Ettens had one of those on the front door of their home in Lake Forest. A device built into the door with buttons above a locking knob that were set in a combination in order to unlock the door. It eliminated the need for a key to the front door. All it required was a memory of which buttons to press, along with a simple turn of the knob to unlock it. The combination buttons were supposed to be on the outside of the door, however, not inside. It was installed above the normal doorknob and lock, too high for a normal deadbolt. Alex must have put this in when he came to prepare the house for this venture.

I closed my eyes, sighed, and looked back at the lock. "You've locked me in."

Alex stood up and noticed my gaze. "Yeah, I prepared for the event that you might resist at first. Don't bother trying the windows and other doors, either. I have locks on them from the outside. Well, actually, go ahead and try them if you want."

"Oh, I believe you," I said, so low I wasn't sure if he heard me.

With nothing else to do, we sat down by the fire for at least an hour, and weariness overtook my body. Never before did I feel such empathy for a mouse in a maze, trapped and halted at every turn. If there was a clear way out, I couldn't see it from this angle. And my mind and body both felt such intense fatigue from the shock.

Alex looked heavy-lidded, as well, and he stood up. "I think we both need sleep. You agree?"

I nodded. He held out a hand for me to grab. I just stared at it and stood up on my own. He rolled his eyes, and led me toward the stairway back to the left of the room near the kitchen. The ceilings of the great room stretched to such a height that the room took both levels of the house.

But in the wing where the predominantly-used bedrooms were located, the stairs led up to a second-story hallway. We climbed the stairs and I followed him to one of the five bedrooms in that hall, the one that was considered Alex's room here. Pale log walls and wooden floors continued as in all of the bedrooms of the lodge.

Alex at least gave me the courtesy of turning away as I changed into the pajamas from my duffle bag. He gestured for me to get in on the side farthest from the door. Then he slipped into lounge clothes and climbed into bed next to me. He curled up against my body, holding me down with one arm again. I faced away, gazing out the large window into the night sky.

Most of the overcast had cleared, moving away with the night wind. The moon hovered in the sky in thin crescent form, a rogue fingernail clipping left behind on a black sheet smattered with dazzling stars. So many stars—so many that I could see up here but could not see in Chicago with the lights of the city hazing them out. I laid under these stars, the same ones my family and friends were beneath back home.

I could see them.

They could not.

I knew where I was.

They did not.

I realized being the only one to see the complete picture had to be one of the loneliest feelings in the world.

CHAPTER ELEVEN

When I woke up the next morning, bright light streamed through the window of the bedroom, hurting my eyes. Alex's arm still weighed down my torso, and my neck felt a little stiff from the unfamiliar pillow. I shifted a bit, and Alex groaned, releasing the burden of his arm from me as he stretched.

"Morning," he whispered, and kissed my hair.

I recoiled and said nothing. I felt him get off of the bed, and then I turned to look at him. He stretched again as he stood upright, and ruffled his hair.

"I made sure to get this pancake mix that you only need to add water to when I stocked the cupboards. So we can have pancakes for breakfast if you want. Or even crepes if you're feeling fancy."

His mood seemed light. He acted like My Alex again, speaking as if things were the same as they ever were. I sat up, and watched him put on some socks.

"Have a preference?" he asked.

"I don't feel that hungry."

"Oh, you will after you see me whip up these puppies. They will be, hands-down, the most delicious plain, just-add-water boxed mix pancakes you've *ever* tasted."

It made me want to weep, seeing him like this. Like seeing the ghost of a loved one, knowing full well it was just a phantom image and that the real person was dead.

"Sounds gourmet," I muttered.

"Sounds like *you* need some coffee."

Sounds like you need medication and a padded cell, I thought. And then I felt a pang of guilt for even thinking it with any sarcasm, because it was probably the heart wrenching truth. It had to be at this point.

Alex let me use the bathroom and brush my teeth. I swallowed down a birth control pill, and then he guided me downstairs and back into the kitchen. He started the coffee pot, pulled out a mixing bowl and the bag of pancake mix.

I fiddled with my hands. "Did you happen to get any tea when you were, um, stocking up? I'm not sure my stomach can handle coffee this morning."

"I don't think I bought any tea. But there might be some here from the last time my mom visited." He searched through cupboards, moving things around and inspecting small boxes of non-perishables. "Ah! Here. It's probably kind of old, but if you like Earl Grey, there you go."

I evaluated the box. It expired about six months earlier. It would do.

Alex whistled as he measured out pancake mix and water, whisked it together, and heated the griddle on the stove. Then the teakettle he'd put on whistled, too. He brought it over with a mug, poured it for me, and then took it away, placing the kettle back on the stove. Again, he stood to the side as he poured out circles of batter, keeping watch over me out of the corner of his eye. I bobbed the tea bag a few times, and took small sips.

Between studying Alex at the stove, I glimpsed out the windows at the sunlight on the snow, at the majestic pines, and at some kind of large bird of prey, a hawk maybe, soaring around in the distance. If I turned my envy for that creature's freedom into pure energy, I could implode the whole house.

"So you are just giving up on school then, I take it?" I said. If he wanted to act like this was a reasonable path to take for his life, then fine, I would pretend to have a rational morning conversation with this madman. With this madman I swore I knew. I still wondered if I truly knew at least some pieces of him, any at all.

Alex flipped a pancake. "Why not? Screw it. I hate school anyway. It's not like becoming a lawyer was some ambition I possessed since dinosaurs roamed the Earth."

I looked down at my tea. "True. Not everyone has those kind of longstanding aspirations... I do, though."

"You can still dance. It's not like New York City is a requirement to twirling around and kicking your legs up in the air. We can move sofas aside so you can dance here."

I actually laughed. The concept of replacing a dream like that with dancing for leisure in a living room was so obscene to me I couldn't take his comment seriously. And then I felt offended, because that was how he saw it: as some silly, juvenile pursuit that could be replaced by an open space of hardwood floor in a large, remote cabin.

"You're a fool if you think that's even in the same universe," I said. "And I want to make a living doing it. I've danced in front of mirrors for myself enough in my life. I want to dance for other people."

"Two things. A: strippers make money dancing, too. I wouldn't hold fast to the idea that making money off of dancing is such an honorable quest. And if you really want money for it,

I'll pay you to dance here. Which brings me to B: you can dance for me every single night. I'm pretty sure I won't get tired of it."

I glared at him with such ferocity that he turned away from me. "Like I would dance for you."

"Oh, you will."

"And where are you going to get the money to pay me, pretty boy? Now that you're far from the safety net of Mommy and her fortune. Who will fill your wallet with all that undeserved allowance now that we're here alone?" I surprised myself by how nasty my tone sounded.

I never felt anything negative toward the Van Ettens and their money growing up, but the entitlement Alex demonstrated since assuming I was his for the taking—like any other material object—turned my unbiased sentiment about it into a sense of revulsion.

Alex shot me an irritated glance. "I've had access to my trust fund since I turned twenty-one. So I'm set."

"Of course," I said, disgusted.

"You, on the other hand, are penniless. And you've just lost your free ride here with that bitchiness. So scoff at the idea of dancing in the living room all you want. But *that* has just become your meal ticket. Or your reason for hunger, if you refuse."

"Then I guess I'll die very, very thin."

Alex shrugged. "Suit yourself." He plated some pancakes and walked over to slide them in front of me. "I already made these, and I can't eat all of them myself. So why don't you consider it your last free meal."

"Why don't you consider the fact that you're an arrogant prick," I said. Part of me *knew* it was pure stupidity to enrage him. But part of me remained in the habit of being casual and honest with him. Unable to believe this was happening. Not with Alex. Not with my best friend.

Alex's eyes scolded me, but he retrieved a bottle of syrup from the fridge and slammed it in front of me. "Canada's finest. Enjoy," he said, his words chipper yet angry.

I ate the pancakes when he turned back to make a few more for himself. We were silent for the rest of breakfast.

After we finished eating, Alex made me follow him into the great room. He went to adjust the dial for the heaters and put a couple more logs in the fireplace, reviving the embers from the night before. As I surveyed him, I felt as if rage were a tangible thing, like a liquid that someone poured down into my torso, filling it so that it spread through my limbs and poisoned my concentration on anything else. I couldn't believe the fury I felt toward him. Alex, who just days earlier I was in love with; who was my oldest and best friend.

It occurred to me I was living Stockholm Syndrome in reverse. Instead of the reported experience of many captives— who learned over time to trust or even care for their abductors—I began this journey in love with my kidnapper. Already knowing and trusting him. Caring for him so much, enough that I didn't even initially understand an abduction had occurred. And over the course of the last few days, that love transformed into anger, and then from anger into hate.

I pondered in my anxious yet bored state what the opposite of Stockholm might be. What existed on the other side of the planet from Sweden? I watched Alex another moment, still tending the fire, and then walked over to the globe next to the bookshelf.

My fingertips caressed the cold surface, inlaid with polished stones. Nothing was labeled on this globe, not the oceans, not even the countries themselves. Each country just had its own semiprecious stone to distinguish it from the borders of others. I tilted the globe and bent over to see what lay on the other side of the world from Sweden. Without measuring to be exact, it looked like if I drilled a hole right through, it would land somewhere in the South Pacific, close to New Zealand. New Zealand, that was close enough. I didn't know its capital, but the first city that came to mind when I thought of the island country was Auckland. In my head I gave a name to my own unique experience: Auckland Syndrome. From love to hate in the hands of my captor.

The rest of the morning we spent taking showers and getting dressed. Alex hung out in the hallway while I showered first, dried my hair, brushed my teeth again, and dressed. Even though he warned me that he installed locks on the doors and windows from the outside, I tried the window in the bathroom anyway. In a hushed manner, I tested the latch, shoving my weight against it and jimmying the knob. It wouldn't budge. I wiped the fog from the glass, peered around to the outside edge and saw that Alex had, indeed, put a lock on it. His thoroughness was obscene. What the hell did he do, get out a ladder and spend hours locking up every possible orifice to the house? I sighed and stared out the window for a moment, and then went to open the bathroom door.

"I need a shower, too," he said. "So you'll have to stay in the bedroom while I am in the bathroom."

"Why would I need to stay in the bedroom?" I asked, but before I finished the question I knew the answer. "You put a lock on the outside of the bedroom door, too, didn't you?"

He nodded. I ground my teeth and went into his bedroom, turned around, and glared at him as he shut the door.

"I'll be back in a jiffy," he said, and winked.

Eww. I knew he wasn't being serious with that wink, but it still made me want to gag. I heard the lock on the other side of the door and I gave him the finger, even though he couldn't enjoy the gesture. I crossed my arms and examined the room in the daylight. He took his bag with him into the bathroom, so I couldn't get to the knife or his phone. But I scanned the walls for objects that could either break a window or cause injury to a human body. He was even more thorough than I originally thought. Spaces on the walls that were once occupied by things I couldn't quite remember from the last time I visited were now bare, as if Alex took down certain things knowing I might think of this very plan. There was just a single tapestry of evergreens on one wall, held up by a flimsy pole and string, and a framed picture on another wall.

The photo was of Camille, Sam, and Alex—the three of them posed outside by some small brook and a few trees. I estimated the picture was taken maybe five or six years earlier. I stared at them, and looked into Alex's eyes. On the surface he looked normal and happy. The slightly rebellious, outgoing son. But looking deeper into those blue eyes gazing back at me, I now saw a wicked, broken mind. I shuddered and took a step back.

Sam sat on the other side of Camille in the picture, handsome and content. Was he the proverbial golden boy, or was he cracked inside, too? He knew something was amiss, even if he didn't know the full situation. So where the hell was Sam? Why hadn't help been there when we stepped off the train? Why wasn't help here now?

I walked over to the window and stared out to the front of the property. Beyond the cobbled footpath, beyond the long driveway, and out onto the road that led over the horizon. Maybe Sam was not as concerned about me as he seemed in his text messages. Maybe it was just a way to cover his ass if the police questioned him and confiscated his phone. They were brothers, after all. Was it crazy to think Sam's loyalty might fall with Alex if he knew what was happening? If Sam thought Alex would keep me alive, but just imprison me up here in this beautiful house, would he rationalize to himself that it was not so horrible that he should just stay out of it? It was conceivable that he was deranged, as well, and didn't see the situation with rational eyes.

Whatever the case, I couldn't depend on Sam to help me at this point. So I discovered a revived determination to get out on my own. I went over to the tapestry, thinking even the flimsy pole could be broken into a point that could injure someone. But I realized it was plastic, and it would not break under my hands. It just kept bending as I curved it back and forth. I went over and inspected the frame of the picture, but it was some kind of solid metal, so I couldn't break that, either. I was about to smash the window with it, considering its solid weight, but then I looked down at the ground beneath the window. We were on the second floor, and below there were only rocks and stepping-stones. I felt certain I would break my legs if I jumped. Even though I was desperate to get out, I figured there had to be a way I could do it without destroying my dance career before it even began.

Then I remembered the secret passage into Alex's bedroom. I hung the picture back up and turned to the wall I knew the passage door was on, and my eye scanned for the seam of the short doorway. I found it, listened to make sure the shower was still running, and pushed against the wall in that spot. The door unlatched and opened an inch. I pulled it the rest of the way open and it squeaked in protest. I hesitated for a second, smelling the musty scent of a closed-off passageway, and stared into the darkness. No time to wait, even though I wasn't sure what my plan was exactly.

I stepped into the passage, having to crouch much more than I ever remembered doing as a child. I felt a cobweb stick to the side of my forehead and brushed it away. I pulled the door closed with only a crack left open behind me for light. I still couldn't see anything. I moved down the stairs into darkness. When I reach the flat floor, I walked forward, forgetting how far it stretched until a person reached the next door. I panicked in the tight space, the lack of light, with time running out. Alex's shower wouldn't last forever. I would have to break out of the front window or something as fast as possible.

I moved faster through the darkness, and crunched one of my fingers when I ran into the door as I reached ahead. I pushed against the door but it wouldn't open. I tried again and again. Then I moved my hands all over, searching for a lock or something. I found one near the top of the small door and undid the slide lock. I pushed again but the door would not open. I threw myself against it, shoving with my shoulder, but it remained closed.

"Asshole," I whispered. There had to be a lock on the other side of the door, too. My palms were sweating, so I left the lock on the inside undone, and hurried back to the stairway, tripping when I stubbed my toe on the first step. I ran back up the stairs and reemerged into the bedroom, flinching in anticipation as I expected Alex to be waiting for me. The shower was still running, so I shut the short door behind me and went to sit on the bed.

I heard the shower shut off in the bathroom a minute later. I waited there for a few minutes before I heard the door unlock again and watched as Alex entered the room. His hair was still a little wet and mussed, but looked good. It pissed me off. He also smelled nice, like he put an effort into attracting me with cologne. I hated him now, God I hated him.

"Can we get outside for a bit today?" I asked. "We've been cooped up for days. I need some fresh air."

He evaluated me for a moment, considering.

"I'll play nice, okay? I just need some fresh air."

"Okay, fine. I could use some, too. I think that storm is on its way anyhow, so it's not a bad idea to get out before it hits."

He held out his hand, I took it with reluctance, to avoid a repercussion, and we went downstairs to the giant coat closet by the front door. There were all sorts of spare goods in there: summer hats, winter gear, cross-country skis, and a golf bag in the back corner. He pulled out some of Camille's winter things for me. As I slipped my own jacket on and the accessories from the closet, he put on a few winter items himself. We walked to the front door and he made me turn away while he did the combination to the lock. When it opened, the blast of frigid air entered, both refreshing and painful, but it felt so good to be outside as we stepped into the light.

We wandered around the house and he gripped my hand without a second's interruption. As if Alex, captain of most of his high school sports teams, wouldn't be able to catch me if I tried to run. Sure, my body was extremely fit, but he was fast if it was a lengthy race. So we walked together and I scouted out my surroundings, trying to find a fragment of hope for a later escape.

Behind the house, off in the distance, a small forest of evergreens loomed. I could see just a bit of the giant pond amidst the trees, frozen over. I tried to erase the mental image of my dead body sunken under that ice as soon as it appeared in my head. Alex reassured me he would not kill me. Could I believe him? I wanted to. But I kept seeing flashes of my own face under a sheet of ice. Would I already be dead? Would I be screaming as I drown in icy water? *Erase it!* I yelled in my head.

Out toward the road at the front of the lodge I knew that other house existed somewhere in the horizon, but I couldn't make it out in the blinding light of sun against snow. I doubted I could run to it without Alex catching up to me unless I had at least a ten minute head start.

The sun shone, but clouds were moving in. The wind pushed at us, whipping the hair that hung below my hat around my face. I shivered, hoping it would just be a light snow that passed in no time, rather than the brutal blizzard the forecast warned of when we were on the train. It was so desolate out here, so isolated. I held Alex's hand, my mitten in his, and I felt a strange emotional pull of resistance yet dependence on him in this remote place. I had no knowledge of surviving in the wilderness, and was used to life near the city. I despised that sensation of dependence, but it remained.

I sensed the oncoming storm, and that was bad enough. As we strolled around the pines for a while, we discovered tracks—the kind that made the weather only one of the concerns outside the lodge. They looked like the footprints of a dog, of many dogs. Alex knelt and examined them closer, and I saw what he saw: how long the claws were, how many of them left indentations in the snow.

"Wolves," he said. He pulled me forward to follow the tracks.

"I don't know if we should," I said. "What if they're still around?"

"The prints are glazed over with a little ice. It's probably been a while since they were here." I drifted behind Alex as he pulled me along, and when a bough from a pine tree brushed the arm of my jacket I moved closer to him. We followed the tracks around a handful of trees until the paw prints became a mess, as if scraping and thrashing had occurred.

"Whoa," Alex said, just before I spotted it myself.

I peeked around his shoulder and saw the frozen, mutilated carcass of what I guessed to be an elk, or some species of deer. The wolves devoured so much of the flesh it was hard to tell. I gripped Alex's arm and my eyes scanned the area around us for predators, then they fell back on the elk again. The frozen blood was dark but striking against the snow. I wanted to cry, both for the animal, and for myself. Getting out of the house seemed hard enough. It hadn't occurred to me that if I managed to get out, I would have wolves to contend with. Many wolves outside, and one wolf indoors, wearing the skin of a boy I loved. I couldn't say for sure which was worse.

CHAPTER TWELVE

When we submitted to the shelter of the house, with cheeks and noses red from the wintry winds, the first heavy snowflakes began to fall. Alex went to the kitchen and made himself a sandwich and looked at me as he spread peanut butter over bread. I felt the wave of obviousness rolling off of him, as if he wanted me to see what he was doing.

"Feel like dancing?" he asked.

"No."

"Well, let me know when you get hungry enough that you do." He ate the sandwich in front of me.

I turned away and watched the snow through the windows of the great room. Each snowflake accumulated like a tiny piece of my own growing dread. The wind brought the clouds in fast enough that you could watch their approach, and by mid-afternoon giant flakes dropped in what looked like a winter downpour. I couldn't even see the end of the driveway from the great window. As day rolled into evening, the gusts of wind rattled the windows and made the soft snow look angry and violent. I watched the flimsy single power line, strung from the lodge out to one post connecting to another, that eventually led to nearby transformers and other homes. The power line swayed and whipped as the wind tested its resilience. As the night deepened, an icy sleet began to fall as well, and my nervousness took on an uncontrollable quality. Heavy ice along with heavy snow was dangerous. I thought about the freezing temperatures outside, and continued to watch that power line. I felt a desperate kind of longing for my mom as the storm increased, the kind that extreme danger or illness conjures in a person, out of an ancient need for nurturing.

One of my only fragments of gratitude toward Alex came when the power went out around ten o'clock that night. The lights shut off as the radiators simultaneously stopped making their rattling and low hiss. I didn't want to be here with Alex, but I didn't want to be here alone in a power outage, either. He tended the fire all evening, and also built one in the smaller fireplace of the master bedroom upstairs.

Even with the fires roaring, however, the cold crept through the walls, faster than I expected. If there existed a drafty spot anywhere in the lodge, the wind found it and beat at it until it almost seemed there was no difference between the outdoors and inside. Alex lit a handful of candles and set them about, and retrieved a flashlight from a drawer in the kitchen. Then we sat by the fire, unable to find the will to move around the house and brave the cold.

"I'm starting to get hungry again, so I know you have to be famished," Alex said after we sat in silence by the fire for about a half hour.

It was true. I was starving, and it made me feel even colder. But I said nothing.

"Stop torturing yourself. Just dance for me a little."

"You're not seriously going to enforce that stupid rule, are you?"

"Maybe not forever, but I want you to dance for me. At least once."

"And I want you to take me home."

"You don't always get what you want," he said.

"Eat your own words. You're not getting what you want, either."

"Yes, I am."

"No."

"Dance, Autumn."

From the corner of my eye I saw a glint of light by his hand. I looked over and saw he had pulled out the knife. The fire reflected against its blade. I didn't even know when he put it in his pocket, in the bathroom this morning, maybe. My shoulders tensed as I eyed the threat in his hand. I didn't argue with him, but I also didn't move.

"Do you think I won't?" he asked, letting my imagination finish whatever picture he started to paint.

I thought about how he'd yanked my hair so hard that I whacked to the floor on the train, and how he had tied me up. My assurance that he would not kill me began to evaporate.

"No. I don't think that you won't. I think you would. I just..."

"Just what?"

I had no answer. I looked at my thighs, and then slowly stood up. "What do you want me to do?"

"Dance."

"I have no music."

"Stop making excuses."

I looked at the blade of the knife again, and then tilted my head to the side, staring at my socked feet as one brushed against the wood floor. I stood there and wiped one of my eyebrows with the back of my forefinger, uncomfortable, trying to think of what kind of movements to make. I remembered a short routine I learned a few months earlier, heavy on technique with almost no artistry. That would be perfect. I didn't want to do any kind of dancing that portrayed even a hint of emotion. I hated to dance without warming up, but I eyed that knife again.

I paced around the open space between the chairs and the fire a couple of times, willing myself to perform when I felt such disdain. I turned to the fire and watched it crackle, and for a moment I was eight years old again. I tried to grab onto the fleeting sensation and hold it in a mental vice, remembering how carefree and light my heart had felt back then. Dancing on my own in front of this same fireplace, for no one but myself. And Sam. I tried to pretend it was just Sam watching behind me. Just Sam. I turned around to face the darkness, avoiding even a glance at Alex.

With the heat of the fire at my back I went up on *relevé*, then down, spun into a *pirouté*, then a deep arabesque, moving into a motion where my elevated leg swung over in an arch as my head nearly grazed the front of my weight-bearing leg. Up again, *ronde de jambe*, then into *fouettés*, a leap small enough to be performed within the space between the chairs and fireplace. After landing, I stood upright and eased my leg up into the air, pointing my toe and continuing to lift it until my knee almost touched my shoulder. I held the position for a moment, staring out into the darkness of the great room. Leg down, spinning into pirouettes again, a turn and into an axle, and then a slide to the floor. I wrapped my back leg around to the front and bent my knees up, wrapping my arms around my legs and putting my forehead to my knees, as if it was the end of the routine. There was more to it when I learned it, but Alex didn't need to know that, and I didn't want to do it anymore.

"Lovely," Alex said. "Now. Let's eat." He got up to endure the chill of the kitchen, and I heard him banging things around in there.

I stayed on the floor with my arms wrapped around my legs. I turned my face toward the fire, still resting my head on my knees. *Sam, please*, I thought. *Please help me. Please don't be broken like Alex.* All evening I missed my mother, and now I felt an intense longing for Sam, as well. If he was sane, unlike his brother, if he really was the person I always thought him to be, I ached for him to come and save me.

My own brother would be doing what he could to help. But my biggest hope for Tim was that he was keeping Mom as calm as possible. That was the assignment I delegated Tim in my imagination: keep Mom calm.

Sam was the one I communicated with since being kidnapped. And my heart cried out for him to do something, to come and meet me halfway, so-to-speak. My eyes watered from frustration and despair. It felt like too much of a burden for me to carry all on my own, getting away from Alex, getting out of this lodge, getting to another person in this isolated place, and getting back home from The Middle of Nowhere, Canada.

Where the hell are you? I thought at Sam. And my longing slipped into despair as I considered the possibility that he was protecting Alex. This was his own brother. He must feel some kind of loyalty to him. I shuddered when I considered that he might be hiding the truth from everyone.

I turned my head toward the bottom door of the secret passage that led up to the door into Alex's bedroom. I glanced over toward the kitchen and still heard Alex moving things around in there. I leapt to my feet, ran in silence to the hidden door, and scanned the wall for a discrete lock. I found it— another slide latch, almost the same color as the wall. A lock that wasn't there when I was a child, installed by Alex in his recent insanity. I slid it undone, and then hurried into the kitchen to find Alex.

CHAPTER THIRTEEN

The snow fell so heavy by the time we went to bed that it covered most of the thick foundation of the lodge. The back door locked us in not only thanks to Alex's contributions, but also by a snow drift several feet deep. The small deck leading up to the front door tucked itself under the drifts as if it were curled up under a thick comforter, so hidden one wouldn't even know it existed if you never saw the house before the blizzard. With the power still out, Alex stoked the fire in the master bedroom and moved our things into there. Camille's bed was larger in this room, and the fireplace here looked more rustic than the great room's, comprised of large stones held together by mortar. Wooden beams crossed the ceiling overhead.

"We'll have to sleep in here until the power comes back on," Alex said.

I nodded, peered out the window, and thought again for a second about breaking the glass and jumping. The snow might break my fall a little easier. But then I considered getting stuck in a deep snowdrift, maybe even suffocating to death, and I scratched that idea. Even if I got out of it, how could I run from Alex through snow that deep? Not a chance. So I slid into the king-sized bed, shivering against the cold sheets. My body racked so hard with tremors that I did not protest when Alex pulled his warm body against mine, holding me close.

Again I faced the window in this room, and Alex slept on the side near the door. He seemed to feel at ease because of the blizzard, knowing I wouldn't try to escape. So he slipped into a heavy slumber right away. I gazed out the window, unable to sleep as I tried to think of a plan. My eyes scanned the room, lit in a flickering orange glow from the flames. Nothing of consequence caught my eye that could be used against Alex, but then I remembered that our bags were in the room with us. I squeezed my eyes shut, bracing myself for the cold temperature and for the risk I would take by slipping out from under Alex's arm, and out of bed.

Little by little, I maneuvered myself out from under his hold and eased myself into a crouch on the floor. I crawled, ever so softly, around the bed and to his bag where it sat next to the door of the bedroom. I glanced over my shoulder to make sure he didn't move, and then opened the bag. It felt like a repeated nightmare from the train, unzipping the bag as quiet as a snowflake falling to the ground.

I could not find the knife, but I located Alex's phone and tried illuminating the screen while hiding the light with my body. It worked. He must have put the battery back in it at some point when I was in the shower or something. There were no bars at all and I was certain roaming charges applied here. That didn't matter, but having no service did. I mouthed the word *shit*, and then noticed Alex had dozens of missed calls and texts. I pressed the messaging icon, and saw new messages from what seemed like everyone: my mother, Camille, Tim, a couple of his school friends, and Sam. Camille was the most recent to send a message, followed by Sam. First I clicked on the most recent message from Camille.

Sweetie, get your shit together and get yourself home. Are you trying to kill me? Do you have any idea how frightened to death I am right now? I've been crying for hours. Alex, please. Remember what we talked about. Please, I love you.

I couldn't compute thoroughly what she meant by her message. What had they talked about? I exited the message, then clicked on Sam's thread and scrolled through his notes to Alex. The older ones seemed very alarmed, and even threatening. One of his earlier texts from a couple of days ago read:

What the hell do you think you're doing Alex? Get your ass home. You think this crap is funny? Are you trying to ruin the holidays for everyone? You're in for a beating if you don't call us or something soon.

There were a handful more that were threatening, and then Sam began to change his approach. As the days progressed, his messages became more accommodating and understanding.

Okay, I get it. You're in love, and you two crazy kids are off on some romantic adventure. You've had your time to do that, now will you both please come home so we can all celebrate Christmas together?

And another.

Alex, I understand now. You're worried she'll run off to New York or something, right? But you know I can be very convincing. I'll make you a deal: bring Autumn home, and I'll convince her to stay in Chicago with you, guaranteed. But for God's sake man, it's me. Will you please just give me a call?

The final one came through on the last day we rode the train. I wondered how many more were sent, and how many missed calls evaporated into the void of cell service since we made it to the lodge. The line of Sam's communications confused me a little. A filament of anger lit up when I read that he would try to convince me to stay in Chicago, but it burned out because the mismatch of thinking he sent through the texts. My instinct whispered consolations. *He's trying to talk Alex off the ledge. Sam is just treating him like a wild animal, trying to calm him down to keep him from resisting.* I sighed and closed my eyes, putting every bit of my energy into hoping and praying that Sam was on my side.

And then I felt a thin line of pressure against the front of my neck, sharp and cold. My eyes opened but I did not move. Alex's breathing moved the air just over my shoulder behind me, and his other hand grabbed my upper arm.

"Worried I might be texting some skank? Autumn, I didn't realize you were the jealous type," Alex said, but his words were facetious.

I swallowed, and felt the pressure of the blade against my neck as I did. "Well, you're good looking. I expect girls to throw themselves at you," I whispered.

"The way you are?" he asked.

I said nothing.

"Don't worry, Sam doesn't stand for Samantha. I have this brother; I might have told you about him before. His name is Sam," Alex said. His tone grew more sarcastic with each word. "Oh, that's right. You've met him. In fact, you looked like you were ready to take him to bed the night we had the party.

Right... Now it's coming back to me. I had this all wrong. You're the one trying to send out a booty call. What's it going to say, Autumn?" Alex seethed more as the seconds ticked by.

He spoke again, this time in a mock female voice, as if imitating me. "Hey Sam, I already had your brother and he was just... Eh, okay. But I'm feeling slutty and would like to see what it's like to be with a doctor now."

I ground my teeth and rage exploded in me so fast I didn't even have time to breathe and control myself, or think about the extent of the danger offered by the knife at my throat. I threw myself back against him, butting him in the face with the back of my head, and then just as quickly, I ducked under the arm that held the knife and scrambled to my feet. Still clutching the phone, I ran for the door. I yanked at the doorknob, realized it was locked on the inside and fumbled to unlock it. He was on his feet by the time I swung the door open, but I made it out into the hallway and ran full speed for the stairs. I slipped and stumbled down a few of them, but caught the handrail in time to keep myself from tumbling all the way down. I heard his feet hit the top of the stairs behind me. After running down another stair or two, I decided to just leap off of the staircase all the way to the bottom.

I hit the floor hard, but landed on my feet and was up and moving again in an instant. It was dark in the house aside from the dim light of the fire, now burned down to coals in the great room's fireplace. I paused for just a second to think of which direction to go, and heard Alex reaching the bottom of the stairs behind me. I bolted to the kitchen, and slid to the floor behind the island. It was so dark that my eyes strained to adjust.

I heard him stop at the entrance to the kitchen, and then his feet moved again—dreadfully slow, exceptionally quiet. I could just barely hear him making his way around the island, and sensed him searching every corner of the room for me. I breathed—in and out, in and out—as silently as I could. I thought my heartbeat sounded loud enough that he might actually be able to hear it. Another subdued step of his foot. And then another. The hairs on my neck stood on end, nerves rigid.

When I heard him getting too close, I rushed to my feet and ran for the cabinet that contained the ceramic plates and bowls. I grabbed a stack of small plates, maybe three or four, and threw the lot of them at him all at once. I saw at least one hit him in the shoulder in the dim moonlight, but the rest of them crashed to the floor, shattering the silence. I grabbed a bowl, threw it, and it smashed against the wall behind him. But I snatched another by the time the bowl hit the wall and pitched that one at him, too. It smacked him on the side of his face with a powerful blow, and in the gloom I could make out the wrath in his expression as his nostrils flared.

I ran to the cutlery drawer, opened it, seized a small steak knife and left the drawer open as I ran out of the kitchen into the great room. I heard Alex slam the drawer shut and follow me out toward the fireplace. I glanced around, trying to decide what to do. If he got close enough for me to use the knife, I knew I would lose. Then my eyes landed on a toss pillow resting on one of the armchairs near the fire. I grabbed it and turned toward him. He stopped running when he realized I stood still, and we glowered at each other. He laughed, staring at me as I situated myself there with a small steak knife and a toss pillow. Alex composed himself, looked at me again, and then another burst of laughter left his mouth.

"What? Is that going to be your shield? A toss pillow? A toss pillow and a steak knife as your sword and shield. That's brilliant. Such a beautiful imagination in that little head of yours," he said, and let out another wicked laugh.

But I glared back at him, eased a step closer to the fire, and lowered the toss pillow toward it. I watched Alex as I held the end of the pillow in the cinders, hoping with every cell in my body that it would ignite. It took a little longer than I wanted, but I glanced down and the edge of the pillow began to smoke. Then a delicate rim of embers burned its way up the corner. I held it there a second longer, and Alex took a step toward me. I backed up, grasping the pillow, and blew lightly on the smoldering edge, stoking the spark into a small flame.

As our eyes met again, a shift of power occurred, as if the control jumped bodies from his to mine. A hint of concern flickered in his eyes, and I felt my face relax as a plan revealed itself to me.

The snow outside halted for the moment, so a helicopter or something could fly out to a house on fire. At the very least it would alert someone *somewhere* in the region that things were amiss out here. It was a huge risk, yes. But so was staying here, waiting to become that body below the frozen lake. The house out on the horizon, someone was probably there... I would take a gamble. I could lose, but someone could be there at home now, and still awake. If so, they would see Tempest Lodge on fire against a dark night. Tempest Lodge, the crooked house of trapped doors and creepy secret passages.

I could burn this whole damn place to the ground.

I felt a wicked smile pull up the corner of my mouth as I envisioned it. I could do it. Just watch the place go up in flames and smoke all the demons out. How would Alex hold me then, if we were both out in the open watching his family's vacation house burn?

I moved as fast as I could over to a tapestry on the wall and held the flame to the edge of it. The tapestry took a moment to ignite, as well. Alex rushed toward me, but I held the pillow out toward him, warding him off with the flame. The tapestry's end turned to a small spot of glowing orange, and the tiniest flicker of flame licked up the woven fabric. That would have to be good enough. I ran to the other side of the room and grabbed the edge of the tall curtain hanging along the side of the giant front window. That lit so fast it surprised me, and I had to jump back from the flame.

"Autumn!" Alex shouted.

He came at me, so I tried to light the Christmas tree, too. That also burst into flames in a flash, but the pillow was burning up so close to my hand that I had to drop it. I stepped back and watched Alex rip the tapestry off of the wall. It burned strong now, and he stamped on it at first, but had socked feet, so he grabbed a blanket from the sofa to throw on it.

I stepped backward, watching the fire light up the room like a sunset. Part of the curtain burned apart, and a piece of fabric fluttered to the ground like a giant butterfly going down in flames. Fire devoured the curtain and I watched the blinding glow stretch its way up toward the wood ceiling. The artificial tree crackled and made strange hissing sounds. A few pops filled the air as ornaments cracked and fell to the floor. I could smell smoke, and realized I needed to get out of the house in a hurry. I scanned the walls for something to break a window with.

There was that decorative boat oar displayed high up on the wall above the bookcase, but I'd need a chair or something to stand on to reach it. I started for one of the dining room chairs, and felt Alex running up behind me. I grabbed a chair and braced myself for some kind of pain when he hit me or knifed me, but Alex ran past me and into the kitchen. I furrowed my brow for a second, but let it go and began to drag the chair over to the bookcase. I coughed and gagged on the smoke as I lined the chair up with the bookcase. The smoke grew thick and the bookshelf sat near the blazing tree and curtain. I could feel the heat radiating off them. I was about to climb onto the chair but looked up and Alex was back with a fire extinguisher. My heart sank.

I backed up as I watched him put each fire out with the extinguisher. It took him some effort to get the higher parts of the curtain to stop burning, but he succeeded. My hands still clutched the chair, and I pulled it with me away from him like a life raft. When the fires were out, smoke and white powder filling the air, Alex stood with his back to me and growled. Then he turned around and stomped toward me. My eyes darted around the room, looking for an escape. I still held the small knife in one hand, and grasped the chair with the other, but before I could react he lifted the fire extinguisher and swung it at me, whacking me in the upper arm.

A grunt-scream left my throat. A blinding sharp pain radiated through my arm and shoulder. It felt like my shoulder joint went loose, and the knife dropped from my hand as I fell to the floor. The pain knocked the wind out of me, and before I could get my breath back Alex dragged me across the floor. I clawed at the floorboards with the hand of my good arm but found no purchase. He hefted me up over his shoulder with my head dangling down over his back, and carried me down the north wing.

"No!" I screamed, because I knew where I was headed.

In the game room was another book shelf. The worst place in the house. The secret room with only a tiny vent on its ceiling. As children we played in the spot once or twice, and I hated it. Too dark, too claustrophobic, too sinister.

I coughed from smoke and whimpered from pain. I pleaded with Alex, but he said nothing. Instead he marched into the game room—a cavernous space with tall ceilings and windows, sickly northern light during the day, a poker table, and musty board games—and walked over to the shelving unit. He dropped me off of his shoulder but gripped the back of my neck so hard it hurt. Then he kicked the shelf, a little taller than him and a few feet wide, and it sprang back, releasing the catch. Like the small door to the passageway, it opened with a creaking sound. A couple of old books fell to the floor and threw dust into the air. I coughed again. He shoved me into the black room, and slammed the shelf-door shut, closing me in.

"Alex!" I screamed. I could hear him walk away, and then it was silent. I stood there for a few minutes staring wide-eyed, feeling blind. Shock. My body shivered and hypothermia became a concern within a very short time. I thought the rest of the house felt cold before. It was a luxury sauna compared to this space. No heat, no light. I started to cry.

After my eyes let go of the phantom image of burning fabric, and settled for the darkness, I could make out the tiny room around me like a shadowy netherworld, granted only the thinnest rays of light through an ancient-looking vent in the ceiling. I didn't even know where in the house the vent connected to, one of the rooms upstairs, but I couldn't recall which one.

I remembered more clearly why I hated this room as a child: once on the inside, there was no way out. Only the mercy of someone outside the shelf-door could free you. I checked the entire door again to make sure of this. There was no handle or button or anything to undo the latch to escape. My fingers pried at the seams to no avail. I sat down and put my head in my hands, my tears still flowing, but growing weaker from the cold. I shivered. I wept. The shivering slowed down into an odd, labored convulsing even though I felt ice cold. Despair worked its way in. I sensed my body shutting down from the temperature already.

I got up again and kept my body moving, trying to keep the blood pumping. I bumped into walls and though I felt like jumping in surprise, my body did not respond fast. I slid my hands over the freezing cold walls to see if there was another way out, cringing the whole time, as if I might find someone standing there in the dark with me, or a skeleton slumped on the ground. There was nothing but some kind of sheet crumpled in one corner.

"Alex! Please! Alex! Why the hell does this house have such a fucked up room?" I yelled, but my voice sounded weaker than I liked.

I paced, cried a little more, and then tripped over my own feet and fell to the floor. My limbs would not work correctly. My arm ached where he'd hit me. I sat up but it took considerable effort. I tried to stand but couldn't feel my legs enough to steady myself.

"Alex! I'm dying! I'm dying. I'm dying..." I crawled to the door and scraped against it, mumbling things even I didn't understand after a while. I have no idea how long I was in there. Maybe twenty minutes, maybe two hours. It felt like an eternity.

When I gave up and decided I was going to die in that claustrophobic space, I went quiet and felt a kind of apathy toward death. I closed my eyes and leaned my head against the door. Then, when I was about to drift off into a numb sleep, the shelf opened. My body slumped down on the floor and did not move. I didn't care. I heard Alex make a frustrated growl again.

"Autumn," he said, and lifted me up. He patted my face to make me open my eyes. "Baby, please, Autumn. Come on, keep your eyes open."

I remained limp from whatever stage of hypothermia I was in, and he carried me upstairs to the master bedroom. Alex tossed me on the bed and my face contorted with the dull agony of my arm, anesthetized by the cold, but still in pain from the fire extinguisher. Brushing a hand over the side of my face, I could feel Alex tremble, as if he didn't know whether to kiss me or hit me. Alex's face flickered between what looked like love, and what looked like hatred. Then he pulled his knife out again leaned over me, whispering as he held it against my throat.

"Don't move. Don't. Even. Move. If you pull another..." He closed his eyes and scrunched up his face for a second before going on. "If you do one more single stupid thing, you're going to make me do something I'll regret later."

"I *can't* move," I whispered.

Alex stood up and kept an eye on me as he went to the closet and found some kind of article of clothing, I couldn't focus enough to look at it. Alex rolled me on my side. He let me stay on the side that wasn't throbbing, but pulled my arms up in front of my face and tied my hands together. Then he tied them to the bedpost.

"No, please," I whimpered. Tears streamed down my face from the intense aching in my arm.

Alex fastened the knot tight, and I let go of the tears, giving into the pain. He threw two thick blankets on me, put another log on the fire to warm up the room, and then looked down at me. He clenched his jaw, shook his head, and then left the room.

I remained there on my side with my arms in front of me bent up toward the bedpost. Amidst the chaos and then the trapped feeling in the cold room, it didn't seem like anything could feel composed again. But the world went silent, and my body settled. I felt so cold. Even though the fire still burned in the small bedroom hearth and I had the blankets on me, it wasn't enough to eliminate the chill left by the power outage and the time I'd spent in the small room. I cried again for a while as I lay there, tied up and suffering, just waiting for Alex to return. Waiting for his wrath.

CHAPTER FOURTEEN

After what felt like hours, Alex returned to the bedroom and got into bed next to me. He saw me shivering, and took enough pity on me to rub the side of my body to warm it. He smelled of chemicals and the smoke from my inferno. After a long time, he removed his hand from me, rolled away, and I heard his breathing turn to the steady rhythm of sleep. I stayed awake from the discomfort in my arm and being tied into this position, so I stared out the window and watched as the bright winter night clouds blew past and a blanket of stars revealed themselves. So many stars. At one point, a shooting star blazed down to earth in the distance, and it was the solitary second of contentment I felt that night. I wished on that star in a way I never wished for anything in my life. As I lay there, another memory of Alex and me from years before slithered up from some shadowy coil of my brain.

~~~

We were young. I was twelve, and Alex thirteen years old. We were out, running amuck around our neighborhood late at night. At least it seemed late. It was early spring, one of the first warm days of the season. The sun still set early. There were railroad tracks not far from our homes, just a couple of miles which we traversed on our bikes. We found a small overpass for the tracks, riding onto the bridge and parking our bikes. We were alone.

"Dare me," Alex said.

"Dare you to what?"

"To jump."

"No. Hell no. Why would I do that?"

"I'll dare myself then," Alex said.

I watched in horror as he climbed over the cement barrier and balanced, facing outward on the guardrail's exterior, gripping the edge with his hands. I looked over the edge and saw that he only had about three inches of space on which to stand, and then one could plummet a couple of stories down to the railroad tracks and the jagged rocks around it.

"Alex, stop! Get back over the ledge. You're scaring me!" I yelled.

He glanced over at me with wild eyes, exhilarated by his position. I decided then that the teenage male brain might be one of the most risky things in the world.

"Alex, come on!"

"Wait for it," he said.

"Wait for what?"

Alex didn't answer me, but a minute later I heard the dinging of the train bell, along with its whistle in the distance behind us. I looked over my shoulder and saw the light of the train coming.

"Alex, I'm not joking, get back over the edge!"

"Feel your freedom, Auttie. Lighten up. Live a little."

"Exactly, I'd like to live. Are you trying to die?" I shouted.

Alex laughed, and I looked over my shoulder again to watch the train's rapid approach. Its whistle blew again. The air felt temperate and damp, dewy on my skin. A wind blew in and it smelled of spring mud. Alex's precious winter snow had melted away. I stared at him as he laughed again.

"Alex, please!"

"I'll do it," he said, looking down at the tracks, looking happy.

"Why? Alex, don't!" I felt tears in my eyes as I moved over to grab his arm.

He didn't look at me as he scooted just out of my reach. The train was so loud as it came up on us and clanked underneath, vibrating the bridge beneath our feet. I don't know if the wind happened to rage at the same time, or if the train brought it in like a vortex of air, but my hair whipped around my face and I brushed it back to see. Alex's hair blew around in a wild way, too. He tilted his head up, as he leaned forward, his hands gripping the ledge behind him. So close to death as the train thundered underneath.

"Alex!" I screamed.

He looked over at me and saw the tears streaming down my cheeks. Something changed in his expression, and he pulled himself back.

"Auttie..." he said, his tone affectionate. He crawled back over the edge just as the caboose of the train passed under the bridge.

"Are you stupid?" I yelled.

"Maybe. I was just joking around. I'm sorry, I was just messing with you."

I smacked him on the shoulder. "Don't!"

"I said I was sorry."

"I want to go home," I said.

"Okay, okay. We'll go home." He wrapped an arm around me and then pulled me into a hug.

I kept my arms in front of me against his chest as he wrapped his arms around my body, but I leaned my head on his shoulder.

"Don't ever do that again," I whispered.

"Okay," he said, rubbing my back, whispering into my ear.

We started to head back home, but I caught him glancing back at the train tracks. I thought it was the thrill of the moment he glimpsed once more to hold in his memory.

~~~

As I recalled that moment from almost ten years earlier, I felt my eyes go wet. It couldn't have just been the thrill he'd looked back at—I believed now he'd glanced longingly at something worse, something more wild. Maybe part of him longed for death with every ounce of seriousness.

Alex was already mad at that point, he was already mentally ill at thirteen.

I'd thought he was just a foolish, wild teenage boy. But every day since he'd abducted me I saw more and more clearly how mentally unstable he was, even back when we were kids. It existed right before my eyes, the entire time. *How did you miss it all this time, Autumn? How?*

Rachel had been right. I really was the worst judge of character in the universe. I cried in silence as I grieved the loss of a personal history I thought I knew well. I didn't know anything if I didn't even know that my best friend's sanity was always on the point of breaking away at the hinges, like a loose door in a fierce storm.

I dozed off in the cold room at last, just as the earliest shades of morning light grayed the world outside. But just before I fell asleep I saw that more clouds were moving in, and flurries commenced their descent once more. By the time I woke up a few hours later, it looked like a snowstorm again. It lacked the wind that yesterday's blizzard threw at us, but the flakes were fat and torrential. At least another foot of snow had accumulated by the afternoon.

Alex left the room when he awoke and kept me tied up all day. My body ached everywhere. I tried to squirm out of the binding around my wrists, but he tied them so tight in last night's anger that I could not slip free. I did manage to twist and lie on my back, though.

Alex came back to the room once, untying me and leading me to the bathroom, where he let me use the toilet while he stood outside the door. As soon as I finished, he forced me back to the bed and tied my hands up again. Then he left the bedroom and did not return until evening. By then I moaned from discomfort, from cold, from thirst, and from hunger. When he returned to the room, he seemed calm, as if his frustration with me dissipated at last.

"Alex, please," I said. "Please. I'm begging you. I'm in so much pain. I'll be good. Please untie me."

He tilted his head, appraising me, as if to say, *You brought this upon yourself.*

"I'll get you something for the pain," he said.

"I don't want any more sedatives."

"It's ibuprofen. I'll show you the bottle if you don't trust me."

Alex left and I heard him going down the stairs, and then he returned a minute later. He had a small glass of water and a bottle of ibuprofen. He set the water on the nightstand, opened the bottle, and tilted the opening for me to see. Inside were pills the color of rusty southern dirt. In my years of dance, I had taken more than enough of those pills to ward off the aches and pains from hours of practice, so I recognized them to be the real thing.

"What about the water? How do I know you didn't drug the water?"

Alex sighed. "Remember, I'm not trying to kill you. I don't know how the drugs react together, so just trust me. I didn't drug your water."

I eyed him, but I felt so thirsty I couldn't resist the lure of the glass on the nightstand next to me. He poured two pills into his hand, set them on my tongue, and then he lifted the glass of water to my mouth. I swallowed the pills down, but couldn't stop myself from continuing to gulp the entire glass of water. Alex lifted it a little more for me, so I could drain all of the liquid. I drank so fast that it spilled down my chin a little and onto my shirt. He stroked my chin with his hand, wiping the water away. His hand continued along my jaw line and onto my cheek as he gazed at the features of my face without meeting my eyes. Alex stared at my mouth, and then leaned forward and placed a small kiss on my lips. I did not return the kiss, but I lacked the energy to fight him off. He pulled back to look me in the eyes.

"Please untie me."

"Not yet. You need to calm yourself first."

"I am calm."

"No, I mean, *calm* yourself down. Like keep yourself calm, all the time. You need to be broken in. I hoped it wouldn't have to be like this, but you're being just absolutely ridiculous, the way you're acting in this house."

"*I'm* being ridiculous! And *broken in?* Like an animal? That's how you see me?"

"We are part of the animal kingdom, my dear," he said, rising from the bed. He stretched back, as if to boast the luxury of being able to move freely.

"You're right. You're a beast."

He shrugged with his eyebrows, and then put another small log on the fire. "Not sure when the power will be back on, but I can heat some soup in a pot over the fire downstairs. I'm guessing you're starving."

I nodded.

"Be back in a bit. Don't go anywhere," he said, and snickered to congratulate himself on his own cleverness.

I glared at him as he left. By the time he returned with a bowl of soup, the ibuprofen was just beginning to work its way into my system. The pain in my arm still throbbed a bit, but subsided enough that I didn't feel like I had to fight back groans anymore. Alex sat on the edge of the bed next to me and stirred the soup with a spoon.

"Open wide," he said, like a mother feeding a toddler.

"How hot is it?"

In response, he took the spoonful himself and swallowed it down without needing to blow on it. "It's perfect." He spooned up another bit and held it out for me.

With some hesitance, I took a sip off of the spoon. It was bland, canned tomato soup, but it tasted like manna from Heaven after going all day without food. Alex continued to spoon feed me, and my body slipped into a state of relaxation.

"The ibuprofen worked well," I said. "I'm not so uncomfortable."

Alex nodded, stirred the soup a little more, and then spooned me another mouthful. "Yeah. And the sedatives should be helping a little, too."

I froze, holding the most recent spoonful of soup in my mouth.

Alex saw the look on my face and tried to calm me down. "Don't worry, it's just a touch. Hardly any at all. I just know you haven't slept much and you need to sleep. It will help ease the discomfort and let you get some rest."

A second passed and then I spat the soup at him. It sprayed all over his face. He paused to control his temper for a moment, and then wiped one hand over his face.

"Stop drugging me!" I yelled, leaning forward against my restraints.

"Autumn, calm the hell down. There are hardly any in there."

"You said you weren't trying to kill me, so you wouldn't mix the medications. And now you're mixing them! Dirt bag lying sack of shit."

"Well, I needed you to get the ibuprofen down so you would stop moaning and whining. It's unnerving. And I already know that the two drugs don't have negative interactions with each other, so don't worry about it. It's not going to kill you. Anyway, you have a nasty habit of trying to sneak around and get yourself into all sorts of trouble in the night, and I want to sleep without having to worry about it."

"Uh, I'm tied up, moron. Can't exactly sneak around now, can I?"

"I like to be extra careful sometimes," he said.

I ground my teeth and whipped one of my legs over at him, kicking the bowl of soup Alex held. It spilled all over his face and shoulder. He jumped up from the bed, and the bowl tumbled to the floor but didn't break. I continued to kick at him, getting in a solid blow to his jaw as he bent over to try and grab my legs, but he managed to wrangle them together and held them down, pressing so hard with his weight it became painful, and then excruciating.

Alex looked at me, seething with resentment. "You want to keep your pretty little dancer legs intact, Autumn? Hmm? Do you?" He moved in, his face close to mine as he pressed on my legs.

I moaned at the torture. "Yes."

"You sure you want that?"

"Yes," I said, louder.

"Then keep them still."

I nodded, and he went to the closet to find a sheet, ripped a strip of it into a thinner piece of fabric, and then tied my feet up, anchoring them to the bedpost at the bottom of the bed. He walked over to me and looked like he might slap me for a moment, but restrained himself. I shut my eyes and heard him walk toward the end of the bed.

After a minute, I realized Alex was not leaving the room, so I turned back to look at him. He sat on the bed, facing away from me hunched over. I detected him making a small sort of rocking motion, and he shook his head a little every now and then, as if responding to some internal dialogue. None of the fear I felt on this entire escapade matched the terror I experienced then, because I saw that Alex was losing his grasp on himself.

That meant I, too, was losing any last shred of my grasp on My Alex. And if I lost all of him, if I lost every piece of My Alex, I knew I'd be murdered out here in this God forsaken place. *Come back to me*, I thought. *Alex, please. Come back to me.*

The two drugs together were a blessing in a sense. Within minutes, the sedative he mixed into the water eased some of my anxiety. Just enough to keep me from complete panic. My discomfort vanished, leaving my body with a pleasant, tranquil, pain-free sensation. I stopped even caring that a disturbed man sat at the foot of the bed. As the night stretched out before us, I fell into a sleep so deep that I didn't even realize when Alex slipped into bed next to me. Only when I awoke the next morning did I see him there, sleeping and peaceful. I stared at the log-beamed ceiling for a while before he woke up. When he did, he got up and left the room.

"Alex!" I called. "I need to use the bathroom. Please, at least let me use the bathroom."

He paused in the hallway just outside the door and sighed, but complied, untying me, grasping me by the arm and leading me to the toilet. Alex stood right next to me in the bathroom but turned away.

I cleared my throat. "You don't want to leave a little mystery between us?"

"I don't trust you," he said.

That makes two of us, I thought.

After I finished and had scrubbed my hands raw, Alex took me back to tie me up again and left me there alone for hours. He came by in the afternoon to put another log on the fire, escorted me to the bathroom again, and gave me a few bites of a sandwich. I almost hoped he'd laced it with drugs at that point. I didn't want to be conscious just lying there, staring out the window. The snowstorms finally ran themselves out, and the sky turned a bright azure, with the sun shining down against the snow. It blinded me if I looked at it too long. The snow shimmered like billions of diamond fragments dusted over a thick white comforter.

The agony in my body grew so intense as the day wore on that I felt almost delusional. I couldn't tell if I were here for days or months. My arms and my shoulders cried out in such misery from being held in that position over my head, I thought the pain might kill me. My stomach felt like it had commenced consumption of its neighboring organs, and the thirst burned in my throat. As the sun began its gradual plunge toward the horizon, I felt like madness would overtake me. Did I ride a train up here, or did I imagine that? Was I tied up, or did I stay here on my own in a self-imposed hell? I tried to yell for Alex, but initially I was unable to muster a formidable holler in my condition. Each time I called out, however, my voice gained a little strength.

"Alex! Please! Help, Alex!"

After what I guessed was five—maybe twenty—minutes, he came up to the room and it seemed like he had a hold on a diminutive piece of his old self again. Alex looked at me with pity and tenderness.

I whimpered. "Please. I can't take it anymore. Please."

Alex nodded and untied me, helping me ease my arms back down to my sides, which felt excruciating after they remained over my head for so long. He rubbed the tops of my shoulders and I winced when he touched the spot the fire extinguisher had collided with, leaving behind a contusion of fantastic proportions.

Then Alex helped me up and escorted me to the bathroom again. I scoured my hands and they trembled. Alex had to assist me down the stairs, too, because my legs shook with such violence from hunger and weakness. He ushered me into the kitchen and sat me on one of the stools around the island. I didn't even care about trying to run or escape. I just needed nourishment. While Alex filled a glass of water at the sink, I noticed that he had a few battery-operated space heaters running in various spots, reducing some of the draftiness. They looked old, as if he'd discovered them stashed away in some storage space from many years ago. I only now computed that I'd seen one in the bathroom upstairs when I used it. Alex handed me a small glass of water and I reached for it.

"Drink it slowly, if you can," he said.

I lifted it with both of my shaking hands and sipped. I set it down, but couldn't resist and picked it up again to gulp down the whole thing. Alex moved about the kitchen, pulling things out of cupboards and drawers. Then he slid a sandwich in front of me, and I ate it so fast I consumed whole pieces without chewing.

"I'll give you more in a bit, but you should let that settle in your stomach first," he said.

"Can I have more ibuprofen?"

Alex nodded and pulled the bottle out of a cupboard, dropping three into my hand. Well, *now* he was going to be generous, after keeping me tied up for two days like he was a monster. He gave me a little more water and I took the pills.

"Do you want a shower?" he asked.

"Yes."

"We have a measly generator from like a thousand years ago. It's not enough to heat this entire place *and* keep the water heater and pump running. But if we use it mostly for the water heater and pump, we should be able to get decent showers."

I wrung my cold hands. "Thank God."

Alex took my plate and glass, put them in the dishwasher, and then helped me back upstairs. I gathered my things from my bag and took two birth control pills to catch up on missed days. When I walked into the bathroom, Alex got the water in the shower running for me, testing the temperature.

"I'm not going to leave the room, since it looks like you're regaining your strength a little. But I'll just sit at the door facing the other way," he said.

The shower curtain was an opaque thing with muted green stripes, but I still didn't like the idea of him in the bathroom with me.

"Alex, I'm not going to do anything. I... I learned my lesson after being tied up for days," I said, hating to stoop as low as submitting to the words, even though I did not mean them. But I had to placate Alex.

He looked at the floor for a moment. "Well, that may be the case. But you're going to have to earn my trust again."

I had to earn his trust? I glared at him for a second, but remembered that I needed to play the submissive role if I wanted a second of privacy anytime soon. I acquiesced and waited for him to turn away so I could undress and step into the shower. There were no razors in the shower now, just soap and shampoo.

"Can you trust me enough with a shaver so I don't feel so nasty?" I asked while giving my body an initial rinse down. "I promise I won't do anything stupid. I just... would really like to shave." As asinine as it was, it was true, I felt a little too mountain-woman for my taste.

There was no answer from Alex for a minute. "If you do try anything, I'll tie you up again."

"I swear I won't."

A minute later his hand slid around the side of the shower curtain and he offered it to me.

"Thanks."

"Yep."

When I finished showering, I grabbed for a towel and wrapped it around myself before stepping out onto the bathmat where Alex could see me. He continued to face away, and I dressed with as much privacy as I could, but I caught him sneaking a few sideways glances in the halfway-fogged mirror. Strange sensation—we were intimate just days before, and now it enraged me if he stole even a single peep in the mirror.

After I dressed, we meandered around the house for a bit. We looked through board games in the game room and I shied away from the bookcase door, feeling sick as I thought of the haunting cold of that space. Alex forced me to play a few rounds of checkers with him.

We moved back out to the great room, which bore scars of the fire and its aftermath. It was a disaster, left to be cleaned by a non-professional. The one curtain was half burned away. A char spot marred the floor where Alex put out the flame on the tapestry. Extinguisher powder, though cleaned off of most things, still dusted a few ledges of the bookshelf and corners of the floor. We sat and stared out the large front window while sipping warm drinks, acting as if the disturbed condition of the room was commonplace, unnoticeable, unworthy of remark.

An hour before we went to bed that night, the power finally returned. The heat coming back on was like the sweetest gift, warming the drafty chill that permeated my bones even when I took a warm shower or sat next to the fire. When it was time to go to bed, I didn't want to get anywhere near that mattress. Two days tied up on it turned the surface into a repulsive place for me, but I had no choice. We stayed in the master bedroom with the fireplace again, just in case the power went back out. Alex held me, and I didn't resist. It wasn't just my bruised arm nagging at me. My shoulders still ached from being tied up, and I was willing to do almost anything to avoid that again. So I let him hold me against his body.

The next day rolled by in uneventful form. We ate at meal times, sat by the fire in the great room for a long time, and attempted to go outside, but could not get any further than a few feet because the drifts were so high. A single step down to one of the porch stairs, and our feet got stuck in about eight inches of snow.

At least the weather began to warm a little, and the sky cleared, allowing the sun to beat down on the snow. Icicles dripped from the overhangs. I prayed for the drifts to melt away in a hurry. For now, however, there would be no escaping outside.

Alex left me no privacy again that day. When I showered, he stayed in the room. Even when I had to use the toilet, he came in with me, but turned away. When we went to bed the following night, I worried about losing track of the days. How many days was I held captive now? *I'm losing myself*, I thought. *I'm not just losing Alex, I'm losing myself.*

I felt madness moving into my limbs, taking over my brain, and stirring sinister places inside me. Stirring, stirring, stirring... A dark cauldron of poison, bubbling up to the rim. Breathing life into parts of me I didn't want to exist. Parts of me that were capable of heinous things.

CHAPTER FIFTEEN

The following morning, I woke up to see Alex crouched by the window of the bedroom drawing on the wall. Alex had always drawn like a skilled artist. I remained still, my eyes simply opening and taking in the sight as I tried not to make a sound. I watched for a few minutes without moving.

Alex hummed quietly. In his hand he held a permanent marker, and he sketched a scene on the wall just below the window. It was the exact view outside the window of the pines, the road, the rolling hills—drawn right underneath the ledge, on the smooth, sand-light wooden wall. The double image was eerie. An echo of the free outdoors, sketched by a madman inside who imprisoned me, imprisoning himself in the process. The tune he hummed sounded happy. I marveled at the perfection of his drawing. I panicked at being in the same room with the artist.

I hadn't made a sound. Perhaps it was the silence as I held my breath that tipped Alex off, but without warning he turned to me as if he knew I was awake the whole time. It startled me. A smile lit up his face.

"Get up. Come on. It's Christmas Eve. I know you did some damage to the tree the other night," he said, his face flickering annoyance for a moment and then returning to normal. "But there are some more decorations in a closet. You'll have to help me fix it up a little. It'll be fun."

I sat up in bed and my forehead wrinkled in irritation and confusion. How could he think anything here would be fun for me? And what the hell? I must have miscalculated how many days passed since the party back home.

"It's Christmas Eve?"

"Of course!"

"That's it. That's it!" I said, and then flung the blanket off of me to stand up. I began to pace the room in a panic. "Take me home, Alex. Take me home right now! Stop this! Alex, take me home! You're going to make us stay here even over Christmas?"

I knew this was his plan already, but the reality of it didn't sink in entirely until now. I just could not fathom that I wouldn't get out, or that he wouldn't change his mind. Or that help would not have come by now. Where the hell *was* everyone? It was silly, every day here had me in a panic, but the marking of the holiday shocked me into a mental tailspin.

Alex's face went dark, and he sat down on the edge of the bed, fiddling with his hands. "Don't ruin this for me, Autumn."

"Don't ruin it for you? Don't ruin it for *you*? Are you effing kidding me?" I said, and then smacked him across the face as hard as I could. Not even a second later I knew it was a mistake, but my anger took control before I could stop myself.

Alex's nostrils flared and I saw the muscles of his jaw tighten. He grabbed my wrist so hard it throbbed. He rose from the bed, squeezing harder and harder. My mouth dropped open in agony, and Alex towered over me as he stood. I began to crumple under the pain. He twisted my wrist, lowering our arms. I felt his breath against the side of my face as he stood over me.

"Do you want to be tied up again? Is that what it is? You like the restraints, don't you? Bad girl... I didn't see it before. You get off on it, don't you? Let me get the stuff to tie you up."

"No. No, please."

He yanked at me, but I resisted and tried to pull away.

"Stop... fighting," he said as he shoved me to the bed. "Stop!" He crawled on top of me and I realized he was about to switch gears, forgetting the restraints.

Alex was about to enforce his control in a more disturbing way, again. But I remembered the night on the train, how well it worked to go along with him. And so I cringed inside as I swallowed my pride in this house—this beautiful, mysterious, disquieting prison. I kissed his mouth.

Alex pulled back a little and looked furious. "No, I'm not buying that crap again. I know what you tried to do on the train. I'm not buying it this time."

I kissed him again, making it so believable I almost believed the passion myself.

"No," he said. "You call *me* the lying sack of shit? You're the worst liar of them all." He squeezed my chin with one hand until it hurt.

"Alex, please. Why do you have to be so angry with me?" I caressed his face, forcing him to look me in the eyes. "Where are you? Alex... I got on that train with you. Even if I was intoxicated, I got on the train with you in my uninhibited state."

I sighed and my breath shook. "Yes, I hate you for holding me captive. I'm so mad at you I could kill you. But I got on that train with you. And we made love. And now you're gone from me." It was a ruse, almost every ounce of it.

Almost.

But I felt it in there, that infinitesimal illumination. A glow, so small and hidden beneath the grime of emotions turned to dirt that it sat like an unknown tumor, biding its time. It was there: the truth. A part of me that I had no time for in all my efforts to flee. A part that I planned to ignore until I got out of the heinous situation.

The reality was that I was in love with Alex when we boarded the train. I wanted him when we had sex that first night and the morning after. He was my oldest and best friend. And I lost all of that in the past week. Furthermore, I wanted to know what happened, where he *went*.

Alex stopped fighting against my efforts, but remained on top of me. He avoided my eyes, looking down toward our stomachs. We were both motionless, his act of aggression halted within seconds. His sudden shift in demeanor surprised me again.

"Alex, I miss you. Where are you? I've been fighting against you, yes. But you're fighting me, too. How can I not be defensive?" As I spoke, that splinter of truth grew and spread, exploding into a splendid array of light inside, and I wanted to weep.

"I'm sorry," he whispered. "I'm sorry, I'm sorry."

I lifted my eyes and realized his own welled with tears. My heart broke for that broken Alex. I hated him, absolutely loathed him. But I loved him, too. My Alex—the old Alex—cracked in the mind, and it stabbed my heart with a deep ache.

"Autumn... I'm sick. I'm sick, and I'm sorry," he whispered, his voice shaking.

"I know," I said, stroking his face.

"I don't want to be sick. I don't want to be like this."

I felt a tear of my own roll down the side of my face and into my hair. My breath hitched in a quiet sob. I opened my mouth to say something, but couldn't. I felt like I would burst into uncontrollable hysterics if I tried to talk about it.

Alex stroked the side of my face, and looked so sad. "I'm sorry I can't be... Normal. For you. I love you, and I want to be, so bad, but I..." His throat tightened at the end and he didn't finish his sentence. His eyes were wet and he closed them.

To my dismay, I kissed him again. It was a soft kiss, quiet and full of sorrow. I scolded myself and told myself to stop. But I didn't stop. I still felt abhorrence toward him, but I also felt like my own sanity was going to pieces, bit by bit, up here in this place. It felt like an outlet for the madness. And that piece of heartbreaking love—the bastard—it shouted at me, too, demanding its own acknowledgment. I still loved him. God, I still loved him, and I hated myself for it.

I pulled back from the kiss slowly and Alex, now psychologically weary, slid off and curled around me as we both faced the window. I stared out into the bright, late morning sunlight on the snow, and silent tears fell to my pillow. My heart hurt for Alex. And I wanted to go home. I just wanted to go home.

The one positive result of admitting those caring words to him was that Alex appeared to have regained a little trust in me, and after a bit his mood lightened. He made us oatmeal for breakfast, and I tried not to cry when I thought about what my mom would be doing this Christmas Eve morning. Talking to the police? Weeping in despair? Posting signs with my picture and the word *missing* on them?

After we finished eating, Alex scratched the side of his jaw and looked at me. "The tree. It sucks. It needs some work. Come on."

I bit my lower lip and followed him down the hallway beyond the main fireplace, down the opposite direction of the bedrooms. In that wing, Alex led me to a closet where plastic storage bins were kept. He pulled out a bin with Christmas decorations and hefted it into the great room. Alex set the bin in front of the tree.

"It's not the prettiest thing ever, but it'll be okay if we tidy it up a bit, right?" he said, as he appraised the half-burnt Christmas tree.

When he looked over at me for an answer, I nodded, attempting to appear enthusiastic. He opened the bin and handed me an extra box of red bulbs. Then he pulled out an extra string of lights and began wrapping them around the tree.

It looked as if Alex had wiped most of the branches clean during my hours of being restrained to the bed, but remnants of extinguisher powder still clung to the tree. If I squinted it almost looked like snow, white dusting a half scorched pine tree. The beauty was lost on me within seconds, though. It was a Christmas tree destroyed by a wicked situation. I found it hard to keep myself from crying again. This couldn't be happening. I couldn't miss Christmas at home and spend it instead up here in this deranged nightmare.

"Come on, help me out," Alex said.

I opened the box and put bulbs on the small wire hooks, and hung them on crispy branches. The smell of boxed Christmas decorations and packing dust caused my eyes to well with tears further. *A lost year*, I thought. If I even made it out alive, this would be a lost year. My chest felt hollow. I sniffed and forced myself to stop crying. This was enough; I had to stop falling into the role of victim. I was going to get out of here, damn it. I focused on the stench of the burnt parts of this room, rather than the nostalgic aromas of childhood, and it helped dry my eyes. It smelled like shit when I paid attention to it. Charred artificial tree reeked in a stench of smoke mixed with what had to be cancer-causing chemicals.

Alex plugged in the tree when he finished his indolent job of wrapping the lights around it, and then helped me put the last few bulbs on the tree. Then we stood back and evaluated our masterpiece of clashing desires: holiday cheer meets desperate arson.

"This is really demented," I said, meaning the whole situation. Meaning it in a sinister way. But I didn't want to bring out Alex's wrath again, so I covered. "The tree. It's a demented tree." I forced myself to chuckle.

Alex laughed and ran a hand through his hair. "Yeah. Yeah, it is. You have yourself to thank for that, though." He looked at me and his expression flashed between genuine irritation and a sort of adoration for my stubborn personality.

"Ah, well. It'll have to do," he said, and packed the storage bin back up, returning it to the closet. He came back out to the great room and turned on Christmas music.

"At least the power is back on," he said.

I agreed.

Most of the day bored me into irritation, like the ones before. The snow continued to melt, and most of the steps up to the front porch were now visible when I looked out the window. I searched the horizon, wondering when a car would drive by. Not that the driver of any random passing car would know what was going on here, but I hadn't seen a single vehicle since arriving here. The isolation of this place frightened me. What would a person do if there were a medical emergency? *Where are you guys?* I thought again. Sam, Mom, Camille, Tim... any of them. Where were they?

In the early evening, Alex made us cocoa and turned up the holiday music. I watched his back, the lines of his muscles through his slate-colored shirt, as he stirred the mugs in the kitchen. His body looked nice, and I thought of kissing him earlier that morning. I stifled my love once more and felt pure disgust at the thought. He walked over, handing me one of the mugs.

"Let's sit by the fire," he said.

I didn't respond, but followed him out into the great room and took a seat in one of the armchairs. We sat there, watching the fire, and he sipped his hot chocolate. I smelled the faint smoke from the blaze, and its warmth heated the front of my body. It crackled and whispered at me like a fellow conspirator. I stared down at my cocoa, and wondered if Alex had drugged it. How could I take anything from him now? He prepared this cup with his back to me, hiding the process.

I realized that if I lived through this, if I ever got home, I would never be able to look at a cup of hot chocolate again without remembering this. I took a measured breath. The fire popped and hissed again. I continued to look at the drink in my hands. When the song "I'll Be Home for Christmas" played over the speakers, I clenched my jaw and tightened my grip on the mug. Home... I wanted to go home more than I ever wanted anything in my life. I felt a spark of rage ignite inside me as I stared at the drink and listened to the song.

That vicious ember in me radiated and pulsed, until all at once it detonated. I lost it, and felt like a wild animal, trapped and feral. I had to get home. I had to get home! I threw the mug against the stone hearth, and it shattered into a mess of liquid chocolate and ceramic debris.

I bolted up out of the chair, and screamed so loud it surprised even me. "Get me the hell out of here! Get me *out!*"

Alex was up in an instant, and set down his mug. He came toward me, but I leapt toward the hearth and grabbed a piece of the broken mug, a nice large, sharp piece. I swiped at him with it, but he dodged. I ran around to the back of the armchair again and we paused for a minute, standing off in a duel. We stood there, staring at each other, that homey song killing me with irony in the silence that lingered between Alex and myself.

Alex came around the chair and I waited for him. When he got just close enough, I used my free hand to shove up with the heel of my palm and bash in his nose. Alex staggered back, grabbing his nose. Blood began to drip from it, and my hand throbbed from the hit, so I knew I struck him good.

Alex groaned, and his eyes flit up to mine with pure rage. I took advantage of his moment of weakness and jabbed him on the side of the face with the shard of mug, dragging it down to slice his cheekbone. Blood pooled up and dripped from his cheek. Then I turned and ran, but the frenzy I started in him was greater than I expected. He was after me so fast I didn't have time to think. All I could compute was terror, a cut on my own hand from the broken piece of ceramic, the voice on the speakers crooning, and the sound of Alex's steps pounding behind me.

I ran to the kitchen in an attempt to grab a knife, but he caught me before I got to one. I tried to reach for the island countertop, but he pulled me away. He yanked at me and wrapped his other arm around my waist, lifting me and dragging me back into the great room while I kicked at him, elbowed his ribs, and screamed. I punched him in the jaw. Alex put a bloodied hand over my mouth to silence me, and I tried to squirm away from the slippery gore against my face that made me panic more.

"Shut up! Shut up!" Alex yelled into my ear.

I stopped screaming and kicking just so he'd stop hurting my eardrum. He dragged me into the middle of the great room.

"You see this? See this beautiful Christmas Eve? See it, Autumn?" He yanked at me, removing the hand from my mouth and holding my face up by the chin to look at the room.

"Such a beautiful Christmas Eve. So beautiful. So perfect. And then, ha! You! You just *insist* on damaging everything in your path. Like a tiny little hurricane in paradise, making people think you're a beautiful place to be, and then ripping shit up by the roots. Tearing houses apart. Ruining people's lives," he said.

Blood dripped from his nose onto the shoulder of my shirt. Then he hauled me toward the staircase.

"No! No, Alex, no!" I yelled. I fought against him, trying to kick and elbow him again. I punched him in the face once more, but not hard enough.

He kept yanking me, and grasping a full grip on my hair, he tugged my head back, and then bashed the side of my skull on one of the stairs. A jolt went through my head, pain like nothing else. I heard the song fading. My vision vibrated, just long enough for it to scare the hell out of me, and then all went dark.

CHAPTER SIXTEEN

The anguish in my head when I awoke in the morning felt like a vice that someone clamped, released a smidgen, then clamped harder again at regular intervals. It made me nauseous. I lifted my hand, which I noted was free from any bindings, and touched the spot on my skull where Alex had bashed it against the stair. I flinched. Rolling from my side onto my back, I let out a groan. I needed painkillers so badly. *Throb, throb, throb*—I could feel my pulse in my head. I tried to sit up a little, but the dizziness made me recline again for a minute. Alex stirred next to me in bed.

"Mmm. Waking up Sleeping Beauty?" he said, intending it as anything but a term of endearment.

"Pain. My head. Alex, it hurts so bad."

"You deserve it."

"Please. Please can I have some painkillers? I'll do anything."

"Anything, huh?" he asked, as if he meant something vile, but he fell silent for a moment. "I'm not in the mood to force you to do anything right this second. I'm not feeling so hot myself."

I looked over and his face reminded me of the transgressions that had earned me the head wound. His nose was bruised, and blood caked around it as well as along the gash I gave him on the cheek.

"We both could use some pain killers," he said. "I'm not so sure I'm feeling very charitable, though."

"Please. Alex, I'm begging you." It hurt to even talk and my stomach rolled from the throbbing.

"Fine," he said, with a sigh and pulled a bottle of ibuprofen from his nightstand along with some water. "I took some last night to get to sleep," he said, answering my surprised expression in seeing the bottle right there.

"You must have knocked me out pretty hard. I can't believe I'm just waking up now," I whispered, noting the morning light coming through the window.

"I diluted some sedative in a little water and made you choke it down while you were unconscious. I'd had enough of your shit and wanted to try and get some sleep because I was so uncomfortable."

I let out a slow, heavy sigh of aggravation. I was losing track of the number of times he'd drugged me, and felt pissed off by that additional lack of control. My head wasn't making my stomach feel great, but the sedative helped explain some of the queasiness, too.

Alex took some pills, drank them down, and then handed me three ibuprofen with the glass of water. I swallowed them and lay back down for a while, counting the minutes until they took effect. Alex remained next to me, soundless.

After maybe a half hour he finally spoke. "Merry Christmas." He sounded dejected.

I stayed silent for a moment, and then I burst into tears. My poor mother. My poor self. *A wasted year*, I thought again. *It's too late.* Crying hurt my head again, but I couldn't stop the tears.

I contemplated my death then. If Alex went astray so much that he would actually steal me away and keep me here, keep us up here while everyone at home spent Christmas morning grieving our absences, I believed he had to be deranged enough to murder me. I no longer had any doubt.

How would he do it? What would he do with my body afterward? Would Mom ever know for sure what happened to me? I imagined the stress breaking down her immune system. As if I needed another thing to worry about. *Damn it Sam, where the hell are you? Help me!* I screamed inside.

When I cried myself out and the throbbing in my head subsided enough that I could get out of bed, I rose and dressed in a pair of jeans and a hoodie, while Alex sat up on the edge of the bed facing the door. I looked at the ground out of the bedroom window. More of the snow had melted, but light flurries were falling again.

I brushed my hands over my face and realized dried blood still laced my skin from where Alex's bloodied hand grabbed me last night. I flinched. "Can I wash up?"

"Yeah. We both need to."

Alex let me use the bathroom without coming in, just standing outside the door, and I took my time. I blanched at the sight of myself in the mirror with the dried blood around my mouth and chin. I washed it off, scrubbing hard. It took me a long time, maybe five solid minutes to stop washing my hands and face. Then I brushed my teeth, combed out my hair, and just tried to locate any feeling other than despair.

Alex came in after a bit and proceeded to wash his own face. It looked painful for him as he cleaned around the gash and his bruised nose. He brushed his teeth and I saw a little blood when he rinsed and spit. Some of my hits must have gotten him in the mouth last night. I felt like I was in a nightmarish, involuntary version of *Fight Club*.

"Come on," he said.

I sighed and followed him downstairs for breakfast. He put the Christmas music on again, and a chill crept up my spine when I remembered hearing it last night as he dragged me across the floor. I wanted to plug my ears, but forced myself to hear it as I always did—as sentimental music that reminded me of years gone by.

"Christmas morning," Alex said. "You know my mom always makes us poached eggs and croissants, but we'll have to settle for pancakes again."

"That's fine."

"Glad you're being agreeable this morning."

I sat silent for a moment. "Don't you miss her? Your mom. Today, I mean?"

Alex went stone-faced, and prepared the pancakes, but said nothing. Maybe he wasn't letting himself think about her, and what he was doing to his mother by being here. We ate breakfast in a tense hush, holiday music filling the air between us. The cheerful tunes in the background mocked our discord. After a cup of coffee and another couple of painkillers, Alex seemed to relax and warm up to me again, just a little.

I finished as much of the food on my plate as I could, which wasn't much.

"Come sit by the tree with me," he said.

I followed him to the damaged tree and sat on the hard floor. Instead of sitting next to me, he went to the coat closet to pull something out. I could still smell the stench of burnt plastic. I always paid close attention to my posture, but now my shoulders hunched in depression. I stared at the snowflakes falling outside the giant window, like celebratory confetti, but sparse enough that it seemed I'd just missed the big drop. Like I had just missed the party.

"I got you a little something," Alex said, handing me a present. Two presents actually. One smaller box stacked on top of a larger box, wrapped in red paper and tied together with a matching scarlet ribbon.

"Oh gee, I didn't get you anything," I said in a flat voice. "Oh, wait, that's right... I did. But it's at *home* in freaking Lake Forest, Illinois."

"Oh, quit your snippiness and just open your present." For a moment, his eyes were those boyish eyes I'd always known. Joking with me at my crabby response.

I cleared my throat. "You already gave me a present, anyway. The passport holder."

"I felt generous this year."

I recoiled at the depth in his statement. I pulled at the satin bow and it slid undone, smooth like the ribbons of my pointe shoes. I missed my pointe shoes. I opened the smaller box first, unwrapping it with care. In my hand rested a thin, square box from a high-end jeweler. I opened the lid and inside was a necklace that shocked me with its exquisiteness. It was short— a collar length necklace—and faceted black stones, shaped into rounded off squares about an inch large, were set all the way around. Sparkling diamonds traced around the edges of each black stone. I lifted it and it felt heavier than I expected, quite heavy.

"The metal is platinum, isn't it?" I said.

Alex wore a little smile. "You could tell by the weight. Yeah, it's platinum, and those are black onyx. And diamonds around them, obviously."

I felt like I couldn't breathe, trying to imagine the price for a piece like this. Probably more than a semester of my tuition, a year even. That kind of money dropped on a stupid necklace when I struggled to get through school. I just stared at it, awed by the beauty, disturbed by the situation in which it was given.

"Open the next one."

I sighed, wondering what more he could give me that his mind could possibly think would seem impressive after the necklace. I unwrapped the next gift, and lifted the lid of a clothing box bearing the name of a couture designer. I pulled back the tissue paper, and then stroked my fingertips over black lace adorned with black beading. I grabbed the straps and lifted out a dress. The top was constructed of nude material overlain with black lace and the beading. The lace was so thick that it would probably give the appearance that the wearer donned a black dress that was just barely see-through. Black tulle made up the attached skirt.

I stood up and held it in front of me to get a better look at the whole piece. The skirt reminded me of a tutu, but the kind that would lay flat and drape to my lower thighs. The dress was gorgeous and well-constructed. It reminded me of a dance costume I might wear on stage.

"Put it on," Alex said, beaming.

I looked at him in surprise. "Now?"

"Yeah. Why not? It's Christmas."

"Because it's freezing cold," I said. I felt chilly in my pants and hoodie. The dress looked skimpy.

"Oh, come on. I spent a lot of money on it and want to see you in it."

My sensibility grimaced at his mention of spending money on me. It was bad enough that he gave me something so expensive when he treated me like a slave. Even worse that he'd go and point it out.

"Put it on. And the necklace, too," he said. His face turned serious, and I knew there would be a consequence if I objected again.

So Alex followed me up to the bedroom and stood outside the door as I stripped down and slipped into the dress. This had to be the most expensive thing I'd ever worn. The straps were thin, and the neckline plunged deep, but not as far as the low-cut back of the dress. I draped the necklace across my throat and fastened the hook behind my neck. The metal felt cold against my skin, and the weight of the necklace pressed against the hollow of my throat. I appraised myself in the full-length mirror in the corner of the room. I squinted. This could be any one of my costumes for a ballet performance. I even had a pair of black pointe shoes I used for a routine a few years ago that would go with it to perfection. I opened my eyes again, and brushed my hands over the tulle skirt. It made me miss being at school, preparing for dance performances. I went up on *relevé* with my arms arched over my head, and then did a single *pirouetté*.

His tiny dancer, I thought. That's what he wanted—just a tiny dancer, all to himself.

He knocked on the door. "Ready yet?"

I sighed. "Yes."

He opened the door and looked at me looking in the mirror. I met his eyes in the reflection.

"It's perfect," he said. "You're perfect. Do you like it?"

I touched the necklace and looked at myself again. "Yes," I whispered. "Thank you."

It felt so hard to pull those two words up and out of me, but I forced myself. Maybe it was frivolous to think this way, but as awful as everything was already, and as much as the day didn't matter at this point, I still held in my mind that it was

Christmas. I wanted Christmas to be scarred as minimally as possible. If I ended up getting away and making it back to some sort of normal life, I didn't want to go through future holidays remembering being beaten, tied up, or enduring any other kind of punishment on this day.

I did one slow rotation for him so he could evaluate the full view of me in the dress, and then I stopped to face him. "Can I take it off now?"

His brow furrowed. "What? Why would you take it off? You just put it on."

"Because it's cold. It's a skimpy dress."

Alex waved his hand as if to brush away the idea. "I'll turn the heat up a little. It's Christmas. You should look nice on Christmas. I want you to wear it." His expression told me it wasn't up for debate. I thought about taking it off anyway, but complied to keep the peace for today. Just for today.

I followed him to the dial in the hall and he turned up the radiators a hair. I couldn't even tell for sure if the dial actually moved, the adjustment was so small.

"That's it?" I asked.

"I'm not going to waste a ton of energy heating this place," he said. "It's irresponsible. Besides, I'll be hot if I turn it up much more than that."

"Well then why don't you walk around in something more suitable for summer, too?"

"Autumn, don't start with me."

Asshole, I thought. But I said nothing.

We went downstairs and Alex put on a holiday movie. We sat and watched it in silence. I pulled a blanket over me, but could still feel the chill of the cavernous room. I tried not to think of my mother as the scenes flashed by on the screen. I attempted to force some kind of telepathy out to Tim to make sure he kept her calm. And then I sent a mental message to Sam: *If I ever see you again, I'm going to punch you so hard in the face, you'll cry like a little baby*. I began to feel a sort of desperation in my mix of longing and anger toward Sam. After the movie concluded, Alex stood up and stretched.

"Well, you know, we always do Christmas dinner early. Why do they even call it Christmas dinner? It should be called Christmas lunch. So we should start making it now," he said.

I stood up, keeping the blanket wrapped around my shoulders. He moved in my direction and took the blanket off of me and set it on the couch.

"What's the point of you wearing the dress if I can't see it?"

I glared at him and goose bumps stood up on my skin from the chill.

"Come on, we'll come up with something creative for dinner. And if not, we'll just order a pizza," he said.

My eyes lit up for a second at the thought of someone coming to the door, another human. But I realized in an instant he was taunting me.

"Ha! Like I would do that," he said, jabbing my arm in a joke, but hard enough that it hurt more than it should. "You think I'm that stupid?"

I didn't answer.

I followed him into the kitchen and he grabbed all of the knives out of the drawer and set them on the corner of the counter. Then he stood in front of them, like a gatekeeper.

"Not going to let you cook with any knives, so go ahead and find something to make without them."

"Oh, so I'm making dinner? Not *we're* making dinner... *I'm* making dinner, huh?"

"Well, someone has to keep an eye on the knives after the nonsense you've pulled in the last few days," he said.

Stupid fool, I thought. *You must think I'm an idiot if you don't believe I can hurt you with anything in this kitchen but a knife.* Common kitchen items that could cause harm to a body flitted through my imagination: forks being thrust at eyes, drinking glasses smashed against the counter and slicing at skin—I pretty much already did that exact thing with the mug—and cast iron frying pans fracturing a skull. I shook the images out of my head, disturbed by the ease with which my mind went to that place. I was losing it. Being held prisoner by a broken mind was causing me to lose my own.

And then I thought: *Tomorrow.* Today would be serene. Today would be spent doing nothing but hoping for those back home who loved me to find me. Had they not even thought of the lodge as a place to look? Okay, the blizzard could have kept them away for a few days. But I looked outside and the snow continued to melt. The morning's flurries even stopped. A genuine optimism lifted my spirit a little for the first time in days. Maybe that was it. Perhaps the snowstorm held everything up. Maybe today they would come because the blizzard was over.

Alex leaned back against the counter with his arms crossed as he watched me move around the kitchen, searching for ideas for a holiday meal. I tried to act normal as I opened cupboards and the refrigerator. With no perishable items in stock, coming up with something good seemed tricky.

I also wasn't great at cooking to begin with. As a dancer who desired to make it in a world of slender bodies vying for the same position, I tried to eat small meals that consisted of vegetables, salads, beans, or just a piece of lean protein baked or grilled. I didn't get much into elaborate recipes or decadent meals. But I managed to find a few things to throw together and I put a genuine effort into creating a decent holiday dinner, because standing near the stove and the heat it gave off helped lessen the frostiness I felt all over my skin.

When I finished cooking, we sat down at the dining table in the great room to a meal of butternut squash soup sprinkled with nutmeg, rice topped with canned chicken that I sautéed with spices and a can of artichoke hearts, and a dessert of chocolate pudding I whipped up from a boxed pudding mix and a can of condensed milk. I even sprinkled a little cinnamon on top. It wasn't the best meal I'd ever had, but it wasn't the worst, either.

When we finished eating, Alex patted his mouth with a napkin. "Not too shabby, Ms. Wright. Maybe you should consider the idea that you've wasted your time on dance and you should've studied culinary arts instead."

I shot him an icy stare.

"That reminds me," he continued. "You haven't paid for your food here in a bit. I think you owe me a dance."

"You're still going to enforce that nonsense?"

"Of course. Why wouldn't I? And in that dress... It's perfect for a little performance."

Tiny freaking dancer.

"This dress is exactly why I shouldn't dance right now. I don't want to tear it or anything."

"Please, don't give me that bullshit. That's a well-made piece of clothing. Your dance costumes are made of what? Velcro, flour sacks, and glittery shit glued together by grunt workers? That dress would hold up better than cheap garbage any day."

"They're not garbage. My costumes are made with elastic materials that stretch, and—"

"Stop making excuses," he interrupted. "Like you'd give a rat's ass if that dress ripped, anyway. I'm not an idiot. Dance for me."

My hand clenched around my fork and my mouth pressed together in a tight line. *Not today*, I reminded myself. *No fighting him today*. I sighed, and then stood up with heavy reluctance and moved to the center of the room.

"Wait, over by the fireplace. I like how the firelight reflects off your body while you're wearing that."

My stomach turned at the leering inflection in his comment. Alex got up and walked over to sit in one of the armchairs by the fire, and I followed. I stood in the same spot again.

"Any requests?" I asked and then regretted it, worrying he might suggest a strip tease.

"Whatever you feel moved to do is fine by me," he said.

I sighed in relief. Then I touched the necklace at my throat as I thought. Ballet seemed most appropriate for the attire, but I didn't feel like doing ballet. I felt like expressing the frustration, and I sort of reveled in the idea of proving Alex wrong, stretching the limits of the dress. I would find some satisfaction in hearing it tear. So I chose a dark modern lyrical routine I remembered from a while back—one that included a few acro tricks.

"I have to stretch just a little for this one," I said.

Alex nodded and waited as I warmed up as fast as I could. It wasn't the best warm up ever, not just because I hurried through it, but also because my muscles were so cold from wearing the dress in the drafty lodge. But I lengthened my body, stretched my neck, torso, hamstrings, and back the best I could. And then I began.

I blocked everything out but the crackling of the fire, and it somehow accompanied my movements well. Burning in a visual way to accent my infuriation. This was a very different routine from the last one I performed for Alex. Lots of body extensions and poses, contorted at times—not the pretty little dancer he probably expected.

At one point I moved onto my stomach, and then rolled my weight forward onto my chest, balancing on my chest, throat, and chin as I hefted my lower body over my head. My feet came around to touch the back of my head for a moment. The dress felt restricted, pushed to a limit, but did not tear. I flattened out again, rolled over, and arched my back up, lifting myself into a sitting position with one leg extended. Then I moved into a back walkover that slid into a pose on my hands and knees, where I began to claw forward along the floor as if in bondage, spot on with how I felt. I held another acro pose, but the dress refused to rip.

When I finished, I stood up and straightened the skirt of the dress for a second before looking at Alex. He didn't look angry, but he didn't look pleased, either.

"Bravo," he said. His voice was flat and his eyes cold.

"Thank you. I guess you were right. The dress is well-made."

"You tried your best to prove me wrong on that, though, didn't you?"

"Maybe."

"Such appreciation for such a fine gift."

"I appreciate it more now."

"Is that so? So much that you'd like to scrape away into the night, into the freezing cold, while wearing it?" He picked up on the storytelling of dance more than I'd given him credit for.

"I didn't say that."

"You sure about that?"

I fidgeted with my hands. "Did you dislike my performance? You didn't give me any requests. You told me to do what I felt like doing."

He shrugged and sighed. "This is true. I guess I have myself to blame for that."

I brushed my hands over the skirt again, looking down and trying to think of what to say. "Really, Alex. What do you intend to do with me? Why are you keeping me here?"

He said nothing for a moment, and just gazed into the fire. "Live with you, and hope that you'll live with me, too."

"Forever? You just plan to keep me here with you forever?"

He had no response, and kept staring at the blaze. I felt the heat at my back, warming my cold skin.

"Alex," I said, and he looked up at me. "I'm not some puppy you can hold to the ground because you don't want it to escape." I felt like I had more to say, something more profound to add, but couldn't find the right words. I supposed it was all I really needed to say.

Alex sat quietly for a long time. So long that I felt awkward about standing there in front of him, and then even longer still that the discomfort passed and I felt empowered by it.

"I know," he whispered at last.

I waited a moment before responding. "And so what's the plan then?"

"We don't talk about that," he said, looking at the fire again, a sort of dazed expression in his eyes.

Who was he referring to with *we*? Him and me? Him and himself? I shuddered.

"It would be in your best interest to learn to like it here, Autumn."

I couldn't move for a long time. I knew what that meant. I knew he implied that I had two choices. Submit, or die. Alex couldn't go on with this struggle forever, either. He would grow tired of the chase. This was not a sustainable state for either of us. And I decided right then that this was it, I had to quit the half-ass resistance. I didn't think of it that way until now, as being so half-hearted. But all at once, I saw that it was. I waited on help to arrive for the majority of this journey. Help was not coming. I couldn't keep waiting. Before me existed three options out of this dilemma.

One: I escape. Obviously the most desirable prospect.

Two: I die. Unacceptable.

In the beginning, I thought these were the only possible paths, but now I allowed myself to realize there was one more option.

Three: I kill Alex. I *kill*... Alex.

I swallowed down the lump in my throat as the reality of these possibilities sank in, making everything feel surreal. Sure, I sliced at his face with a broken mug, but had I intended to kill him? To end his life? No, not really. I wasn't sure what I was doing all this time, once I had set foot on that decisive ground. It didn't matter, though. The time had arrived to make a watertight plan.

Alex grew tired of sitting there in silence and moved about the room for a few minutes before settling for another Christmas movie. He said nothing to me, expecting me to just come and join him.

After a bit I did so, deciding I could think about my plan as the film played out. I wanted to escape. But I knew I couldn't without Alex catching up to me. At least not without me severely wounding him or slowing him down first. I'd have to do something—try and find the sedative he'd used on me. And if that didn't work, injure him in some way. And then get out.

Get warm clothes and get out. Run to the house far off on the horizon, hopefully avoid wolves in the process, and get help.

Adrenaline coursed through my veins as I planned away in peace. I pulled the sofa blanket over me, but I couldn't keep the chill away. The leather of the couch felt so cold against my skin. This time, however, it felt like more than just the temperature cooling my bones. An iciness, a severance of something inside me hardened my cells.

After the movie, Alex rose and ruffled his hair. I stood up, too, unsure of how to proceed now that my mental direction was so focused. I wanted to seem compliant, unchanged. I did not want to give off the air of someone who schemed away into dark thoughts.

"I'm freezing, Alex. Can I please take a shower? God, a hot shower sounds so nice. The dress is pretty, but I'm so cold."

He looked at me for a second, and then nodded. "Fine. Whatever."

He led me upstairs and waited outside the bathroom door as I showered. It felt like paradise, like standing in a hot rain after being pulled from the arctic. I felt like I could stand in that cozy shower all evening and I'd never get quite warm enough. After a while I heard him pound on the door, and then it cracked open and his voice cut through the steam. *Go away!*

"Save a little hot water for me. I'm going to take one, too."

"Okay." I stood there for another thirty seconds or so, savoring every last drop, and then shut off the faucet. I dried off and slipped into some lounge clothes from my bag. It felt blissful to have warm clothes on again. I dried my hair, and then left the fogged bathroom with my bag.

"Where are the necklace and the dress?" Alex asked.

I lifted my bag in response. The dress was draped over the top. "The necklace is inside, so I don't lose it."

"Put them back on. You don't have to wear them forever, but it's still Christmas, and I enjoyed seeing you in them."

My mouth dropped open in protest. "But... I just got warmed up, and it's so cold."

"Put them back on."

My body cringed at the thought. My shoulders slumped. "Fine," I whispered. *I hate you.*

"I'm going to lock you in my bedroom while I shower, so you don't get into any trouble. Please be back in the dress by the time I'm done."

We walked to his bedroom, and then he left me alone. I heard the door lock from the outside. I exhaled a deep breath, and then reluctantly removed my clothes and slipped the dress back on again. I winced when the cold necklace touched my skin.

Then I got to work as fast as I could, riffling through the closet for anything I could find that would help me in an escape. I stuffed two sweatshirts into my bag. I still had my shoes in my sack, but I grabbed a thick pair of socks from a drawer to compensate for their lack of insulation. Then I found a hat and threw it in there, too. The knit of the hat was thin, but at least it had ear flaps. *Good enough, take it.* I didn't see any mittens or the like in the closet here, so I grabbed another pair of socks to keep my hands warm.

I looked at the small passage door, remembered that it was unlocked on both sides at the bottom now, and was just about to bolt through it and downstairs to escape when I heard the shower shut off in the bathroom. *Shit. Thanks for taking the shortest shower ever, Alex.* I stuffed everything down and zipped my bag, and then sat on it to flatten it a bit so that it wouldn't look any fuller than it had before. The warmth from my own shower already began to dissipate from my body with the damn dress on again, and my nostrils flared in anger. The cold itself—everything else aside—started to make me insane.

I tried to act natural when Alex came back in the room, wearing a thick collared rugby shirt and fresh jeans. A bit of moisture still clung to his hair, and he set his own bag down next to the bed on the side toward the door.

Why do you have to look good? You asshole. I loved you. God, I loved you. I hate you. I hate you so much for leaving. I shook the thoughts away.

"See, you look so nice in that," he said, appraising me. "I'm getting hungry again. You? Should we make something small to eat?"

"Sure. I could eat a little." An echo of our final evening on the train resonated in my mental plotting. I needed to stock up on a hearty meal to prepare for what might be ahead of me. At that point in time, I still hoped for rescue. Now I *knew* I needed to rely on my own resources, so I forced myself to conjure an appetite.

Alex wanted to move our stuff back to the master bedroom because he enjoyed the fireplace in there, so we took our bags down the hall, dropped them off, and then went down to the kitchen. Alex opened a can of chili. I didn't even like chili, and I was going to have to choke it down again. As he began heating it over the stove, I thought about the other things I saw in the cupboards while making our meal earlier.

"I'm super hungry, probably from the cold draft," I said. "Do you want some peanut butter on those crackers in the cabinet? I could spread some for us."

"Sure, sounds good. But how about you do your best to spread it with a spoon instead of a knife," Alex said as a statement rather than a question, and fetched me a spoon from the drawer.

I went to the cupboard and pulled out the peanut butter and crackers, as well as a bag of mixed nuts and an electrolyte sports drink in a small plastic container. Alex dished up the chili and then looked at the small spread I had in front of me.

"Stocking up for a famine?" he asked.

"Just hungry. I haven't been eating enough."

"You *are* on the pill, right?" he asked.

It took me a moment to catch his meaning. "Oh. Yeah, yes. I've missed a couple of days of them here and there because of... all of this. But I'm on it. Besides, I don't think cravings would set in quite that fast," I said, and my voice trailed off as I fell into an abyss of odd, sad, and disgusted thoughts.

I downed all of the sports drink, ate all of my chili, consumed as many handfuls of mixed nuts as I could, and ate five or six crackers with peanut butter on them. Compared to my usual diet, I was stuffed to the point that it felt ill, but I reminded myself this was to sustain me out in the freezing temperatures.

We sat by the damaged Christmas tree for a little while before bed. My insides rocked in turmoil, like a tiny ship thrashing at sea. I wanted to weep for my mom, who was no doubt in hysterics. I trembled with terror, though I tried to hide it. The next twenty-four hours had to be it. One way or another, this had to end. I hoped I wouldn't have to flee into the night when the temperature was even colder than the day, but if I had to, I would. Somehow I had to get the sedatives out of Alex's bag while he slept, and the times I'd attempted a stunt similar to that had offered less than ideal results. I also considered what I might have to do if forced—breaking a window and jumping from out of the bedroom if cornered. I wanted to sustain my dance career before, but now that I comprehended how much my life was at stake. Given the choice between the two, preserving my life obviously won.

We wandered upstairs to the master bedroom. I went to grab some pajamas from my bag, but Alex told me to wait.

"Just for the night. Let me just enjoy it for the night. Tomorrow you can wear whatever you want," he said, eyeing me in the dress.

I gaped at him. "But you'll be asleep. What does it matter?"

"Just, humor me. I love the idea of you sleeping next to me. Wearing that."

I stood there staring at him in clear fury, but he ignored me. He put on his own pajamas and crawled into bed, and then patted the spot next to him. I sighed, tried not to scream, and got in, too—pulling the blankets up over me as tight as I could. *I'm going to burn this damn dress the first chance I get.* Alex wrapped an arm around me and kissed the back of my shoulders. *Get your lips the hell off of me!* He brushed my hair aside and kissed me a few more times, but I guess he picked up on my vibe and didn't feel like pushing it. *Fall asleep, asshole. Just go to sleep, so I can make you sleep longer—so much longer.* It must have taken him an hour to go to sleep. I remained there, staring out into the night sky, waiting... waiting... waiting. I watched the reflection of the fire flickering against the windowpane.

When at last I felt confident he was in a deep sleep, I slithered out of that bed with more stealth than any of the previous attempts. *I'm becoming an expert at this.*

I set my own bag close by so I could grab it in a hurry if needed. Then I moved to his bag and searched through it painstakingly slow. So slow. *Where are you, stupid drugs?* I investigated each item in the weak light of the fire, squinting to see what it was. Finally, *finally*, I found a bottle. I lifted the prescription bottle, read the name of some drug I didn't recognize, and realized this must be it. It had to be the sedative. I glanced back at Alex to make sure he still slept. *Sleeping beast.* Then I raised the white-topped orange bottle up to the light of the embers in the corner to see how many pills were inside.

It was empty.

I bit my lip hard and let all of my antagonism contort my face into pure terrible irony. For the love of all that was holy, the bottle was empty. *End this!* My heart sank, because I searched again to make sure I had not missed another bottle or plastic baggy, but I knew I hadn't. And I knew there was only one other option in there, an object my hand grazed over a minute before. When I found no other evidence of something containing any kind of drug, I went back to that object. I sighed, closed my eyes for a moment, and mustered the toughest, darkest, most ruthless part of me. *End this, Autumn. End it now.* I swallowed, opened my eyes, wrapped my hand around the handle, and pulled out the knife.

CHAPTER SEVENTEEN

I held the knife in my hand for a moment and just looked at it, pondering my options. I could inflict a major wound on Alex, but that would either just kill him gradually, or result in another bashing of my head against the stairs. More probable, this time around, it would end up with me dead. The other option I did not even want to put into thoughts, but they appeared there anyway. *Kill your best friend.* The perverse paradox: it was the option I knew I had to select.

Kill him, Autumn. You have to. I felt the lump in my throat, the chill of the night against my skin, the silkiness of the dress fabric against my lower back and the front of my thighs as I crouched there. I had to—I had to do it. This was it. I took a deep, trembling breath, and then rose. I could feel the soft heat of the dying fire behind me, too faint to warm me much at all. I moved like an apparition toward the bed, and looked at Alex as he slept, the knife in my hand. *It's his life, or yours*, I told myself. *His life, or yours. His life, or yours.*

I eased around the side of the bed, feeling sick to my stomach, feeling like my feet were not attached to the floor. Feeling like I was about to kill myself, too—forever tarnishing myself with the mark of a murderer. One of those decisions in life one cannot undo. *Go there, and you're never, ever coming back.* I'd never again not be a murderer. *His life, or yours.*

Creeping onto a bed never happened more silently than it did at that moment. I gripped the handle of the knife so tight that my hand ached and sweat. I had to strain to even hear the gentle swoosh from the skirt as I straddled myself on top of Alex. My arm shook, and I held my forearm out parallel to me, in a position to slit him across the throat. *Do it.*

I was going to do it. For a moment in time, there was no hesitation. Just the wicked part of me that would do something like this if necessary. It frightened me to realize that she was in there. Good God, she was actually in there. *It's Alex.*

And then I saw him, sleeping at peace, and it wasn't Alex holding me hostage anymore. For a second I saw My Alex. *My Alex.* And a memory of us as kids running after the ice cream truck surfaced out of nowhere, hitting me like a punch to the gut. I saw his boyish smile turn to me with ice cream around his mouth. Following right after was a memory of sitting with him at my high school graduation party, laughing about something I couldn't remember, as we drank the Coke we'd slipped a little booze into. The images came so fast I couldn't stop them. I thought of him last summer, when we were home on vacation from school, him taking me out for a day at the beach and joking about all the sand in his crotch as we packed up our things to leave. His eyes had been bright and innocent looking as he'd shaken his swim trunks and smiled at me.

My free hand suddenly came up to cover my mouth, and my chin quivered. My vision went blurry with tears. This was Alex, broken, yes. But it was Alex, and I was about to end his life. He needed help. But he was Alex... A boy who had a place in my heart my entire life. I held my breath, holding as hard as I could, like a feeble dam against a flooding river. I couldn't hold it all back, though. One small sob slipped through my mouth, and Alex's eyes shot open. He did not move, he just stared at me—one second sleeping, the next wide-awake—as I straddled him holding a knife to his throat. I still held my other hand over my mouth, and realized my tears were now a detriment to my position, obscuring my vision. I blinked them away and they fell to my cheeks, one or two of them dripping down onto Alex's shirt.

"Autumn," he whispered.

Oh, how I'd fucked up. How marvelously I had really fucked this up. In an instant his hand gripped my wrist holding the knife, squeezing until I dropped it. Somehow I twisted my wrist out of his grasp, and was off the bed faster than I thought possible. I snatched up my bag and ran for the door, but realized it was locked. Thank goodness it was the master bedroom, not his bedroom where he'd installed the door with the key lock. I fumbled for a moment with my shaking hands to unlock the knob.

As I grabbled at it, I heard Alex rush off of the bed and come after me. Just as I unlatched the door and swung it open, the blade of the knife sliced through my skin on my back, a line of searing pain along my left shoulder blade. I let out an agonized noise, and swung the door open, stepped halfway into the hall pulling it with me, and then I whipped the door open again to smack Alex in the face and chest with it. It hit him hard, and with an already damaged nose from my previous attack, it must have hurt like hell. While he was distracted, I kicked him as hard as I could in the stomach. I could feel the impact, and knew it would knock the wind out of him for a moment.

I started for the staircase, but changed my course at the last second and dashed into Alex's bedroom with the secret passage door. I hung onto my bag like it was a part of my own body. I tried to be silent as I opened the small door and slipped inside. I was about to pull it shut behind me, but heard Alex coming my way, so I started down the black passageway staircase. I couldn't see anything, and tripped, tumbling all the way to the bottom. Stair after stair knocked against me, a couple of times thumping against the knife wound on my shoulder. I bit my lip to avoid crying out, and tasted blood. Any chance of this secret passage actually *offering* me a secret passage vanished with that loud tumble.

I could hear Alex entering his bedroom upstairs just beyond the small door at the top. I picked myself up, limping at first—wanting to cry in agony—and ran for the bottom door. For a second I panicked and wondered if I'd just imagined I unlocked it from the outside. *If you only imagined unlocking it, you're dead. Dead within the next few minutes.*

I sprinted so fast I ran into the wall when I got there, but I ignored that pain and searched the wall for the door. I found it and pushed it open just as Alex began running down the stairs behind me. I bolted out of the door and yanked it shut as I heard him reaching the bottom of the stairs. My fingers fumbled, but I slid the lock on the outside of the door closed, hoping it would buy me a few extra moments.

I stepped back quickly as I heard him running for the door. He yelled my name. And then the door rattled as he threw his body weight against it. My eyes widened and I took off running for the opposite side of the great room, toward the south wing. The door took a beating again, and I glanced back to see if the lock would hold. It wouldn't restrain him forever—it was just a small piece of metal. But it sounded like Alex judged it to be a waste of time, and I heard his footsteps carrying him back up the passage staircase to come out through the main hallway.

I paused for one second, realizing I needed a hiding spot to at least get on some kind of winter gear before attempting to break through a window. But I also wanted to throw him off, so

I grabbed the closest thing to me, some decorative stone figurine, and when I heard him exiting his bedroom into the dark hallway upstairs, I threw it toward the kitchen. I aimed well through the large doorway, and it hit a cabinet or a countertop, something in the kitchen, with a loud crack. Then I ran without a sound down the hall straight ahead, where the storage closet with the Christmas bin was kept. I hurried into one of the guest bedrooms, glanced around, and slid under the bed, pulling my bag with me. The wooden floor felt ice cold against my skin, and it was a tight fit under the bed frame.

I stopped to listen for a moment, my ears pricking like a wild animal's trying to detect a predator nearby. I could just make out Alex's soft footfalls down the stairs to the great room. He tried to be quiet now, which made his approach even more terrifying. It took a lot of my energy to control myself from going into a full nervous breakdown.

I had to be quiet, but I also couldn't waste time. I pulled a sweatshirt from the bag and somehow managed to get it over my head and slide my arms through the sleeves in the confined space under the bed. I stopped and listened again. It sounded like Alex was maybe in the kitchen, so I hurried to get pants on, along with the thick socks. I stuffed the extra pair of socks in the pocket of my jeans to use for my hands once I got outside, and rolled up the hat and stuffed it in the waist of my pants, under the skirt. I didn't have time to get the dress off before layering on the winter clothes. I took hold of my shoes, pulled them out of the bag, and slid myself in silence out from under the bed on the side away from the door. As fast as possible, I slipped the shoes on, and then slid under the bed again. My shoulder felt like it was painted with a strip of lava where Alex had knifed me, burning and oozing.

I heard him moving down the hallway in which I hid, and my pulse roared in my ears. I had to think of a way to move, to get out of here, and into an area he had already looked for me, because eventually he would check this very spot. I needed to slide past him, into a room he already swept through. Then when he came to look in here, I might be able to get to a window to make my escape.

So I listened. I lay on my stomach, with my head facing the door, and heard him enter the room to my left—the office den. Then he whipped open the storage closet, as if hoping to surprise me, shut it again, and moved into the other guest bedroom across the hall from the den. I squeezed my eyes shut, fought back the urge to be sick, and moved out from under the bed more lithe than the world's finest prima ballerina. I almost left the bag behind, but then realized he would catch onto my plan if he saw it under here, so I brought it with me. I bit my lip and winced from the cut my teeth had left in it before. *Now or never*, I told myself.

I took a deep breath, stood up, and skimmed the wall of the hallway. Pausing for a second, I heard Alex opening the closet door in the bedroom he currently searched, and then I continued into the den to my left. I stayed near the wall and moved around to the far side of a bookshelf, hiding behind it as I stood there to reassess my situation for a second. Alex padded slowly into the hallway, and then into the bedroom I'd just been in. *I'd be dead now. This is where I would be caught, and I would die.* I felt the wetness of my blood on the back of the sweatshirt, and swallowed.

"Sweet girl..." Alex called. "Come out, sweet girl. Come out and stay with me, won't you?" There was an eeriness to his sentiment, like he meant something so sinister I didn't even want to imagine it.

"We've had a rough go of it, haven't we, Auttie?" he continued, and at once it was My Alex talking again. As if it wasn't the same person who spoke two seconds earlier.

"But look, we're going to get it worked out. Just trust me, and stop running. We're going to get it worked out."

Two people, there were two different people inside him. Three people in this house. I swallowed down the acid climbing my throat. I worried a little about the condition of my heart, it beat so hard against my chest.

I looked around the den, and then moved fast to the desk. It had an elegant wooden front panel on it, so I could crouch underneath and remain unseen as long as he didn't come back in here to check this spot again. He moved down the hall to the bathroom in this wing of the lodge. I heard the shower curtain rings as he tugged the curtain back in a swift motion. I heard another cabinet open, and then shut. Then he came back down the hall, and I closed my eyes and held my breath as he passed the den.

Alex continued back out to the great room and went to check some other area of the house. I took a few moments to breathe, trying to slow my heart rate and calm myself. Then I used the opportunity to readjust some of my clothing, and again noticed the pain of the wound on my back. The strap of the dress chaffed against it here and there, so after listening for Alex's presence again and deciding it was safe for the moment, I removed the sweatshirt. I shivered violently. I pulled the dress off over my head, careful not to brush the fabric too much against the still-bleeding gash, and then put the sweatshirt back on again. I stuffed the dress into the bag to hide it.

There was a large window facing out of the den toward the front of the house. It wasn't floor-to-ceiling like the one in the great room, but large enough that I could make out the far end of the long driveway if I got up on my knees and moved my head out from under the desk. The night sky looked cloudless, and I saw the moon. Even though it was just less than a half circle, it shined so bright I could see the outline of the road in the distance. Snow still blanketed the ground, but much of it had melted away. Good news for me. But also good news for Alex if a chase ensued.

I stayed crouched there under the desk for what felt like an eternity. I continued to listen to Alex move about the lodge, and I thought for a while about slipping into another room to change my location again. But after a bit, I heard him slump down in an armchair by the fire, perhaps trying to wait me out.

Apparently Alex was good at waiting. I didn't hear him move all night. I wished that I could get up and peek in on him, to see if he fell asleep. *Don't do it, he's still awake. You know he's awake.* I imagined him out there, staring at the fireplace, holding that knife. Just waiting.

I huddled down, wrapping my arms around my knees, gazing out at the stars. Wind blew in, rattling the windowpane. Even in the sweatshirt and jeans, I shivered from the draft. At moments I thought about smashing through the window during the night, and just risking it. *Go ahead, just break the window and run for your life.* But something about daylight seemed more survivable. Not just the temperature, but also the sobriety of daytime. It felt less possible that Alex would kill me during the day. At night... Well, all of the worst things in the universe seemed possible at night.

Though I thought there was no way I could, I ended up half-way dozing off for a bit sometime right before dawn. I awoke with a start when I heard Alex get up and stomp around again. At last his patience wore itself threadbare, and he lashed about the house again, knocking things over, and opening and slamming shut closet doors. I went from sleep, to paralyzing fear within seconds. From the light outside, I could tell it was early morning. I heard him coming down the hall again where I hid, and I held my breath. More slamming of doors. I heard the bed that concealed me last night shift as if he kicked it or moved it somehow to look under it. He stomped back out into the great room again, and he yelled loud enough that I'd be able to hear him from any hiding spot in all of Tempest Lodge.

"Go ahead! Keep hiding like a sniveling little rodent! You'll starve that way, though. Every bit of the food in this house will be under lock and key, so enjoy the feeling of famine, cupcake. And if you're thinking about somehow getting out and making a run for it..." He trailed off and let out a wicked laugh. "Go right ahead! Be my guest. I'd almost enjoy watching you try. The temperature out there right now? You know what it is? It's fucking negative twenty degrees Fahrenheit. Did you hear that? Negative twenty! You'll have hypothermia before you even *see* another house."

I looked outside and felt the concern on my face. After sitting on the floor all night, with the weather testing against the windows, I already felt like I was freezing to death. Maybe he was bluffing. *He's lying.* But the sky was clear last night and this morning, and when the sky is clear in winter, that usually means more frigid temperatures. No atmospheric blanket to hold the heat to the Earth. *He's not lying.*

"If you're going to head out there, why don't you strike one of your elegant dancer poses for me? That way, when you freeze to death, you'll be my very own pretty little statue."

Disgusted shock contorted my face. There was a minute of silence, and then I heard his footsteps moving upstairs. After a few more minutes, I heard the shower turn on.

Again, I wondered if he tried to deceive me by turning on the shower, thinking I'd come out of my hiding spot with a false sense of safety. I did not give into it until I strained and heard actual movement in the shower—a bottle being set down here, the shifting of falling water there. Then I eased myself out from under the desk. My whole body ached, and my joints felt stiff after sitting in a stooped position all night. The skin on my shoulder blade blazed and the dried blood tugged when I moved. I hoped it wasn't a very deep wound. But if I didn't get something on it soon, it could get infected. I needed to clean it. Fear surrounding the remoteness of our location trickled down my spine yet again at the thought.

When I stood up, I continued to move in hushed progress, and watched the door. I peeked into the hall to make sure Alex wasn't standing right outside the den, and I breathed a sigh of relief when I heard him moving things around upstairs in the shower. I turned back toward the den window and walked over to it. *I can do this. God, negative twenty out there*, I thought. But I shook it off, and told myself I could do it. I looked down at the ground. It might hurt a little, but I could manage it, only five or six feet. Maybe seven at worst. I took a deep breath, braced myself, and then glanced around for something to break the window with. At first, nothing stood out to me. The desk was bare, since it was pretty much stupid to have a desk up here at an isolated vacation home anyway. There were books, but I doubted my ability to break a window with them.

I turned back to the window in an effort to gauge how thick it looked, and that's when I caught sight of a car. The first car I laid eyes on since arriving here, barreling down the road far off in the distance. I leaned forward as it traveled closer, heading for the bend in the road near the lodge. I had to get outside! I had to get out there now! If someone passing by could see me, maybe they would stop to help a frantic young woman running toward the highway. My eyes darted around the room again, searching for something to break glass, and I began to panic that the car would be gone before I could get outside.

Then I remembered the boat oar in the great room above the bookshelf. I ran, giving up on trying to be quiet. Before going for the oar I saw the stone globe on the stand and tried to lift it, but had underestimated it weight. It was too heavy for me to lift and swing or throw effectively.

So I bolted for the dining area to grab a chair to stand on. I thought for a second about using the chair itself to break the glass, but the legs looked too thin, like they might break before the window would. I needed that thick oar. I hefted the chair over to the bookcase, and when I sat it down two things happened at once. I looked out the main giant window, past the mangled artificial Christmas tree, and realized the car was turning onto the driveway leading up to the lodge. I squinted and discovered it was not just a car, but a police car. And then I heard the shower upstairs shut off, and the shower curtain whip open.

CHAPTER EIGHTEEN

My heart sped with both hope and with terror. I moved that chair into place as fast as a star streaking across the sky, and then I was up on it, reaching for the boat oar. I had to strain, and even then it remained a little out of my grasp. So I climbed onto the bookshelf with half of my bodyweight. The chair wobbled beneath the foot holding me there. With my other foot I elevated myself just enough to reach the oar, but as I yanked on it, I realized it was hooked to the wall in such a way that I couldn't quite get it loose. I heard a few things banging around upstairs, and I glanced out the window. The squad car moved so slow up the driveway, aggravatingly unhurried. As if it were keeping a distance on purpose, being cautious.

I heard the bathroom door open and Alex's footsteps coming down the hall toward the stairway. I released all prudence and climbed onto the bookshelf, putting all of my bodyweight on it and wrenching the oar, trying to lift it over the hooks it rested on. It was as if it resided there for so long that paint on either the oar or the hooks had caused it to stick in place. The bookshelf was a sturdy thing, but not quite stable enough. It leaned forward in my direction, flirting with the idea of toppling over.

"Shit, come on!" I said with a grunt, and just then I yanked the oar free over the hooks. I fell backward, at first catching myself in a balanced position on the chair, but then the chair fell backward to the floor. I landed on my feet, but the momentum knocked me on my back. I had the oar, though, and I was up on my feet again by the time Alex made it halfway down the stairs. I looked up to see the bookshelf leaning forward, and I didn't hesitate. I ran for the giant window and swung the oar back like a baseball bat, and then whipped it forward against the glass. I felt the blow through my shoulders, radiating pain through my left one in particular where I was knifed and still had the bruise from the blow of the fire extinguisher. The glass shattered into a massive spider web, but there was no hole to escape through yet.

A thunderous noise from behind me followed, and my back went rigid, startled, although I shouldn't have been. I took a second to glance back and see the entire bookshelf on the floor, books splayed around it. Alex stood at the bottom of the stairs, blocked momentarily by the bookshelf, and his eyes looked as if they were from some evil place. I didn't want to turn my back on him again, but I did, swinging the oar once more and shattering the glass into a rain of daggers and diamonds.

The gust of arctic wind that blew inside took my breath away. I hit the window once more to widen the gap, and I looked down to see the ground below. The snow melted enough that I could see some of the stones showing through. I heard Alex running; it sounded as if it were in the direction of the front door. Without thinking, I dropped the oar and jumped out of the window, scraping myself on a couple of shards before hitting the ground. The jolt that went through my ankles hurt, but I was up and running within a second or two. I heard the front door swing open, and I looked back to see Alex coming after me with something long in his hands. A golf club—the bastard stopped at the coat closet long enough to grab an iron before coming out after me.

The rapid crunch of our feet on the ground made my ears prick. My lungs tried to keep up against my heart rate, and against the negative twenty degree air. Alex hadn't bluffed about the temperature, at least it felt like it could be that cold. As I ran I tried to wave at the squad car to get their attention. God, I was so close. The car picked up speed, but the driveway stretched such a long distance, so long. I heard footsteps and glanced back to see Alex only about two yards behind me. He was so fast.

I tried to scream out for help, but the cold air... the adrenaline... the pace of my pulse. I couldn't seem to get a sound out. My feet slipped on ice, but I kept my balance and kept running. The car wasn't going to make it in time, though. I could feel him on me, just a couple of feet away. And then I saw the passenger door to the police car fly open, and a figure bolted out and came running toward me, as if trying to stop the scene from happening.

Too late, though. Too late. The golf club came down and around, swiping like a wrecking ball against my right ankle.

In the first second, the shock of pain was in my right shoulder. Maybe from a jerking movement on my part, maybe from some kind of related pressure point. But then the shattering exploded inside my ankle, breaking into a million pieces like the glass of the window. One second I had an ankle—solid bone, solid forms. The next, Alex destroyed it, turning durable bone into crushed fragments with nothing to hold onto. I fell to my hands and knees against ice and stones and snow. Everything went white, more pallid than just the snow, blinding white from anguish. I scrambled forward, hearing the golf club slice through the air again with a hollow kind of sound, and a familiar voice met my ears. The voice of someone other than Alex yelling, "No!"

I turned over and saw Alex holding the club over his head, ready to bring it down on me again. I rolled out of the way just in time as the head of the golf club smashed the ground next to me, right where I had been. I saw a decorative stone about a foot from me, the size of a softball. I grabbed it, having to yank for a second to free it from its frosted spot on the ground, and then chucked it at Alex. If he were any farther away, I probably would have missed; but his proximity was a lucky thing in that moment. The stone smashed him on the side of the face. Not hard enough to knock him down, but long enough to halt him for a moment.

I reeled myself over onto my hands and knees again, and clambered forward. I tried to get up, using my good leg for almost all of my body weight. But even the lightest feather touch on my bad foot brought me down on all fours again, and I vomited right there on the snow from the pain.

"Autumn!" the familiar voice yelled. I looked up, and realized the person who had jumped out of the passenger seat of the police car was Sam. *Wait... Sam? Sam!* I computed the thought for a second, and then my body rocked with heat and dizziness, and I thought I'd pass out from the agony in my ankle, radiating up my leg. I forced myself to keep moving, crawling onto the cobbled path.

A second later, Sam was at my side, lifting me up with a shoulder under me, holding all of my weight. My body went limp. There was some other kind of shouting. I looked up and saw two police officers, navy jackets and navy police hats with a yellow band. One had brunette hair and fair skin and pointed a gun just past Sam and me, yelling at Alex to stop, yelling to get back.

The other had dark skin and moved cautiously toward Sam and myself, keeping his eyes ahead on the situation. I looked over my shoulder and saw Alex, a trickle of blood running down his face where the rock had struck him, as it happened, in the same spot that I'd left a gash on him before.

"It reopened the wound," I mumbled, my head lolling a bit.

Alex stepped forward slowly, and still clutched the golf club in an offensive position. He glared at me. Alex's face turned into that of someone I did not recognize, all of My Alex evaporating into the dryness of the winter air.

"Alex, stop! Just stop! Calm down," Sam said.

I still felt limp, but then adrenaline flooded my system, bringing some of my alertness back.

"It's going to be okay, Alex. Just calm down, okay?" Sam continued.

I felt frozen aside from the fire burning its way up my leg. I felt detached from my body, and yet the pain was like nothing I'd ever experienced before. My face twisted from the misery, and a freezing wind bit at my skin.

"Sir, put the weapon down," the police officer with the gun said, easing closer. His thick Canadian accent rung in my ears. He continued to hold the gun on Alex. Alex continued to glower at me.

"Come on, get back," the other cop said in a hushed tone to Sam and me. He held something in his hand I didn't recognize when I glanced back at him—sort of the shape of a gun, but boxier.

"Alex, come on. Calm down," Sam said.

I could feel Sam pulling me toward the police officer and the squad car, down the cobbled path.

Alex shifted his gaze to Sam then. "She's mine," he said. "All this work, and you're just going to take her away. Just easy like that, like everything else for you, damn golden boy. Just going to take her like your own little precious doll. So easy for you, huh? Like every other thing in life."

"You're not making any sense, Alex. Just take a breath," Sam said.

"Sir, lower your weapon," the police officer with the gun said.

Alex took another step forward.

"Lower your weapon! If you don't lower your weapon we will have to disarm you," he said.

Alex took one more step forward, and then the police officer's voice turned into a commanding shout.

"Stop! Lower your weapon!" Alex took another step forward, a little faster this time, and then one more.

The crack of the gun going off was so loud it made my ears ring, and its echo sounded through the open winter landscape. My whole body startled at the sound, and my head whipped over to look at Alex. I expected for a second to see him dead on the ground, that quick. But he wasn't. Alex looked down at his leg, where a bullet wound left a macabre hole in his pants, and blood began seeping down, wetting the fabric. The police officer hit him on what looked like the edge of a thigh. It didn't seem real, seeing the blood. The blow made Alex stumble back a little, but he still held onto the golf club.

"Adams! You do not fire your gun unless all options have been exhausted!" the cop with the darker skin shouted to the other.

Alex lifted the club again, shaking but enraged, and stumbled forward a step or two. He swung the club as Sam pulled me back, and it missed my face by a few feet. I heard a strange sound to the side of me, and then a thin cord shot out, hitting Alex on the lower part of his rib cage. I looked back and forth, watching the officer holding the strange device connected to the cord, and then back at Alex as he jolted. A Taser gun—my brain computed a second later what was happening, as I glanced from the cop back to Alex again. The sound... I'll never get that sound out of my head. The rapid clicking. Alex's chest lifted in a thump and his face contorted. His body jerked back and he slipped.

"No!" Sam and I screamed at the same time, because we both saw it happening before the actual impact occurred.

But it happened too fast. Alex's body weight, combined with the force of the volts from the Taser throwing him backward, shoved him onto one of the wooden spikes that lined the cobbled path. It went through him too easily. Alex, like anyone else close to me, was supposed to be invincible in my still-juvenile brain. In a logical sense, I knew people died; but it seemed impossible that they really would, especially like this. Alex's body broke as easily as my ankle, though. The wooden spike ventured through the inside of him and came up to tell the daylight all about it, slick with gore as its souvenir.

I watched for a second as his body continued to writhe from the Taser, making the ghastly sight of the spike become even more gruesome. Then I quickly turned away in revulsion, because it was terrible, and because I didn't believe it was true. The rapid clicking stopped, and I heard the cops mutter a few curse words. I moved, again to my hands and knees and crawled a foot closer to Alex. I tried to whisper his name, but nothing came out. Sam was at Alex's side then, his words of shock turning into a kind of sob, as his doctor hands fluttered around looking for something to do. But there was nothing to do. Steam rose from Alex—from his mouth, from his wounds. I thought I heard Alex mumble an apology to Sam, and then after just a gurgled noise, he was gone.

Broken Alex was gone.
And My Alex was gone.

CHAPTER NINETEEN

A strange lag of time bridged the gap between Alex leaving us and further help arriving. The police officer who fired the gun stared at the scene with one hand over his mouth in shock, and then he spoke into some kind of radio unit on his shoulder. Through my haze I noticed how young he looked, perhaps a rookie. Fear painted his face. Whether it was from what he witnessed, or from the repercussions he might endure, I didn't know.

Sam huddled over Alex, murmuring things. Silent tears flowed down my cheeks. Sam brushed Alex's hair back off of his forehead, and closed his eyes for him. I couldn't make out everything Sam said, but there were words of love in there, and he repeated Alex's name many times.

After a minute, the older police officer who had held the Taser helped Sam up, coaxing him away from the body. Sam did not want to leave Alex, and I did not want to see the full picture of the destruction when Sam no longer blocked part of my view.

It felt a little like the night I boarded the train. Fragments of time vanished from my memory. I thought I could remember Sam trying to comfort me before the ambulance came, stroking my hair, saying things that I couldn't concentrate on. An ambulance arrived, and paramedics lifted me onto a stretcher.

Sam had to stay behind to be questioned, and a different police officer rode in the ambulance and tried to pull coherent answers out of me. The physical shock wore off by the time we arrived at the closest hospital. In my writhing anguish a doctor ordered a painkiller so strong that it knocked me out. Somewhere in the mix I was taken in for surgery on my ankle. When I woke up, feeling sick and groggy, a doctor came in and tried to explain things to me. I missed parts of the details, but got the gist of it. There were pins in my foot and ankle, metal connections holding things together.

"We had to clean some of the bone fragments," he said. "There were a lot of small fragments floating around. What we did today will help build back a basic foundation, but you're going to need at least one more surgery before your foot is even close to normal, Ms. Wright."

I stared at his hospital ID tag, and then up at his hair, and at the lines on the mocha skin of his forehead.

"Another surgery?" I repeated.

"Yes, at least one."

"Close to normal."

"Well, yes. You may end up with a limp. But you have good muscle tone, and people can pull off some amazing things if they put their mind to it. With the right care and physical therapy, you may be able to walk just fine in a relatively short amount of time."

"Walking. Close to normal, in regards to... walking," I whispered.

In one fell swoop, Alex had ended the dance career that I'd spent my life building. I stared at the wall, nearly catatonic, for what felt like hours.

Mom and Tim were there during my hospital stay. Mom cried an incessant stream of tears of rage, gratitude, grief, and emotions I was sure I couldn't even comprehend. At one point, I heard Camille in the hallway outside my hospital room, and my mother consoling her. It sounded like she wanted to see me, but for a multitude of reasons couldn't bring herself to enter my room. Then she tried again, and broke down. Mom told her it was all right, that she didn't need to push this. I didn't even want to think about what Camille was going through. For a fleeting minute I imagined her despair, her heartache, her guilt, and maybe even the blame she assigned to me. I didn't know for sure. I didn't want to know. I couldn't deal with Camille's turmoil, too.

When my foot was elevated in a firm brace, and the drugs in my system settled into a balance of pain relief and lucidity, Sam came up to see me. At first he waited outside the door as he gave my mom another minute to spend talking to me and brushing my hair back with her hand.

"Autumn, I would have died," she murmured, tears in her eyes. "I would have died, too, if anything happened to you."

"I know, Mom. But I'm okay, alright? I'm alive. I'm okay, I'm okay, I'm okay." I repeated the phrase too many times, and knew I was trying to convince myself of it.

"Thank God. My sweet baby," she said, leaning forward to hug me again, holding me tight. "I'll let Sam see you now. He... did a lot to help, sweetie," she whispered, and then let go of our embrace.

I looked up at her, wanting more of an explanation.

"He did everything he could. He was in a panic about you."

I lifted my brow in surprise.

She kissed my cheek. "I'm just going to get Tim and go down to the cafeteria to see what kind of awful hospital food we can find," she said.

I nodded. She looked as if she didn't want to leave the room, afraid to let me out of her sight for even a second. But finally she released me, patting Sam on the shoulder as she passed him in the doorway. Sam came in, pulling a chair up next to my bedside, and we sat alone in my room. His face was grief-stricken. He looked a mess. Sam ran a hand through his hair and then wiped it over his face. He looked like he had wept for hours, looked like he was coming apart at the seams. His buttoned shirt seemed disheveled.

"I know, you probably never will," he started, and took a shaking breath. "But I hope that you'll forgive me, Autumn... I tried. You have to know..." He drew in another unsteady breath. "I tried so damn hard. I had an idea. When I got your messages," he said, and ran a hand through his hair again.

Sam sat up straight, uneasy, and then leaned forward again. "We went to the police. But then in the first couple of days they were slow to do anything. And I remembered something a day or two after he took you. I remembered him saying something a long time ago. Like, years and years ago, when we were just kids visiting the lodge, about how he was going to steal you away and take you up here." His voice choked a bit, and he cleared it. "It sounded far-fetched, you know. Like he was joking. How the hell would you ever take something like that seriously, from a kid to another kid?" Sam wiped a hand over his face.

"But then I finally got them to track where the phones were, where the texts were coming from when they were sent, and I knew it was exactly what he was doing. I knew you guys had to be up here. And I couldn't get them to help fast enough." His eyes welled up.

I felt my own eyes welling with tears, too.

"And then the damn storm of the century hits," he said, and lifted his hands in exasperation. "It blew through the whole region. I was going to drive up here myself. I was starting to feel so desperate. But the conditions were terrible. People couldn't get anywhere. We couldn't even get cars out of the driveway." He trembled a little, and I put my hand on his forearm.

"I saw it, I know," I said. "I know. It knocked the power out... for a while." My voice trailed into a weak finish.

Sam ran the back of his hand across his eyes to dry them. "I failed you. I failed you, and I failed Alex. And I'm sorry. But I tried, Autumn. Please, at least know that I tried."

"I thought you'd abandoned me for a little while there," I said.

"Never," he said. His face was stoic. "Never."

We were quiet for a while, and Sam laid his head down on the side of my bed. It felt like an offering of humility or regret. I couldn't blame him for not being able to get there sooner, and knowing that he did everything he could, my heart broke for him. Sam lost his brother, and had to witness it happen. He carried guilt he didn't need to carry.

I put my hand on the back of his head, running it through his brown hair. It felt strange to do something so personal, to touch him like that, but touching someone who was not out to harm me—someone who had tried to help me—felt like a different kind of anesthetic. One I needed, but that the hospital drugs could not help me with.

Sam nodded toward my ankle. "Are you in pain? Do you need the nurse to come and administer something for it?" His voice was still drunk with grief and regret.

"Physically, not too much right now," I said, and then tears began streaming down my face in such masses that I couldn't contain them or wipe them away fast enough.

"It's over, though. It's over."

Sam knew what I meant. He nodded in consolation and leaned forward to hold me while I cried. My dream of being a dancer, everything I ever wanted from the time I was a child, Alex stole from me. He stole so much more from me, but it was the most tangible thing I could label at that moment. While drowning in the middle of the sea, departing the sinking ship and establishing a life raft were my first concerns. Getting through the waves and back to shore would have to come later.

CHAPTER TWENTY

The first weeks that followed my rescue seemed to be a time of just taking one breath, followed by another. Each step back to the world of the living, and each step toward burying the event—marking it with a solemn memorial on the disrupted ground of my psyche—took considerable effort. There was the physical aspect: healing from the first surgery that left my ankle full of metal. I also had stitches for the gash over my left shoulder blade, and a round of antibiotics for both.

Four days after my rescue, they transferred me to a hospital in Chicago, Sam's hospital by chance, where I had to stay another handful of days. Sam only returned to work the last few days I was there, but he came to my room every chance he got, bringing me food and making sure the doctors and nurses assigned to me were on top of my pain medication. Sometimes he simply sat next to my bed looking dazed. I took to running my hand through his hair a few times if my drugs were strong enough, or if he looked especially despondent. When I was discharged they sent me home with a wheel chair, and a set of crutches for later use.

The police found my bag at the crime scene. I'd dropped it in the chaos of trying to escape the house, and after examining it for evidence, they returned it to me. I finally opened it after it sat on an end table for a few days. The first thing my eyes fell upon was the dress. I brushed my hand over it, trying to decipher if all of it really happened the way I remembered. There was still blood on the back of the dress from where Alex had cut me.

"Mom, can you please start a fire in the fireplace?" I asked, still staring at the dress.

She just nodded and did so without asking any questions. I wheeled over to the fire once it was in full blaze, a little repulsed by the sight of a fire itself, and threw the dress into it. Mom stood back, her mouth trembling. I wasn't sure if she didn't want to prod for my sake, or if it hurt her too much to even know what the dress was all about. Maybe she couldn't handle the idea of the disturbed memories that provoked me to burn it. To my eternal gratitude, she did not ask any questions about the dress.

I wanted to both smirk wickedly and weep as I watched it burn. The tulle of the skirt curled up into fine ashes quickly. The rest, however, took a little while to smolder. Bit by bit I could hear the tinkling of beads as they fell through the coals and grate to the fireplace floor. Crackling fire with little pings dropping faster and faster as the material burned away. Quality construction indeed, those were no plastic beads.

That night I awoke from a nightmare in which I burned while wearing the dress. I could sense Alex near me, somewhere in the lodge, as I stood inside its giant fireplace, feeling my skin smolder. My entire body shook when I woke up from that nightmare.

It was just one of many, many nightmares in those early months. Most of them were unique, not the exact same scenario each time, so each one was a new terror to discover. Wolves coming for me as I escaped through the broken front window, dragging me off into the pines before I could reach the police car. Alex throwing me into the secret room behind the bookshelf door, and the ceiling slowly dropping down to crush me. Kissing Alex as he stroked the expensive necklace with his fingertips, touching my collarbones, and then cinching the necklace around my throat to strangle me. I now hated nighttime, and suffered from insomnia for months.

The necklace, which I'd still had around my neck during my escape and the initial trip to the hospital, I handed off to Mom to give to Camille. Camille could do with it whatever she liked: donate it, bury it, keep it as a reminder of Alex. I didn't care. I just didn't want to see it again.

And, of course, there was the pink glittery passport holder. The police had gathered that with my other belongings from the lodge. When I first set eyes on it again I felt queasy and plunged into quiet sobs. But after a while, I forced myself to touch it and pick it up. I couldn't decide what to do with the passport holder. I brought it with me to a corner of the living room, set it on the arm of Mom's sofa and stared at it. It hurt me profoundly to look at it, but I forced myself.

It was one of the very last memories I had with Alex prior to my abduction—going to the mall and watching him buy it for me. I think I kept it for that sole reason. But the passport holder also became such a symbol to me of the change from my previous life to boarding the train. Somewhere deep inside me, I felt like I would never really leave that train.

I finally decided to pick apart the passport holder, one crystal at a time. I kept a small dish next to it, and for each step in my recovery, I would dig one of the crystals off and set it along with others in an accumulating cluster. I counted everything as healing—nightmares from which I calmed myself down, surgeries on my ankle, evenings that I cried myself to sleep and let myself feel the grief, and speaking about anything that happened to anyone.

Rachel came by the house with some food and a face full of sorrow the first week I was home. She started crying when she looked at my leg, but wiped the tears away for my benefit. After giving me a long, almost suffocating hug, she pulled a few containers out of a paper grocery bag and set them on the counter.

"Hungry?" she asked.

"Moderately. Not a whole lot, but I need to keep food in my stomach with the painkillers they gave me."

"Okay. I brought you some cookies and a sandwich and some chili."

I almost gagged. "Rach, don't take this the wrong way, but if I ever see chili again, I might puke."

She looked at me, concerned. "Should I even ask?"

I shook my head no.

"Okay, to the garbage it is," she said, and tossed the whole thing of chili in there. "Are cookies acceptable?"

"Yeah, cookies will be fine. Thanks."

She opened the package and sat next to me to eat a few herself. "What do you want me to do? Do you want to talk, or do you want me to distract you?"

"For now, just distract me. We'll get to it. We'll talk eventually. But right now, please just entertain me."

"That I can do, honey," she said.

Rachel amused me the best she could. I watched her hands fly around in animated gestures as she recounted standup comedy sets she remembered. She talked for so long about a girl who lived next door to her parents I began to think maybe she was making up some of the stories. Like how the girl still had a Halloween wreath on her door at Christmas, and how she left a dish of milk on her front porch in case any cats wandered by, even though the milk froze in winter. When Rachel went home, I was left with my thoughts to riffle through again.

Going to Alex's memorial... Now that was a tricky decision to make. He was cremated, and for whatever reason—legal issues, border-crossing regulations, maybe even to just let the dust settle over the situation—Camille opted to hold the memorial a full two weeks after his death. That left me fresh out of the hospital and forced to decide whether or not I should go. My first thought was along the lines of, *hell no*. Stay as far from it as possible.

But then Sam came to visit me in the afternoon the day before the funeral. Mom let him in. She'd taken all of her vacation time off of work in my earliest weeks of recovery to help me get around the house. And she left Sam and me to ourselves in the living room. The television was on, but I paid little attention to it.

"So how are you managing?" Sam asked quietly.

I brushed my hand over my thigh on my bad leg, which was elevated to lie outright in front of me in some fancy contraption on the wheelchair.

"I'm hanging in there. I'm not going to lie and say I'm doing well. I'm just... hanging on."

Sam nodded and scratched his jaw. "It would be pretty obvious you were lying if you said you were doing well. But I'm glad you're hanging on. Whatever you need, anything. Any way I can help pull you up onto the ledge so you don't have to hang there. Tell me."

I turned off the TV with the remote sitting on the end table next to me. "If I think of anything, I'll let you know. But I'm sure you're suffering, too."

He nodded and looked down. I hated seeing the grief on his face.

"Not like you are," he said.

"He was your brother, Sam."

Sam exhaled a heavy breath. "He was like a brother to you, too."

I turned my head away, knowing the truth in that, but unable to listen to those words. I couldn't hear them just yet after the torture. I couldn't hear them just yet after the pleasure that had come before the torture.

"How is your mom coping?" I asked.

Sam sighed. "Not well. I think every last vintage we had in the wine cellar is gone by now. I'm trying to keep an eye on her. But I still have to work so I can't be there all the time."

I swallowed. "My mom has been over there a lot, too, when you're not. She's been hovering so close over me that I've insisted she go check on her sometimes to help both your mom and myself."

"Do you want me to go?" Sam asked. "If you need more time to yourself right now, I understand."

"No, no. Stay. This is nice. Please."

"Okay." He stared down at the floor, and his blue-green eyes looked heartbreaking.

"There are things..." he began. He paused a moment, and then continued. "Things I've learned about that *I* didn't even know, Autumn."

"What do you mean?"

Sam took a heavy breath and picked a piece of lint off of his jeans. "Things about Alex. My mom, she's been telling me things. I knew little bits of it, but not much. I hardly knew anything. He... struggled. But I had no idea how much. He'd been diagnosed with actual conditions, forms of mental illness.

My mom was too upset when she was telling me about this, so I haven't asked her what they were yet. But he struggled his whole life with stuff. I thought it was really mild, common little things, like A.D.H.D. I always thought that was it, nothing else. I knew he took at least one medication. Millions of people have stuff like that and deal just fine. I figured he was one of them, and it was just one minor flaw in the larger picture of Alex that was otherwise awesome." Sam took a moment to keep himself composed before continuing.

"Apparently it was much worse than I knew about. He had much more terrible things up there than just A.D.H.D. scratching at his mind. Apparently, Alex tried a lot of different medications over the years, and was supposed to be on at least two for the last year or so. My mom said he had an argument with her over the phone a few months back. He didn't want to take them anymore. She said he didn't want to have to be all medicated his entire life. But she thought she'd convinced him to stay on the meds after that talk. She ordered him to, and said she'd threatened to take away his trust money and such if he stopped them. But it's clear he didn't listen after all this."

Sam looked away out the window for a moment, and I let him have his minute to keep himself together. I thought about the bottle I found in Alex's bag the night I planned to drug him. Maybe it wasn't a sedative, but one of the medications he needed, run dry. Was it empty before the journey, or at some time after it began? Did he hide his internal fight in the beginning of the abduction, or did he genuinely slip farther away from me as medication withdrew from his system? I supposed I would never know, not that it mattered at this point.

"I don't think my mom and Alex kept it a secret to be dishonest or anything," Sam said. "I think it was just shame on

Alex's part. And I'm sure my mom just wanted to protect his privacy. Why *I* never knew about all of it, I don't know. He was my own brother, for God's sake. I'm trying not to be angry about it. If I had any idea about it, I think I could have watched him closer—kept an eye out for him."

I cleared my throat and wrung my hands. "Maybe that's exactly why. Maybe Alex didn't want you watching him all the time. Pitying him, or whatever."

Sam nodded a little. "That could be. But I should have known. I'd like to think I could have kept a closer eye on him the night of the party, with you two."

"Would you ever have suspected he'd do something like that, though? Even if you knew?" I asked.

Sam sat silent for a moment. "No. You're right. I would've been blind to it. I still can't wrap my head around him doing anything like..." His words trailed off, leaving his thought unfinished. He fidgeted, looking uncomfortable.

"Autumn... How much did he hurt you? I mean, I saw the ankle thing happen, obviously. But..."

I stared at nothing in particular for a moment while flashes of memories moved past like a silent montage. Alex forcing himself on me on the train, and later crouching over me with the knife in the darkness of the dining car. The fire extinguisher swinging through the air to collide with my arm. The door to the claustrophobic room being shut, locking me in. A knot being synched around my wrists and a bedpost. The sight of my hands reaching for anything just before my head was bashed against a stair. I flinched as I remembered the last visual with more vividness.

"I'm sorry," Sam said. "I didn't mean to pry. If you don't want to talk about it, I understand. I apologize."

"No, no. It's okay. I don't mind you asking. Let's just say, obviously I left there battered and bruised. You saw part of that." It took me a long moment before I could continue.

"He drugged me a few times. He locked me in the secret room. He got violent with me a couple of times. And yeah, there are going to be mental scars. A therapist would probably define one event as rape. I think the psychological stuff in the lodge was even worse. The betrayal was worse. But... it could have been even more terrible than it was. I'm alive. I'm alive. It just... it wasn't great. But more horrific things have happened to people in the world."

I swallowed, feeling naked from the vulnerability of my admission. It felt awkward to talk to Sam about something like his brother raping me. But Sam had asked, and he was close enough to me that I figured he might as well know. He'd already had enough hidden from him concerning Alex in the past, and I respected Sam enough to allow him some knowledge of what happened. Embarrassment colored my face, though. For some reason I didn't want Sam knowing I'd been with Alex. But there it was, and then the moment passed and I couldn't take it back. And I didn't have to worry about him finding out later.

When I let go of my shame enough to look back up at Sam, he rested one elbow on the sofa as he covered his mouth in thought. His eyes were wet. I questioned my decision to say what I had about my experience for a second because of the look on his face, but then he cleared his throat and spoke.

"I'm sorry, Autumn. God, I'm so sorry." He moved over to me, sitting on the very edge of the couch next to my wheelchair. He fiddled with his hands and looked down at them with such remorse. "I'm so sorry I didn't get there sooner."

"Stop apologizing. Don't blame yourself, okay?"

"He was broken. I know in his normal moments, when he was really himself, he never would have ever... It will never be a consolation, I know. But he was so broken," Sam said.

I ran my hand through his hair, and he leaned into me.

"I think I know that. I think," I whispered and felt the warmth of Sam as he hugged me.

CHAPTER TWENTY-ONE

When Sam left for the day, I still teetered back and forth about going to the memorial. For a second I thought I might. But then all of my fury came back and I would think, *Fuck you Alex*. Once that evening, I looked at the wall and actually screamed out a kind of groan, pure rage spilling forth from the depths of my soul. Rage at Alex for what he did to me, and anger that it had to end this way, because for the love of God, it was my lifelong best friend's funeral! And I couldn't go because of how he'd left this world. I couldn't go because I hated him so much. How the hell could I attend my kidnapper's memorial, when he ruined our friendship, ruined his family, and ruined my life?

I went upstairs to my bedroom with the help of my mom, and when she left me alone, I riffled through some old things in a box from my closet. I knew I had some pictures in there of a few ex-boyfriends, and I thought looking at them might be a superficial distraction, enough to ease the ache in my gut that the night before Alex's funeral left throbbing inside me. I forgot, however, that I also had a card in there from Alex, a get well card he gave me years ago.

~~~

I was fifteen. I came down with the flu so badly after Alex and I had stayed out too late acting like riff-raff around town, that I'd ended up getting pneumonia for a couple of weeks. Alex came over, one of the handful of times he came through the front door so I wouldn't have to get up out of bed and open my window for him. His face looked so sweet when Mom let him in my bedroom to see me.

"Hey, I brought you something," he said. "I have soccer practice, so I can't stay long, but I keep thinking about you, and just wanted to give you this." He handed me a yellow envelope, and it felt bumpy, like there was something inside the card.

"Just open it when I leave, don't worry about it now. I just wanted to make sure you were going to live, and were feeling okay," he said.

"I'm going to live. Don't worry, I'm a fighter, I'm going to live," I said with a laugh, and then coughed. "The antibiotics are kicking in, and I'm starting to feel better."

"Good, good," Alex said, and stared at me for what felt like a long time, our eyes just holding each other's gaze in a comfortable silence.

He sighed. "Okay, well I'm gonna be late for practice if I don't get going, but you better feel back to normal soon, alright?"

"Alright."

Alex turned to leave, but stopped. "And hey, really... I just thought that bracelet was pretty. I bought it, legit. Didn't steal it or anything. Anyway, don't go trying to tease me about friendship bracelets and shit, okay?"

I raised an eyebrow at him, and realized the lumpy object inside the card must be the bracelet he referred to.

"Even if it is one," he mumbled with a small smile.

I burst out laughing as he walked out of my room, and he pointed a finger at me as if to say, *Don't do it! Don't tease me!* His eyes had looked so lighthearted. When he left, I opened the card and stroked my finger over the picture of a cartoon bear holding a flower on the front. Inside, the card was printed with the standard "get well soon line", and the bracelet slid out onto my lap. I picked it up and examined it. It was woven leather in cobalt blue with a toggle clasp—probably authentic white gold knowing Alex—and white gold beads along with small rhinestones were woven into the leather strands all the way around. It was the most beautiful friendship bracelet I'd ever seen, if that was what we were calling it. I laughed again, then I put the bracelet on, admiring it, and read the note Alex had written in the card in his unruly, boyish handwriting.

Auttie,

I saw this and thought it was pretty. Thought you might like it. I really hope you get better soon. Just makes me realize how important you are to me, you know? You're my best friend in the world. I mean it. I care about you so much and want you to know that you'll always be my best friend. I'm an idiot sometimes—messed up—and I'm sorry if us staying out too late made you get run down and caused this. But you can always lean on me. No matter what, I'm here. I'll always be here.

Yours… always,

Alex

~~~

I covered my mouth as I read the card for the first time in years, and wiped a tear from my cheek. I still had that bracelet in my jewelry box, and had still worn it often, whenever I put on something that matched it. Reading the card again, I felt like the depth in his words went much farther. Aware now that he'd known about his condition even then, that he'd known he struggled with mental illness, I read the note in a new light. It was as if from ages ago, he tried to tell me he was there. Even if a time came when it seemed he wasn't himself, My Alex was real. He wasn't perfect, but he couldn't tell me just how imperfect he was. I was his best friend, yet he couldn't tell me. The shame. The talk with Sam earlier in the day, and finding that card—it broke down my defiance.

I hated Alex, yes. I hated him for what he did to me, I hated what he stole from me, I hated the entitlement, and that he would have likely killed me if help hadn't arrived. But somewhere under that deranged layer, I believed Sam, and I believed that note from years ago. I believed that My Alex did exist in there. I wanted to trust that there were pure moments throughout the years, when the best friend I always thought he was might have really been that best friend. Maybe I deluded myself and maybe it was just a way of coping. But I decided to believe it.

So I changed my mind about going to the memorial for a few reasons. One was for Sam. Sam got help to me just in time, and I felt like I owed him for that. If I detached myself from the link between Sam and his brother, I wanted to be there for Sam. I thought of him with those sad eyes earlier in the afternoon, and thought of him sitting next to me while I was still in the hospital, looking so lost. Yes, I wanted to be there for Sam.

I also decided to go for myself. I didn't want people to think of me as some weak victim, slinking off and hiding after what happened. I wanted to feel empowered by facing that gathering.

And as I read that card over and over again that night, beneath my raging fury, I wanted to go for My Alex, too. I sat for an hour looking at that card, brushing my fingers over it, tracing the bear on the front. Tracing the lines of the letters Alex had scrawled inside. If he'd been a pure version of My Alex at any time throughout our lives, I had to go to my late best friend's memorial.

I knew there would be talk, for certain. So when I went into the funeral home the next day, I stayed at the very back of the room. It was a large space, the kind of parlor for memorials of the wealthy. Elegant ivory curtains, beige and cream wallpaper in tall stripes, fancy sofas, and end tables with granite tops. People filed in, faces full of shock and confusion and sorrow. Faces that caught glimpses of me and whispered to other faces as I tried not to meet their eyes. But I stayed. I came in with the crutches, refusing to look even more the victim in the wheelchair, and sat with Mom and Tim in the rear.

The urn and a spray of white and yellow flowers rested on a table up front, along with a photo of Alex. A few people sent flower arrangements, but not as many as I expected for someone as popular as Alex. It was as if no one knew what to do. How does one handle the tragic death of someone so young, who abducted and tried to kill another young person in the process? I understood their confusion. I felt bewildered about it myself.

The funeral home smelled of flowers, and also of that sick scent of preserved death. My ankle throbbed a little, even though I took medication for it before leaving the house. It was hard to pay attention to the man leading the memorial service. I just kept staring at Alex's picture and asking *why* in my head. Over and over... Why? *Was it ever you, or were you always damaged? Was I always deceived?* No, I would not believe it. He was there with me through the years. My Alex was there, turned to ash with the other Alex in that small container up front. My throat felt dry and closed off.

When the service concluded, people proceeded past the urn up front as if it were a casket to say their final mystified goodbyes. Camille sat in the front row sobbing, which made me cry silent tears. Sam sat with her, trying to console her.

"Just go help her," I said to my mother.

"I need to be here for you, too," she said.

"No... I need a minute. Just go help her."

"You want me to help you out of here?" Tim asked me.

"No, you go ahead, too."

"You sure?"

"Yes. Go. Please, she's a wreck up there."

I sat in the back and watched as the last of the crowd left the room. Then Mom helped Camille walk up to the urn, where she broke down again, and then ushered her out into the hallway. Sam tried to help, too, but my mom told him to take his time to say his goodbye, as well. My brother put a hand on the table where the urn rested for a moment, and then walked out with a mix with sorrow and anger in his expression.

And then it was just Sam at the front of the room, and me sitting in the back. Sam did not look back to see me there, but he must have known I was still in the room. When I saw him leaning with one hand on the table—his shoulders gently shaking—I rose, adjusted myself onto the crutches, and limped up front.

There was no surprise in his expression to see me as I moved up next to him. He just glanced over, his face a mess of misery, and he looked back at the picture of Alex. I wiped the tears from my own cheeks, and leaning my weight more onto one crutch, I put a hand on the back of Sam's shoulder, feeling the thick fabric of his dark suit jacket beneath my skin. After a moment, Sam turned toward me and we ended up clutching each other, weeping silent tears on each other's shoulders as we grieved the loss of a brother, a best friend, and the Alex we thought we knew our entire lives. Any distance that ever existed between Sam and myself evaporated for good in that moment, vanishing like a wisp of vapor on the breeze.

Sam ended up being the light that came out of the darkness. The friend that made life afterward seem like a journey worth continuing rather than a dead end. For a month or two after the memorial, in the deepest part of our grieving, we gave ourselves the occasional solitude we both required. But I would check on him, and he would check on me.

After those bleak first days, there was no one else who could ease the discomfort in our souls better than the other. No one else understood the loss of Alex in quite the same way. So when we needed to talk about Alex, we would call. When we needed to talk about anything *but* Alex, we would call. And we often told each other how much we needed and looked forward to the calls.

As it turned out, Camille did not blame an ounce of what happened on me, at least so she claimed. She carried a lot of guilt and grief, but she was pleased to see Sam and me spending time together. I thanked the heavens that she still treated me like she always had, only more gently.

My final semester of dance school slipped by as I stayed at home to heal. A couple of months after the initial hospital stay, I had to undergo another surgery, and then heal again. Physical therapy often made me want to cry more from emotion than the pain it put me through. The clinic was sterile aside from a few posters of France, which always made me shudder and look away. They reminded me of the French Canadian staff on the train. But I focused the way I did in dance classes. I sweat through the exercises, bit my lip as the therapists forced me to move my ankle in various painful ways, and grimaced when they worked on pressure points. I powered through, and was walking again without crutches within eight weeks.

Sam drove up to Lake Forest to visit me whenever he had a long enough break between shifts at the hospital. We would play cards or watch movies, and we saw winter melt away into spring. When I had just began to walk around the house on my own on a regular basis, he came up for an afternoon to watch nothing in particular on television. It was sunny, and water dripped from the icicles of a late season ice storm as they hung off the eaves of my mother's house.

"Up for a stroll?" Sam asked.

I looked outside, and thought about my ankle, contemplating the weakness I felt in walking on it for much more than five minutes or so. But I loathed the frailty, and wanted to eradicate it from my body.

"Sure," I said.

We put on our coats, and I eased on my boots, struggling for a second with my bad ankle. We walked down the street and to the nearby park. Sam kept a slow pace with me, glancing down once in a while to check how I was. The sunlight shined into his eyes, making them look more green than blue. It smelled of delicious spring—mud and flowers and thawing fallen leaves— and birds chirped in the sunlight. My ankle hurt by the time we arrived at the park, but I thought of it as physical therapy in a better environment than the clinic.

"You doing okay?" Sam asked as we passed a swing set.

"Yeah. Once around the park, and then we can head back."

"You sure?"

I nodded. "How is the hospital?"

"Fine. Same as ever."

"I'd ask you something else about what's happening in your life, but all you ever do is work and then spend time with me."

Sam rested his hands on the top of his head and laughed. "True. So I guess I should ask you how the physical therapy is.

That's pretty much all you do right now. Other than spend time with me, too, of course."

"Ah! You're missing TV... I spend a lot of time with the TV, too." I felt a smile pull up my cheeks for the first time in what felt like ages.

"Oh, yes. I almost forgot. You should send in reviews to all of the networks telling them how they should tweak the good shows, and which ones need to be scrapped."

"I could do that. I could come up with all sorts of letters to write to all the companies of products occupying my time right now."

Sam laughed. "You could write the next *Wilber Winkle Has a Complaint.*"

I giggled. "Yep. Oh, and mental therapy. There's that. That takes a little time each week, too."

We walked a few strides before Sam said anything.

"How is that? Is it hard? Is it helping?"

"Yes, it is hard, and yes, it is helping. I think. I hope. It better be. I think it is... It's smoothing out the proverbial scar tissue a little, I'd say."

"That makes me happier to hear than you know."

My ankle ached by the time we headed back to the house, and when we were about fifty yards from the front door I gave in and accepted Sam's shoulder as a crutch. He tripped a little over the curb as he tried to help lift me onto it.

"Walk much?" I said.

Sam laughed hard, and the sound—of his light heart, of birds singing in the sunlight, the sound of hope—made me laugh, too.

Seeing my counselor did aid my road back to a normal life. I purged the emotional toxins, and as with any cleanse, it made me sick at first. I thought I'd started to swing back up into the light for much of springtime. But early summer was, at moments, a time of despair. I experienced flashes of pleasant memories, or times when I wanted to talk to the old Alex, and then I would burst into tears.

The worst was seeing his name still in my phone contacts. Though he'd destroyed my phone on the train, my cell carrier was able to transfer all of my backed up contacts to a new phone. I sucked in a breath when I began to scroll through and found Alex's name near the very beginning. It was a haunting word, his name in my phone. I couldn't do anything with it for weeks and weeks. I'd pull it up, stare at it, think about deleting it, and then hit the home button to ignore it.

After a couple of months of this, I pulled his number up while standing in my bedroom. I grazed my thumb over his name, and then held it down. A menu popped up: edit, delete, join contact, etcetera. My eyes glanced up to my bedroom window and I envisioned Alex crawling through it with an easy smile, happy to spend time doing nothing in particular. I closed down the number on my phone and returned to the home screen as usual. I heard my counselor's voice in my head, telling me to push myself when I could—but also to listen to my gut. To challenge myself to move forward with small baby steps. Baby steps when I felt ready.

I sighed, reopened Alex's number, and held down his name again. My hand shook. Water filled my eyes. I sighed once more. I looked over at the spot under my window where the floor mat used to be for Alex to put his shoes when he came into my bedroom. I threw the floor mat out the first week I got home, during my initial days of rage. The number, though; the number was hard. I watched my hand shaking through the water over my eyes. *Goodbye Alex*, I thought to him—wherever he was. I hit delete, and then confirmed it before I could change my mind again.

A second later, part of me wished I could have it back, but I couldn't put his name and number back in my phone. It would be a fraud. It wouldn't be the name and number I'd entered when he was still living, it would be a contact reentered after his death.

I dropped the phone onto the carpet of my room and covered my mouth with one hand while my other arm wrapped around my torso to hold me together. I moved to my bed and laid face-down, sobbing into my pillow for a good hour. Sobbing harder than I had at any other time since he stole me away on that train. Removing that number from my phone was the pinnacle of letting go of My Alex, and the grief hurt like ripping a part of my own soul out of me.

Through times like that, it was good to have a counselor to lean on. I not only dealt with what happened—with the betrayal, the trauma, the loss of my friend—but also with the residual mistrust. I had a month or so where I panicked and worried that Sam might try to hurt me, too. But Silvia, my therapist, helped reassure me time and time again that most people did not suffer from extreme mental illness. She repeated reassuring statistics. Silvia even had Sam come in for a few sessions with me. I think those were good for him in a way, too. They helped Sam's healing a little, and brought us closer. I eventually let go of the mistrust, because I could see it myself in the complete oppositeness of their personalities. Sam had always been, in many ways, nothing like Alex.

Silvia helped me deal with the issues surrounding Alex, and also with the acknowledgment that I would never have a career as a stage dancer. There was never anything for me but the dance world. When I told this to Silvia, she helped me work through accepting that I'd now have to focus on working in that world in some form other than on stage. As part of my counseling homework, I went to my dance school to see if they would hire me to work in an administrative position somewhere. They offered me a job in the office of the registrar with more delight than I felt in accepting it.

The school also helped place me in a gig as an assistant dance instructor alongside a company competition team with girls ages ten through thirteen years old. The first time I walked through the doors into the studio, it felt like a flashback from my middle school and high school days. Girls ran down the hallway laughing and joking with each other in squeaky voices.

"I'm here for the—" I began to say to a flamboyantly dressed young man at the front desk.

"You must be Autumn Wright," he interrupted, and held out a hand.

I shook it.

"Just come with me down this way." He walked around the desk and waved me down one of the halls to its third door.

"This is the class you'll be working with. They're still filing in," he said, brushing a hand through one of the girl's hair as she walked through the door and smiled up at him.

"Ten minutes to go before it starts. But Miss Fox is over there." He pointed to the corner of the giant dance studio room, where a woman was writing in a notepad on a small high-top table.

"Thanks."

"My pleasure," he said.

I walked across the room to the woman, Miss Fox, who appeared to be in her late sixties. We did our meet and greet, and then she introduced me to the girls one by one as we strolled around the room.

"And this is Emily, Courtney, and Madison. And then, ah, just coming in now, this is Finnegan. Finnegan, this is Miss Wright. She's going to be our assistant instructor for a while."

I stopped breathing, remembering the name.

The Finnegan that stood before me looked like a little Irish lass: red hair, freckles across her nose and cheeks, and blue eyes. They were not as bright blue as Alex's, but they still made me think of him.

"Hi, nice to meet you Finnegan," I said, trying to speak louder than a whisper.

When she shook my hand and returned the greeting, it felt like shaking hands with a child of mine I would never have— the child Alex and I could have created if he had been mentally healthy, and if we had ended up married. God, her freckles even looked like mine. If she'd had blonde hair, I think I would have had a stroke.

I watched Finnegan walk over to her friends in the corner and set down her bag. I ran a hand over my forehead and felt faint. My palms were sweaty. I took a few breaths.

"You okay, darling?" Miss Fox asked.

"Uh, can you just excuse me for a minute? I just need to use the restroom. Where's the restroom?"

She pointed the way, and I hurried down the hall to the bathroom. Fortunately, it was empty at the moment, and I stared back at myself in the mirror. My face looked sheet white, and I still felt faint and a little queasy. I rested my hands on the countertop and breathed. My vision went blurry as tears covered my eyes. I attempted to place my feelings the way Silvia had taught me to. I felt angry, as always, because Alex left me with such disturbing memories. I felt sad—such an understatement—because I would never be able to have that normal life with Alex. I felt despondent that he'd been mentally ill. I felt despair, because I missed him. I missed him so much, and acknowledging that made me cry.

I had to lock myself in one of the bathroom stalls to weep for a moment in case anyone else came in the bathroom. I allowed myself two minutes to cry, to feel that despair, and then I shut it off. I wiped my eyes, and discovered one more small feeling as I dabbed my eyes with a piece of toilet paper. Hope. I felt a strange sense of hopeful excitement that surprised me. I never gave children much of a thought, and in truth, assumed I would probably never have any if I acquired the stage career I'd trained for. I always wanted that career to last as long as possible, and I'd figured by the time I was done dancing onstage, I would be old enough that I wouldn't want to risk the complications that having a baby at a later age. For the first time since that day Alex took my future onstage away from me, I realized children were now an option to consider in the coming years. At first, I felt unsure about it. But the sensation of hope was a welcome feeling in a string of terrible ones.

In the beginning, it was hard for me to look at Finnegan, hard for me to talk to her. But as the weeks passed, I warmed to her, and she warmed to me. Whenever I watched her, I tried to hold onto that hope, rather than the despair in my gut. It got easier with time, and that optimism grew into a new aspiration for my future. One less shiny than the "big time" on Broadway, but one that gave me a quiet happiness. Possibilities. New possibilities for a different kind of future. Sometimes as I watched Finnegan dance, the crook of my mouth pulled up into a small smile, and I saw that future like a new door opening.

One I never bothered looking at before, but suddenly felt peace and anticipation about.

CHAPTER TWENTY-TWO

I did return to school in the fall for my final classes to finish my program, no longer with the hope of moving to New York, but to have credentials to become a dance instructor. The assistant instructor position helped me change in this direction with a little less gloominess. I loved that job, and although it wasn't my initial dream, I did have a lot of fun working with the girls.

It was under Camille's endless insistence that she pay for my final semester that I was able to go back. I declined at first, but she persisted, and both Sam and my mom told me it would help ease some of Camille's grief. When I decided to finally accept her offer, I walked over to her house—limping along the path lined with her lovely boxwoods—when I knew Sam would be visiting. I called him before I headed over, and he let me in their front door before I even rang the bell. He gave me a grateful smile, a quick but warm hug, and led me to their sitting room that looked out over the rear of the property toward the birch trees. Camille sat in a chair, staring out the window, with a glass of wine in her hand.

"Mom?" Sam said.

Camille looked up slowly, and when she saw me her eyes brightened, but I also saw them sadden for a second, too.

"Autumn, sweetie. Come sit with me," she said, patting the chair next to her.

Sam nodded to me with a quiet smile, and left Camille and me to ourselves. I sat down and fidgeted with my hands. I adored Camille, like an aunt. But I never felt entirely comfortable around her since the kidnapping. I sighed, and examined her face. She had more lines around her eyes, and a few gray hairs at her temples I'd assumed were previously touched up with color to blend with her beautiful auburn hair, I'd assumed. Her skin lacked the glow it used to have. A portion of life drained from her, and I knew she would never get it back. She would never be quite the same Camille I grew up around.

"I hoped you would come visit. How are you feeling, sweetie?"

I pursed my lips to the side. "I'm getting by. How are you?" I asked, but I didn't want to. How do you ask a mother who lost a child how she is doing? Wouldn't the answer, in truth, always and forever be something like, *Every breath, every day, hurts... Every single breath*. I didn't even have children and I could only imagine the constant ache she must feel in her chest, the sickness in her stomach. The way every heartbeat must feel like a knife—stabbing, stabbing, stabbing.

In response, Camille took a long sip of her wine and stared out the window for a minute before she spoke.

"I do believe I can understand what madness feels like now. And that makes it worse," she said. "Which makes me more filled with madness. But I have my wine, and I have Sam, thank God. You mother is a life raft, too. And you, sweetie, we still have you. I just—" She swallowed back a tiny piece of her grief. "I'm just thankful we still have you, too."

"I don't want you to resent me," I whispered.

"Never," she said turning to look at me. "Never, Autumn. Never. I feel more guilt than you can imagine. People should have known—" She choked down her pain again.

"You can't blame yourself," I said, and felt so cliché for saying it.

She tilted her head in an *I'm not so sure about that* nod, sipped her wine again, and cleared her throat.

"Oh trust me, I most certainly can. People should have known. The people close to him. I thought I was protecting him by holding onto his privacy. You learn things sometimes, and then you can't go back and undo them. That's the irony. Lesson learned. I can't do anything about it now, so what was the point in learning the lesson, really?"

"It might not have made a difference if people knew," I said.

Camille didn't respond to that, but I saw the jaded, inconsolable expression of age shift across her face.

"Are you going to let me pay for your schooling, or do we have to keep up the charade of your polite refusals, and the endless insistence on my part? Sweetie, I'm too tired for games now. Please just let me pay for it. It's nothing for me where the bank account is concerned. And yet it's everything to you to be able to finish school. You know I'm not going to back down. I have nothing left to bother with anymore."

I sighed and looked out at the birch trees, with their small verdant leaves fluttering in the breeze, and thought of so many memories with Alex in that backyard. I could only imagine what Camille saw when she looked out there—a little boy running and playing, growing up, becoming a man, and then vanishing.

I blinked my eyes to clear the accumulating wetness. "If it makes you feel better. But only if it actually makes you feel a little better." I watched her face lift with a small smile, one that met her eyes just a little.

"It would… It would. Thank you for letting me do this."

I thanked her many times in return, and sent her a giant arrangement of flowers the next week in bright shades of pink and orange. I hoped the colors would brighten her day. But I knew they probably wouldn't do much.

To say it was easy returning to those studio classes as a student myself would be a lie. Again, the physical part challenged me, but not as much as the emotional side of it. I watched girls who used to try to keep up with me in classes surpass my skill level. I saw the new students trying not to stare as instructors helped me with modified positioning for my bad foot. I would clear my throat, lift my chin, and look forward, determined to finish out my program. Sometimes after a class, I'd limp out, feeling like such damaged goods, and then stare out my window in depression when I returned home.

But every week I acclimated more, and as the leaves on the trees turned from green to gold, I felt a quietness come over me. It was in that fall—during the peace of my favorite season—circling around to almost a year since my abduction, that I finally found my proverbial footing again. That I started to let go of what happened. That I accepted my altered plans. That I found my heart again. For nearly a year, it seemed I could not thaw from the chill that the lodge left inside me, but eventually I did. The ice melted away, one drop at a time, as if I was an ice sculpture, placed against the heat of the warm earth. Slowly the sharp edges of ice turned to liquid, and soon enough, no ice remained.

CHAPTER TWENTY-THREE

It was late springtime again, about a year and a half after the abduction, and Silvia closed her notebook and sighed. It was our final counseling session together. I would have gone on seeing her forever, just for the comfort she brought to my world, but I was leaving.

"I wish I could take you with me," I joked. "But don't worry, I won't abduct you."

Silvia laughed a little, out of relief that I could finally think on the topic without falling into the depths of depression. It wasn't her favorite thing for me to joke about it, but she acknowledged it as a way for me to cope with the issue without it always taking up such a dark space in my head.

"So are you guys heading out tonight or in the morning?" she asked.

"In the morning. The moving truck is loaded, for the most part. We just have a few last things to pack in there and then we'll get a good night's rest, and start off early tomorrow."

"Which emotion is stronger for you at this moment, sadness or excitement?" Silvia asked.

I looked at my hand as it rested on the arm of the chair, and I traced the paisley pattern in the upholstery.

"Excitement, for sure. Sadness is there, but it's negligible. I think I've cleansed as much of it from my system as I could at this point. I had a little bit of a relapse last week, knowing that the move was happening; knowing that I was headed to a job that's not what I envisioned growing up. But I've made some peace with it now," I said.

I had accepted a job as an instructor at a prestigious dance school with a good competition team in Miami. In the moments where I really let myself release the old dream of the stage, I did look forward to the job. At least I would spend my days in a dance studio—among the wood floors and mirrored walls I felt so comfortable with—selecting music, choreographing routines, and showing younger girls how to shine.

"I'm sad to leave my mom behind, too. But she and Camille are each other's rock, and they'll take care of each other. They've both agreed to move to Miami at some point in the coming years if they miss us too much."

"That's good. And Sam?" she asked.

I nodded and smiled as I watched my hand trace the pattern. "He can't wait. He's looking forward to the job. He was so ready to be done with his residency, and he can't wait to start at the private practice down there. They sound like good people that he'll be working with. So there's that. But also, for him, I think the demons are louder around here. I hear them, too, for sure. But for me, a lot of them are still on that train, and are still in that lodge. Almost all of his are around his childhood home every single time Sam visits his mom. He's there every second for Sam," I said, and Silvia knew I referred to Alex. I'd gotten to a place where I could say his name on a regular basis in our sessions, but sometimes it still felt more comfortable not to.

"The fresh start is exciting for Sam," she confirmed.

"Yes. For both of us," I said.

She chuckled. "Sam... What a happy little twist of fate."

I continued to trace the pattern on the chair, but my mouth couldn't help but smile. It was true. Sam, the one who always seemed so far off to me, ended up as my perfect match. After the months of spending time together—at first in calm hangouts just to keep each other company, and then later with more smiles and increasing laughter—it became routine to spend most of our free hours together.

~~~

When my labored, final fall semester had come to a close, I prepared my routine for the December Showcase once again. I felt more of a sense of accomplishment in finishing that one semester than in finishing my entire dance school program as a whole.

Sam and my mother came to my final dance performance to watch what I knew was likely to be the last time I would ever danced on stage. My entire routine had to be choreographed in such a way that I would land every leap and balance every pirouette on my good ankle.

I cursed Silvia as I walked out onto the stage for that performance. She had suggested I take this one last recital and in some form make it an artistic expression of how I felt about saying goodbye to my childhood dream. To honor it with that last show as a sort of goodbye. So I decided on a modern lyrical piece, and picked a song echoing the words I felt.

When I stepped onto the stage to actually perform this, however, it felt like too much, too painful. My hands trembled as I posed with them in front of me in the darkness just before the stage lights came up, and I could feel my breath on them. Rapid, trying to hold it together. I held a white scarf as a prop, and my breath caused it to billow in tiny gusts. The dance hadn't even begun yet, and I could already feel it being over too soon. This was it. It would be gone, just a memory, in less than two minutes.

My music began and the stage lights brightened. I wore a white costume—the soft fabric of the skirt floating out around my hips as I spun, pointing my bad foot as well as I could as I whipped it around to propel my body in circles. To me, it seemed obvious how I had to baby my ankle, and I could only hope the audience would not see it.

The routine was choreographed to be slow. It began hopeful. I held onto the small scarf as a symbol of my desire. When I eased down to the stage floor, arching my back as if hope—dangling the scarf above it—lifted it upward, the fingertips of my free hand grazed the stage like the final caress of a lover. One that was about to leave my life forever.

My movements changed with a conversion in the music, the tracks switching course and taking my story somewhere else. I didn't need to force expression onto my face during this performance. It was already there. I tried to hold back the tears, which blurred my vision. I hated that they made my last view of the dark auditorium hazy. It was my last time, and I couldn't even see it clearly.

I dropped the scarf on cue, near the front of the stage, then I reached forward and grabbed toward those stage lights, knowing I had to let them go. I did not want to let them go. I felt an actual tear drop to my cheek. And then my choreography moved into a tiny run on *relevé*, toward the back of the stage. I blinked and took the second it afforded me to discretely wipe away the tear along with another that fell, hoping it wouldn't smudge my makeup. I finished with a string of *fouettés*, spinning in place, spotting the audience and then, slowing my pace, I walked toward the stage lights. Stop. Spin into a switch leap, roll to the floor, and then rise up. I gracefully walked backward off the stage into the wings, portraying my reluctance to leave as the music and lights faded.

In the darkness of the wings, I let the tears fall, and just nodded as fellow dancers hugged me and praised my performance. They knew what it meant. I found a secluded corner when the condolences and compliments finally stopped, and wept silently. I didn't hurry myself, I just let myself cry. Then I went to find my bag, used eye drops to get rid of some of the redness, and changed into normal clothes. I let out a heavy sigh as I picked up my bag, looked around, and left the backstage area for the last time.

In the lobby, Mom handed me a bouquet of mixed flowers— larger than any she had ever given me after a recital—and Sam also had two dozen pink roses for me. After hugs and compliments on my routine, Mom had to leave to make a conference call for work. Sam looked at me.

"Up for making pizza tonight?" he asked.

"Yes. I could go for not being alone right now."

"Then pizza it is. And if a homemade one turns out crappy, we can just order one to be delivered," he said.

I smiled.

Once we got back to his apartment, I removed a little of the excessive stage makeup, brushed my hair out, and we made pizza dough as we sipped wine and played music. I adored Sam's apartment. Something about it felt so warm and homey. It was a nice apartment, sure, but I realized over time that it was Sam's presence that lent it the ambiance I loved so much.

"Olives on the pizza?" he asked, holding a can with a questioning look.

"Sure, yes," I said, and sipped my wine again.

I sprinkled the rolled out dough with cheese and sighed, surprised at how light and content I felt after bidding farewell to my final performance. Sam set the can of olives on the counter near me and went to retrieve a can opener. He then set the can opener by the olives, and turned away again. I thought he expected me to open them, but he just turned for a second to grab a paper towel. We both reached for the can opener at the same time. His fingers had felt warm as they accidentally touched my hand.

"Oh, sorry," we said at the same time, and our hands retreated.

After pausing for a second, I grabbed the can opener and the olives and lined them up. I saw Sam's hand move in again and rest on mine, saying so much with that single action. The gesture said that he wanted to touch me, that he was brave enough to try it knowing I could refuse his advance, and that in all these hours together he felt more than just a platonic sensation for me. My heartbeat quickened and the world took on a surreal quality.

For months, flashes of something like this happening had danced in my head, but I'd beat the feeling down because, at first, it just didn't seem right after everything that happened. And then later on, because I didn't think I could handle being wounded by another Van Etten brother, regardless of whether it was only by rejection. But the flashes kept coming back, flashing the way they wanted to.

I watched Sam's hand on mine for a long moment, taking in the knowledge that he was doing this, that the spark I thought I'd felt between us was not imagined. Then I moved my eyes to meet his, and he was close. He looked at me with a gentle, affectionate expression that asked if this was okay. I must have communicated that it was indeed okay, because he moved in very slowly and our lips met. I felt his hand on the side of my head, his fingers making their way through my hair. Then his other hand was also in my hair, moving down my back to pull me in. Sam smelled so good. So damn good.

He leaned against me as I leaned against the counter, and our tongues met. I wrapped my arms around him, and he kissed me slowly, so excruciatingly slow, that I thought I might lose my mind. It was a pleasurable kind of agony, waiting for him to do more as he made the most of each caress our lips made. When I couldn't stand remaining in the kitchen any longer, I pushed against him, directing him toward the bedroom. He pulled back and looked at me, tenderness in his eyes.

"You sure?" he asked.

"Very."

We kissed as we moved into his bedroom, and he lay me down on his plush down comforter. Sam eased himself over me as he kissed my neck, my jaw, and my mouth. We kissed for what seemed like hours, a wonderful mess among sheets and hands and lips. I ran my hand through his dark hair, and grabbed the back of his neck. His hand grazed up the back of my leg, soft and unhurried, pulling it up around him. We proceeded in a leisurely way, moving at the pace of two people who knew each other forever, and had been through all the grief together, month after month. We hesitated at moments, because of our situation. But Sam never seemed rushed, just calm and deliberate as he kissed me and stroked his warm hands over my skin. But the passion won out over any hesitation we felt, and somewhere in the wee hours of the morning, among the tangle of sheets, we found each other.

Afterward, we stayed there in bed, on the edge of sleep, me curled onto his shoulder, Sam brushing my cheek with his fingertips. I had a lot of things I wanted to say to him, but they were things I could not say. How it felt right to be with Sam in a different way, as if all our lives Sam had stood off in the distance, with the fates preparing us to be together this way. As if he'd intimidated me from a young age because of a deeper, subconscious attraction. Alex—I had grown to have feelings for him—but most of my life he took the place as my friend. Sam was always... Sam. Always unintentionally making me feel self-conscious, and now I understood why.

"You still awake?" he whispered.

"Yes."

"I hope I didn't make you uncomfortable."

"Sam. I'm here because I want to be."

"That's good to hear," he'd said. Sam remained quiet for a moment before speaking again.

"I've sort of been in love with you forever," he'd said. The words sounded surreal and delicious.

"What?" I whispered. "Impossible."

He laughed softly. "Why would that be impossible?"

"It just is." *Sam*—older, attractive Sam. Impossible.

"It's true," he said. "From the time I watched you dancing by the fire up at the..." He didn't finish the sentence, and I felt his throat move as he swallowed. The lodge. We didn't like to talk about it.

"You're messing with me," I said.

He smirked when my eyes lifted to see his face. "No. Well, okay, I wasn't exactly in *love* with you back then. You were kind of a kid to me. I guess a better word would be... fascinated. I adored you ever since then. And then when you got older..."

"You wanted to jump my bones?"

He chuckled. "Uh, I guess. In a little nicer way than that. But yeah."

"Why didn't you?"

"Why didn't I jump your bones?"

"Well, you know what I mean. Why didn't you pursue me then?"

I felt him swallow again, and there was a beat of silence. "You were Alex's."

I couldn't find the words to respond, but I understood what he meant. So I just waited for him to continue.

"I knew Alex had a thing for you for a long time, too. He made it obvious, so I kept my own thoughts to myself. You guys were always, you know... close. And I took that to mean you'd already picked him, anyway. I didn't want to betray him by moving in and trying to win you over." Sam cleared his throat, uncomfortable to admit these things, and to talk about Alex.

We remained there quiet for a minute.

"Now I wish I had," he whispered.

I curled up closer to him, caressed the side of his face, and kissed him. I couldn't speak, so I just kissed his lips to comfort him, to comfort me, to do anything to move forward. It was the last time we talked about anything like that, and I tried to make it clear to Sam every day since that I chose him. Maybe getting there was a battered, scarred journey. Maybe it didn't seem like I had the choice. But in my mind, I did. And I chose him.

~~~

I forced myself to stop tracing the arm of the chair and looked at Silvia again, still smiling as I remembered that first night with Sam. This was it, the last time I'd meet with Silvia, and part of me didn't want to leave this office.

"I really am excited for the move," I said. "I'm bracing myself for that moment when the moving truck pulls away; I know that's going to hurt. But I'll let myself feel it, and then once we're over the horizon, I know it's going to be about looking forward. There are things I'm so, *so* excited about in

Miami. The warmth, palm trees, and the water. The culture. I feel pretty confident that it will be good overall."

"I do, too," she said. "And you know I'm here if you ever need to do a phone session, or if you come back to visit and want to have one while you're here. Don't ever hesitate to call me."

"For sure," I said.

Silvia looked at me with an expression full of hope and a little nostalgia. Her mouth set in a line that was almost a smile. As if to say, *well, this is it,* she sighed, and her eyes lifted to the clock on the wall.

"That's our time, sweetheart," she said.

I nodded and lifted myself out of the chair. Silvia stood up, too, and after pausing for a second, decided to open her arms to offer me a hug. I accepted it.

"Take care of yourself down there," she said, and then released me.

"I will. Thank you. You know... Thank you," I said. I didn't want to weep, so I just let my simple words resound with the weight of my meaning.

She patted my shoulder. "I know. And you're welcome."

As I exited the office, I saw Sam leaning against his car, right on time to pick me up. We'd sold my car to make the move easier. One more thing I looked forward to in Miami, picking out a new car. The sun rested so low in the sky that it turned into a giant orange glow levitating just above the horizon. I squinted against its radiance and held a hand over my face to shadow my eyes as I walked toward him. Sam looked like paradise with that light behind him—tall and handsome, with his brown hair illuminated in gold against the sunlight. He took a step toward me and held out his hand.

"Ready?" he asked.

"Couldn't be more," I said, taking his hand.

Sam drew me to him and wrapped an arm around my waist, caressing his other hand against my cheek and into my hair. He brushed his nose against mine, and then kissed me. Even with my eyes closed, I could see the warm light of the evening sun through my lids, and it burned around us like a fire; a fiery light that touched everything, every part of us. We stood in it, letting it warm us as we kissed. Then we got into the car and Sam held my hand as we drove home to put the last few things in the moving truck. The sun dipped below the horizon behind us, the fire vanishing—like Alex, burning out both its beauty and its scorching blaze—and yet Sam and I remained, holding fast to each other. Never letting go.

ABOUT THE AUTHOR

Heather L. Benton is the author of several novels, as well as *The Obliging Fairies* series of picture books, on which she collaborates with her autistic sister. The pair have been featured on Fox Detroit and CFX radio for the series. In addition, Heather has written for *The Oakland Press, Real Detroit Weekly Magazine,* and blogged for the highly popular *Hunger Games* movie websites—through which she was featured on Reelz TV's *Hunger Games* special. She has also worked as a freelance editor, book coach, and in professional copywriting. To learn more, visit **HeatherBentonBooks.com**

OTHER BOOKS BY HEATHER L. BENTON

 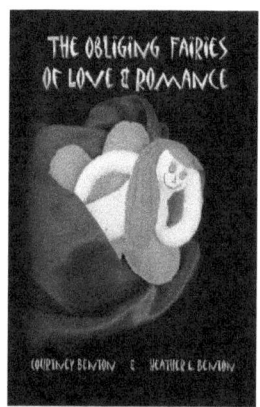

CONNECT WITH ME

Website
www.HeatherBentonBooks.com

Twitter
twitter.com/theheatherleigh

Pinterest
www.pinterest.com/HLBenton

Instagram
www.instagram.com/fairy_and_the_mermaid